She'd been so careful. He couldn't have found them yet. Please, not yet.

"What do you think they wanted?" She glanced over her shoulder and saw Jake still at the outside door, his gaze riveted on her. Her hair. Could he tell that this nut-brown wasn't her natural color? That it was a dye made from walnut leaves and husks?

It hit her then that her hair was down, plaited into a braid that lay over her shoulder and against her clothes. That all she had on was her nightrail and wrapper. And that all he had on were...denims.

There was a fluttery sensation in her stomach that she didn't understand. She forced herself to look away from his chest, but she could feel his gaze traveling slowly down her body....

* * *

Whirlwind Baby
Harlequin® Historical #859—August 2007

Whirlwind Baby

DEBRA COWAN

HARLEQUIN®

TORONTO • NEW YORK • LONDON
AMSTERDAM • PARIS • SYDNEY • HAMBURG
STOCKHOLM • ATHENS • TOKYO • MILAN • MADRID
PRAGUE • WARSAW • BUDAPEST • AUCKLAND

ISBN-13: 978-0-373-29459-6
ISBN-10:   0-373-29459-X

WHIRLWIND BABY

www.eHarlequin.com

Printed in U.S.A.

To my aunt, Sue Warren Green

Chapter One

West Texas, 1885

Jake Ross would rather eat barbed wire than have anything to do with a kid, but thanks to the supposed "dying woman" who'd left a baby at his door three days ago, he was interviewing applicants for a baby nurse and housekeeper.

On this hot August afternoon, everyone except his cousin, Georgia, had taken off faster than a six-legged jackrabbit. She and Jake were in the large front room of the ranch house. Georgia sat in one of the wide leather chairs at the end of the deer-hide sofa as Jake spoke to a tall woman with a British accent. Miz Alma Halvorson was the first person to respond to the ads that he and his uncle had posted in Whirlwind after determining no one there could or would take the infant.

Jake let Georgia keep an eye on the little girl sleeping on the bearskin rug in front of the rock fireplace while he asked questions. Which was a chore because he could barely think past the hammering in his head. He'd spent Saturday afternoon in a bottle, just as he did every other Saturday and he was still feelin' the misery a day and a half later. The pounding in his head only throbbed harder every time he looked at that kid.

After church yesterday, he had asked around the small near-by town of Whirlwind about a family for Molly. Riley and Susannah Holt couldn't take her because they'd just had an-other baby. Riley's cousin, Jericho Blue, and his wife, Cath-erine, couldn't take in the little girl because they'd just learned they were expecting. And Jake hadn't been able to bring him-self to ask Davis Lee and Josie Holt. They had just lost a baby and asking them to take Molly so soon after hadn't seemed right.

After speaking to several other families, he'd driven out to Fort Greer and spoken to Dr. Butler about possibilities. No luck there, either. He'd wired two doctors in Abilene and the marshal about families who might take the child, but no one could help right now. Nor had any of the doctors treated a dying woman who'd been of the age to have an infant.

Jake needed to find some help *today*. Because, if he didn't, he'd be stuck taking care of it and he just wouldn't. Couldn't. Of course, with only one good arm, Georgia couldn't, either. His uncle and brother might not mind caring for the child, but they did have a ranch to run.

"Whose baby is that?" the persimmon-faced candidate asked.

"I don't know." Jake looked down at the blond-haired in-fant, his heart squeezing. After fussing and crying most of the last three nights and on the trip into town yesterday, she had finally fallen asleep on the ride home. "I thought I told you I found her at the door last Friday night."

"No, I meant—" She cleared her throat as her gaze skipped away from his. "Does she belong to you? Is she your illegitimate—"

"No, she isn't," Jake said sharply, "and what difference does it make if she is?"

She was an innocent child. Jake might not want her, but he didn't think she deserved to be thrown away. No kid should be left at someone's door like last week's laundry.

He still couldn't believe someone could actually abandon a child. As if the baby picked up on his dark thoughts, she began to cry.

Jake gritted his teeth and walked over to pick her up, handling her just as awkwardly as he had since she'd arrived. She'd been left in one of their wash tubs along with a blanket, some flannels for changing her, a nightdress and two day dresses. A paper had been pinned to the gown she'd worn, with a letter written on the front and feeding instructions on the back.

After reading the thing at least twenty times, Jake didn't have to pull the paper out of his trouser pocket and look at it to recall the words.

I am a poor friendless woman dying in a strange town. I have no close family or husband and I noticed your kindness to a lost little boy in town. The only way I can bear to part from this life is to leave my Molly with you, not at a baby asylum or foundling hospital. You seem the kind of man who would not let a child starve or be sold. She will be a year old on October 7. I leave her in your care and pray God will forgive me.

The mother had chosen him. Who the hell was she? Had he seen her and not noticed? Her words made him feel responsible for the baby, responsible for yet another person, and Jake didn't like it.

But he knew how it felt to be abandoned and he wouldn't do that to anyone. He'd advertised for the right family, but in the meantime, the kid was stuck here. The baby's crying didn't stop even though he held her. The throb in his head worked down his neck. He had to find a baby nurse and double fast.

Miz Halvorson's gray hair was pulled into a bun so tight it made her scarecrow-thin features look even more stern. She stared haughtily at him as he tried to find a position for the baby that wasn't awkward.

"She'll never learn to stop that if you give in to her."

From the corner of his eye, Jake saw Georgia look up from her chair with a frown. His gaze leveled on the older woman. "Are you saying we should let her cry?"

"Unless you teach her how to behave, she'll never learn to settle down," the woman said in a tone that clearly intimated he was witless. "She'll cry every time she wants something."

Letting her cry sounded mean to Jake. From the tight line of his cousin's lips, he could tell she felt the same.

"Well, she can't talk!" Jake carefully settled the kid into Georgia's good arm, understanding her look that said she didn't like Miz Halvorson any better than he did. "How else is she supposed to tell anybody what she wants?"

The woman started to say something, only to be interupted by a knock on the door. Jake hoped it was another applicant. There had to be someone better than Miz Halvorson.

Baby Molly cried louder and Georgia patted her back with her unwithered hand, just as she had been doing when the baby had finally given out last night from sheer exhaustion. But this time it wasn't working. The knock came again and Jake started across the planked pine floor toward the heavy front door. "Thanks for coming out, Miz Halvorson. We'll let you know if we have any further questions."

She huffed, following him.

"Goodbye, ma'am." He opened the door and got his first pleasant surprise in more than two days.

Framed in the soft amber light of the setting sun was a young woman. Her brown hair was up and she wore spectacles. She was petite and a trifle skinny, but she had skin like cream. *Lady, please open that pretty mouth and tell me you've come about the ad.* Unless she was lost, she had to be here for that. He hadn't had a woman at the Circle R since Delia had passed. Neither had his uncle or brother or the ranch hands.

"I've come about the ad—" She broke off, looking stricken as her solemn gaze landed on the British woman. "Have you already filled the position?"

"Not yet," Jake said quickly.

Miz Halvorson swept past him and out the door, then stopped to say in a low voice to the new arrival, "They don't know anything about raising children and don't believe in discipline."

Holding on to the porch railing, she stepped onto the ground and stomped to her buggy, which sat between the house and barn. The younger woman turned to Jake with uncertainty on her face.

He noted slender curves beneath a blue-gingham bodice and bustled skirt. "I'm Jake Ross. Come in, Miz…"

"York. Emma York." She cast one last look over her shoulder at the departing Miz Halvorson, then stepped inside, watching carefully as he shut the door.

As she followed him to the center of the room, her gaze went to the baby. Molly still fussed and Georgia bounced her gently on her shoulder. Jake gestured to the woman with dark, silver-threaded hair. "This is my cousin, Georgia Ross."

Georgia rose and nodded, since she was unable to extend her hand. "Hello."

Jake gestured to the deer-hide sofa, special made to accommodate any of the Ross men stretched out full-length. "Please have a seat."

"I'd rather stand, if—if that's all right," she said softly, as if afraid he might take exception.

"Of course." He backed up against the sofa and eased down. She was a pretty thing, with more of a fullness to her breasts than he'd originally thought. And, behind those spectacles, he could tell she had green eyes. Pretty green eyes.

Though, it would suit him just fine if Emma York were ugly. He hadn't noticed much about a woman's looks since his wife had died five years ago.

From her spot in front of the fireplace, Georgia asked, "What's your feeling about babies crying?"

"Ma'am?" Miz York glanced from the woman to Jake, looking confused.

"Before you got here," he said, "Miz Halvorson was giving us her views on what to do when a baby cries. What would you do?"

Emma York's fingers twined in the folds of her skirt. "I'd check to see if something was wrong, if she was hungry or needed to be changed."

The baby twisted and squirmed in Georgia's arms, and she spoke in a low voice, trying to calm the child.

"And you'd pick her up?" Georgia prompted.

"I imagine so." She searched Jake's face as if trying to guess the answer he wanted.

Still wiggling, the baby cried out. "I guess since you found your way here, you know this is the Circle R," Jake said. "Someone left this baby at our door last Friday night and, until I find a place for her to go, I need a nurse. Right up front I should tell you we also need a housekeeper, someone who'll cook and clean. Ours was gone Saturday when we returned from Abilene."

As if Jake's biweekly visit to his brother-in-law weren't hellish enough, he'd gotten home to find his housekeeper had taken off and left this baby with Georgia.

"I can do both," Miz York said with quiet determination.

"Are you sure?" Jake thought she barely looked sturdy enough to fend for herself, much less another person. And cook for all of them.

Georgia gently bounced Molly on one arm. "I would do more, but as you can see, my left arm is crippled."

"I'm sure I can do the job." Understanding and compassion darkened her eyes before her anxious gaze settled on the child and softened. "If I may ask, why did your housekeeper leave?"

"She ran off and got married. I don't think the baby had anything to do with her decision." Jake tried to keep the tightness out of his voice. It wasn't Miz York's fault that Louisa had chosen to leave at the worst possible time. "I've advertised about getting a family for Molly. I don't want to send her to Buckner Orphans Home in Dallas or anyplace like that."

The baby's face screwed up and turned red; she let out a scream and Jake moved away, wishing she'd be quiet.

Miz York frowned. "You're planning to give her away again?"

Jake's eyes narrowed at the words. Said that way, they sounded hard and ugly. He grunted, seeing no reason to answer to a woman who might soon be in his employ.

She seemed to realize her place and changed the subject. "What kind of food do you all like?"

"Biscuits, gravy, ham. Sweets." So far, the lady didn't seem put off. He spoke loudly enough to be heard above the baby's cries. "Nothing too fancy, but something that sticks with you."

"So you'd want me to cook and clean? Laundry, too?"

That wasn't all he'd like. Surprise shot through him at the fleeting thought. He hadn't wanted to do anything like that with a real lady, in years. Women didn't distract him, even when he'd been a long time without one. There hadn't been a woman since his wife, who had insinuated herself into his thoughts.

He jerked a thumb toward the squalling baby in his cousin's arms. "Yes, and take care of her. We'll give you room and board. You'd need to live at the ranch. Will that be a problem?"

She twined her fingers nervously and, for the first time, he saw the dull gold band on her left hand. He was stunned to feel a prick of disappointment. Why did he care? He wasn't getting involved with her. Or any other woman, for that matter. "I guess you'll want to talk to your husband about that, first."

"No," she said quickly, glancing at the distressed baby. "I mean, it won't be necessary. He isn't with me."

Jake didn't like the instant relief that jabbed at him. He also didn't examine it. The baby lurched toward him and he took her reluctantly. Her sobs grew louder as she twisted to look at Miz York. Jake juggled the infant from one shoulder to the other in an attempt to shush her.

"But your husband will be here?" Jake asked.

"I'm...I'm a widow." She pulled her gaze from Molly, raising her voice to be heard over the child. "That's why I need the work."

He wanted to ask how her husband had died and how long she'd been alone, but those things had nothing to do with whether or not she could do this job. "Where you from?"

Her knuckles showed white as she gripped her purse strings tighter. "Up north."

That could mean anywhere. "Up north?"

"Illinois."

"And you wouldn't have a problem living at the ranch?"

She glanced at the child as she pushed the spectacles up the bridge of her nose. "No."

The baby jabbered something he couldn't understand, trying to lunge out of his arms. "Whoa, there. You're a slippery one."

The woman stepped around the sofa and closed the distance between her and him, moving so quietly, with such still grace that the air didn't seem to stir. Even her skirts didn't make a sound against the floor. She held out her arms. "May I try?"

Jake didn't need any urging. He did little more than lean toward the woman and Molly went willingly, looping her chubby arms around the lady's neck and burying her face there. That kid hadn't taken to anyone in his family like that. After a couple of gulping sobs, she drew in a deep shuddering breath then hiccuped. The sudden silence was startling.

"What the— How did you do that?" he asked.

"I'm not sure." She hugged the baby close, speaking to her in a low voice and looking…relieved? "What's her name?"

"Molly." Jake glanced over his shoulder at Georgia, who nodded. *Yes.* "Name your price."

"Wh-What?"

He stepped forward. "You're hired, Miz York."

"But…you don't even know if I can cook." As the baby grabbed for her spectacles, the woman shifted the little girl to her other hip.

"I guess we don't. So, *can* you cook?"

"Yes."

"And you're interested in the job? Caring for the kid, the house and cooking in exchange for room and board and a decent wage." He named an amount he thought was fair. Judging by the flash of surprise in her eyes, so did she.

"That's very generous."

"I would ask if you have experience, but it's plain that you do."

She looked at him then at his cousin. "Are you just going to take my word that I can cook?"

"Yes," Jake said, thinking how soft her hair looked. "You don't strike me as someone who would misrepresent herself. Besides, I'm sure we'll like your grub."

Georgia murmured agreement. "And it will be nice to have another woman around."

Miz York rubbed the baby's back and he noted that her fingernails were short and ragged. "How many will I be cooking for?"

"Sometimes a couple of the hands might eat here at the house, but usually it's just Georgia, my uncle Ike, my brother Bram and myself."

After a moment, she nodded. "All right."

He realized she hadn't smiled once since she'd arrived. And, still, she was more pleasant than Miz Halvorson. "We need you to start pretty quick."

"Now?" she asked hopefully.

"Yes, good." The relief he felt was mixed with an unidentifiable emotion. But the baby liked her and so did Georgia, whose spells of tiredness were getting more frequent. "Did you bring your luggage?" he asked.

"Yes. I don't have much."

"I'll fetch your things and Georgia can show you to your room."

"Thank you." Her gaze moved to his cousin.

"We're glad to have you." Georgia motioned for her to follow as she crossed the big room toward the dining area.

As Jake moved toward the front door, Emma asked, "Where will the baby sleep? With me?"

He stopped, frowning. "We hadn't much considered that, but, if it's okay with you, that would probably be best."

"Oh, yes." The tightness in her voice eased for the first time since her arrival. "That would be fine."

Jake nodded, struck by the solemn look on her face. He watched her follow Georgia past one long side of the heavy dining table and stop in the doorway on the right.

"This is Louisa's old room," Georgia said. "You'll be directly across from the kitchen."

Miz York glanced over her shoulder, looking past the table and chairs to the room beyond.

"We sleep upstairs," his cousin said. "You'll want to take a look in the larder to see what you need."

"Shall I cook tonight?"

"We'd be obliged."

She nodded, stepping inside the room.

Jake noticed again how carefully she moved. Almost as if she could make herself become part of her surroundings.

That baby was quiet now and still stuck to the brunette like a cocklebur, her little eyes closing occasionally.

Jake's gaze traveled slowly over the nurse, from her hair down the delicate line of her spine and gentle flare of her hips.

Impatient with himself, he turned for the door. He didn't want to notice Emma York. All he wanted was to hire someone to care for the baby and he had.

Emma could barely keep from sinking to the floor in relief. She'd done it. She'd gotten the job.

The slightly plump older woman stepped aside so Emma could go into her new room.

"Take a minute to settle in and let us know if we can get

you anything." Her brown eyes were kind. "When you're ready, you can have a look at the kitchen."

"All right."

"Would you like me to take the baby while you unpack?"

Emma could tell the other woman was tired and that had to affect the strength in her good arm. "That's all right. We'll need to start getting used to each other."

Muted red light filtered into the room as the sun sank lower in the sky. This room had two glass-paned windows, one looking north and the other looking west. A large wardrobe covered the length of the west wall from the window to the corner. A wash stand with a cream pitcher and bowl sat on the opposite wall, a rocking chair between it and the north window. A blue, yellow and white quilt covered the bed that looked almost as fluffy as the one Emma had back home.

Jake Ross appeared in the doorway, holding her valise and small satchel, which he set just inside the door. "Is this all you have?"

She nodded.

"I'll take care of your horse."

"Thank you." If either he or his cousin thought it odd that Emma had ridden rather than driven a buggy, they didn't let on.

During the interview, she'd been too anxious to notice much more than Mr. Ross's size, but it hit her now that he was handsome. He was the size of a mountain with pure black hair and eyes that were just as dark.

He pulled a piece of paper out of his trouser pocket. "Here's the note that came with the baby. It says how old she is and what she can eat. And some things about her ma."

"There were some flannels for changing her and a couple of dresses," Georgia added.

Mr. Ross muttered something under his breath that

sounded like a curse. Did he not like the baby or was his dislike over the fact that someone had abandoned the child?

The little girl looked well and fit. Still balancing Molly on her left hip, Emma took the note with an unsteady hand and glanced at it.

Jake gestured toward the heavy bureau with two deep drawers along the bottom and a pair of doors that closed to conceal hanging clothes and shoes. "If you want, we can make one of those bottom drawers into a bed until the kid's arrives. One of them would be plenty big enough for her."

"You ordered her a bed?"

At the surprise in her voice, his gaze shot to hers. "Yes, in town today."

The town he referred to was Whirlwind, a small community several miles west of Abilene where the stage had brought her. "She needs a place to sleep, after all."

"Yes," she murmured. How sweet.

"It was Georgia's idea."

Oh. "The drawer will do just fine. I can make a little pallet in there."

"Looks like you're set, then," he said brusquely. He walked away and Georgia followed, smiling at Emma as she left.

Still holding the child, Emma shut the door then backed up against it, closing her eyes.

The baby gurgled, tugging on Emma's lower lip. She opened her eyes and smiled. After shaking out the little girl's blanket, she spread it on the floor and sat Molly there so she could watch Emma unpack.

The weight of the derringer in her skirt pocket provided a small sense of security. For the first time in the two weeks since she'd fled Kansas, Emma thought she might be able to escape the hell of home.

With the uncertainty of getting the job—*this* job—behind her, she suddenly felt light-headed. Clutching the night rail she'd just pulled from her valise, she sank down on the edge of the bed, her legs shaking.

Intending to be the only applicant, she'd gathered up every flyer Jake Ross and another man had posted in Whirlwind. Or thought she had. Finding that other woman here had nearly caused her to faint. If Miss Halvorson had gotten this job, Emma's plan would've been ruined.

You don't strike me as someone who would misrepresent herself.

Jake Ross's words echoed in her head.

Misrepresent herself? Emma had flat-out lied. She wasn't a widow. She'd never been married. Her last name wasn't York; it was Douglas. And she wasn't a baby nurse.

She was Molly's half sister and she was the one who had left the baby at the rancher's door.

Chapter Two

The next morning, Emma stood just inside the kitchen door and tried not to bite her nails. It was a bad habit she had thought broken long ago, but she'd had to stop herself more than once last night, too. And during the days before she'd been hired and fretted about what Jake Ross would do with Molly; about what she herself had done with the baby.

The Ross family sat at the large dining table, Jake on the end closest to her, his brother opposite him. His uncle sat between them with his back to her and Georgia sat across the table. Behind Jake, the pink of early morning light filtered through the large glass-paned window that looked into the dining room and front room to the staircase beyond.

The men wolfed down the eggs, biscuits and ham Emma had set out so she took that to mean they liked the food all right. But they ate breakfast as fast as they had eaten supper. The meal could've been boots and gravy, and she doubted they would've noticed.

Last night she had dreamed that Jake Ross had changed his mind about hiring her. That he'd found out nearly everything she'd told him was a lie.

Just because he acted as if things were fine this morning, she'd lived long enough with her stepfather to know that a man's temper was as unpredictable as a twister and could come up just as fast.

So she watched her new employer carefully, looking for a sign, a change in his temperament that so far seemed quiet and even. If she had to leave in order to protect Molly, she would. While it would be inconvenient, it wouldn't pain her. Certainly not like what had happened two weeks ago when she had found their mother dead. Murdered.

Emma had no proof, had witnessed nothing, but she *knew* it was murder. And she knew who'd done it. Her stepfather had abused her mother since their marriage two years ago, especially when Nola had put herself between his fists and Emma. When Nola became pregnant with Molly, she knew she had to get the baby and Emma away from Orson. Despite endless threats from Orson to use any means necessary to stop his wife from leaving him, Emma's mother had prepared, anyway.

After Molly turned six months old, Emma and her mother began to carefully make plans to leave Topeka and Emma's stepfather. A month ago, he found a stash of money and assumed, rightly, that his wife intended to use it for her and her daughters' escape.

Orson Douglas didn't take any action at the time. Probably due to the risk that, just before an election, he might have to answer questions about what had happened to his wife and eight-month-old baby. Most people admired the politician, looked up to him. But not his stepdaughter. Senator Orson Douglas scared Emma witless.

And one afternoon two weeks later, she returned from the seamstress in Topeka and found her mother dead. Mama lay in her bed with Orson standing over her crying that it must have happened because Nola had taken too much of the laudanum she used for relief from a back injury due to a recent fall. A fall caused by her husband.

Horrified and frightened, Emma'd managed to give away nothing, but she knew Orson Douglas had killed his wife. And she knew what Nola would want her to do. Two days later, as people filled their grand house after the funeral, Emma had used the excuse of putting her half sister down for a nap, then had slipped out with the child.

Jake Ross turned his head then, his black gaze locking on her. She straightened, her fingers curling in the hem of the worn white apron she'd found.

His uncle Ike, as tall as Jake and lanky, picked up his cup of coffee as he looked over his shoulder. "We sure lucked out when Jake found you, Miz York."

She doubted he would think so if he knew *she'd* found *them.* After reaching Abilene by train, she had seen Jake Ross there. Emma would've noticed him, anyway, because of his size and rugged good looks, but what had her deciding he was right for Molly was the patience and kindness he'd shown a lost little boy. No one else had paid a whit of attention to the child except to order him out of the way, but Jake had helped him find his mother.

Emma had included that in the note, hoping the mention of it would make the rancher less inclined to send Molly somewhere else. "So everything's to your liking?"

"Everything's wonderful." Ike nodded.

"Yes, ma'am," Bram declared.

"Especially the coffee." Georgia smiled.

The older woman had told Emma that Bram and Jake had been raised by their uncle. Though both were dark haired and strapping, Bram's eyes were blue rather than black like Jake's.

Jake glanced over, making her stomach flutter the way it had when she'd first seen him last evening.

"Yeah, the coffee's real good," he said gruffly.

Bram took another biscuit, split it and slathered butter on it. "These biscuits are better than Pearl's."

At her frown, Jake explained, "She's a lady in Whirlwind who owns the Pearl Restaurant."

The relief that moved through Emma was so strong it made her chest ache. *Thank goodness they liked the food.*

The elder Ross squinted at her. "Did you sleep all right?"

"Yes, very well."

"And the baby?" Georgia asked. "Did she keep you awake?"

"No. She slept, too."

Her employer looked surprised, but said nothing.

"Is she up yet?" Bram asked.

"Yes." She inclined her head toward the kitchen. "She's in there."

"She sure is quiet," he said.

"She's a good baby," Emma said mildly.

"So she hasn't scared you off yet?" Jake's voice was flat.

"No, not at all." The way everyone's gazes went to him then immediately skipped away had her wondering again if he disliked the baby. "I was going to make flapjacks, but wasn't sure how many."

"None for me." Bram grinned, reaching for the platter of biscuits and bacon. "I've got all the food I need right here."

"What he's got is plenty for everyone, Miz York," Ike said dryly.

Jake said nothing.

She smiled. "All right, then."

"Aren't you going to join us?" Georgia patted the empty place next to her.

The invitation took Emma by surprise. If circumstances had been different, she would've liked getting to know them, making friends, but leaving was going to be hard enough when the time came. She should do her job and keep to herself. "Thank you, but I've eaten."

"I'll share the biscuits with you," Bram cajoled with a charming grin that revealed a deep set of dimples.

Aware of the sharp look Jake threw him, she turned for the kitchen. Mr. Ross obviously didn't like his family being friendly with the help, which was fine with Emma. "If you're sure you don't want the flapjacks, I'll start cleaning the dishes and I'll bring more coffee."

"But—" Bram began.

She fetched the coffee then returned, using the skirt of her apron to hold the hot handle. After pouring a cup for the elder Ross, she moved to Jake.

He passed her his cup and when she returned it to him, their fingers brushed. She pulled away quickly.

"Thank you," he murmured.

Her gaze caught on his and she felt heat creep into her cheeks. She stepped behind Ike to go to Bram, wishing she weren't so aware of the way Jake's pale gray shirt molded shoulders that were as wide as the door. Of his dark hair and black eyes. He was handsome in a rugged, rough way that made a woman think he could protect her. Well, Emma knew better than to trust such sentiments.

As she moved around the table to Georgia, he didn't look at her. And yet she *felt* his attention on her. Weighing, considering. Her guard immediately went up. She wished she could disappear.

As she stepped into the kitchen, she surreptitiously cast one more glance over her shoulder and her gaze crashed into his.

Their new housekeeper acted nervous, Jake thought. Because of him? He didn't mean to make her nervous, but, well, he couldn't stop looking at her.

Bram looked at Jake. "She acted worried that we wouldn't like her cooking."

"I think she was."

"She's every bit as good a cook as Louisa. Don't scare her off."

Jake glared at his brother and shoved a biscuit in his mouth. Something about Emma York compelled his attention and it wasn't that she was taking care of that kid. He'd woken several times last night thinking about her. Not hot, sweaty-type thoughts, but curious, bothered-type thoughts.

He'd decided that was on account of all the alcohol working its way out of his system. He drank to forget and she was a much more pleasant image to contemplate than the reason he'd been drinking. Quentin. Thoughts of his brother-in-law—*former* brother-in-law—made Jake angry and uncomfortable and chute crazy. The quicker he finished breakfast, the sooner he could get some space.

Under the table, something grabbed the left leg of his jeans, startling him out of his thoughts. He registered a tiny hand just in time to stop himself from shoving his chair back. Knowing what he would find and knowing it was inevitable that he would sometimes have to be around her, he bent and looked under the table.

The baby stared back at him with big gray-green eyes. She grinned, revealing two teeth. Clutching his knee, she pulled herself to her feet.

Dammit.

"What is it? The baby?" Bram ducked his head to get a look.

Jake wanted out of this chair right now, but, if he rose, the baby would fall. She took a lurching step forward into the vee between his legs and latched on to him to keep her balance. One chubby little hand hit his thigh, the other one his man parts.

He didn't want to hold her, but he didn't want her looking at him with those big eyes, either. Easing his chair back, he sent a pleading look to his brother, who was occupied with scraping his plate clean.

Jake picked her up, holding her stiffly out in front of him. He had every intention of handing her off to Georgia or his uncle when Molly grabbed his face between her hands and jabbered something. Her sweet baby scent drifted around him, pricking at memories he kept ruthlessly tucked away.

Sheer reflex had him surging to his feet and thrusting her toward Ike. Before the older man could take her, Miz York eased the baby out of his hold.

"I'm sorry." She sent Jake an apologetic look. "I didn't know she'd gotten away from me."

Heat searing his nerves, he stepped behind his chair, putting some distance between them. The knowing look in his uncle's eyes had him dragging a hand across his nape.

Puzzlement slid across the nurse's fine-boned features.

"We don't know much about babies—" Bram stood, drawing her attention "—but we like 'em."

Her uncertain gaze darted to Jake then fixed on his brother. "I'll try to keep her out of your way."

"She's not in our way," Ike said jovially as he rose from his chair. "We like having her around."

Jake caught the flash of skepticism on Emma York's face and knew he should try to reassure her, but he couldn't do it. Her light soap scent joined with the baby's and he felt as if his chest were being crushed.

"We didn't hire you so you'd keep her away from us," Ike said. "We just need some help taking care of her."

Jake wanted to say he had definitely hired Miz York to keep the baby away from *him*. That he was the one who made the final decisions around here, but he wasn't. And he didn't want to be responsible for that baby. Fine with him if Uncle Ike wanted to raise the orphan the same way he'd raised his nephews. That didn't mean Jake had to.

"It's just that some of us are better with little ones than others of us are," Bram explained.

Miz York nodded, her face pale as she cuddled the baby.

"That was an excellent breakfast, Miz York." Georgia folded her napkin and set it beside her plate.

"Yes. If we don't watch it," her father said, "you'll have us all fatter than peach-orchard boars in no time."

Her lips curved in the closest thing to a real smile that Jake had seen since she'd arrived. "Thank you."

The way her face lit up put a strange tightness in Jake's chest. But, when her gaze shifted to him, her smile faded and a wariness moved into her eyes. She turned and walked into the kitchen.

Dammit. Compelled to make an effort at reassuring her, he asked, "Is there anything we can do for you before we leave? Anything you need?"

Her voice drifted from the kitchen. "I need to do the laundry. If you could just show me the washtub—"

"We'll haul the water for you," Bram volunteered.

"And start the fire," Jake added.

Coming back to the doorway with the baby on her hip, she looked at Bram, not Jake. "Thank you, but—"

"I'll get the basket Louisa used to carry the laundry." His brother went into a small alcove between the housekeeper's room and the outside wall, returning with a large round basket. After setting it in Jake's chair, he moved toward the door. "That was a fine meal, Miz York."

"I'll start the fire on my way out," Jake said.

"That's not necessary," she said stiffly. "You did hire me to do the job, after all."

He looked at her. Did they all make her uncomfortable or was it just him? "It won't take a minute for me to get it burning."

"I can do it."

"We can gather up our clothes for you," Bram insisted.

"I'm supposed to be here to help you—" she looked ill at ease "—not the other way around."

"All right." Bram grinned. "You can gather the clothes, but we'll haul the tubs and the water."

"And rig up the clothesline," Ike added.

"Thank you," she said quietly, though she acted more uneasy than pleased about it.

Bram went outside and Jake started to follow. Now that he was getting some space from her, he could breathe just fine. "We'll be riding in the west pasture today. If you need anything, for any reason, there's a gun behind the front door. And there's a bell hanging right outside the kitchen door and the barn. We can hear both for quite a ways."

"Do you expect trouble?" Her eyes went wide with worry.

"No, not at all. But we're not expecting visitors, either." He'd mentioned the weapon and the bell to reassure her, but it obviously hadn't. "I wanted you to know about the gun for protection and how to signal us if you needed to."

"All right, thank you." She studied him as if she were trying to determine how he was put together.

"Is there anything particular you'd like for supper?" she asked tentatively.

"Whatever you fix will be fine." He needed to get outside, *now.* "If we get held up, don't wait on us. You and Georgia eat while it's hot."

She nodded as Georgia came around the table. Emma and

his cousin followed him to the door, and Jake could feel the nurse's anxious gaze locked on him.

Just looking at her pale face made his chest tight. That baby and Emma York made him feel responsible for their welfare. The minute he'd seen the brunette, something inside him had gone still. He didn't know why. He didn't care to know.

He was sick to death of feeling responsible for everyone, dead and alive. He'd done the right thing by not dumping that baby on someone else, done the right thing by hiring Emma York. He didn't need to do anything else, but, for some reason, *right* didn't seem like enough this time.

Jake Ross had buzzed in Emma's thoughts all day like a pesky insect. She wasn't sure if it was because of the hard look on his face when he'd held Molly that morning at breakfast or because of the quiet way he had studied Emma. As if he knew more than she'd told him. Thankfully, she hadn't seen him again today. He and the two other men hadn't returned until late tonight, well after supper and after Emma had gone to bed.

Now it was past midnight and she stood in the kitchen over the stove. Soft amber light from the lone kerosene lamp behind her pooled on the floor. Molly had been fussy since supper and nothing Emma did had helped. She had finally decided the little girl's stomach hurt and come to the kitchen to make the onion tea that her mother had sworn was the best remedy for upset tummies or a mixed-up sleeping schedule.

As she added another pinch of finely chopped onion to the heating water, Emma couldn't help recalling the look on Jake Ross's face this morning when he'd picked up her sister. It hadn't been disgust or blatant dislike, but she wasn't sure exactly what it had been. *Did* he dislike the baby? Everyone in his family had given him odd looks, but she hadn't been able to decipher those, either.

Had she made a mistake by choosing him, by coming here? The rest of his family seemed to like the little girl just fine, but Emma wouldn't leave her sister in a household where she wasn't welcome by everyone. Still, Emma had no money to take her sister and go farther west. Until she did, she would have to stay here and try to help the Ross family become attached to Molly.

When the onion-and-water mixture began to boil, Emma turned to take a folded cloth from the long counter to her right. And gasped. Jake Ross stood in the doorway, wrapped in shadows. In the shift of gray light, she could see he was shirtless. His denims were unbuttoned and he held a gun. How long had he been standing there?

"Shh." He put a finger to his lips, lamplight slanting across the strong angle of his jaw. "I heard something outside."

She swallowed hard, nodding to let him know she'd keep quiet.

"I'm going to check. Don't go anywhere."

She couldn't have moved, anyway. Her legs felt like water. He walked past her and silently opened the door on the opposite wall that led outside.

Emma's heart thundered. He'd startled her, but that wasn't why her pulse spiked. Gracious, the man was…impressive. His shoulders and chest were hard, solid muscle, only a shade lighter than his face and arms, making it obvious that he worked outside frequently without a shirt. Dark hair on his chest narrowed to a thin line below his navel.

As he went out the door, Emma stared. She couldn't help it. She'd never seen a man's bare back. Or bare chest. Or bare anything. One time, she'd seen her stepfather in shirtsleeves, but she'd never laid eyes on a half-naked man.

A funny feeling clenched her stomach. He looked so huge. Intimidating.

She wasn't sure how long she waited. Realizing she was without her spectacles, Emma slipped them from the pocket of her wrapper and slid them on. Very carefully so as not to make any noise, she reached again for the cloth and lifted the boiling pot from the stove, setting it on the long counter.

After several minutes, the kitchen door opened and Jake moved back inside. He shook his head as he quietly closed the door. "Someone's been out there, but they're long gone. Found footprints, but no other sign."

Though she cautioned herself not to jump to conclusions, Emma's shoulders tensed up. There was no reason to think that whoever had been out there had been looking for her, but she couldn't help it. There was no doubt her stepfather would've already assigned one of his men, probably Sharpton, to start searching for her and Molly. Orson wouldn't risk hiring a reputable detective agency like the Pinkertons because he'd be afraid Emma would tell the lawmen about his violent behavior. And she would, if she had the chance. No, Orson had to be discreet and that meant sending one of his own men to find her and the baby.

She'd been so careful. He couldn't have found them yet. *Please, not yet.*

"What do you think they wanted?" She glanced over her shoulder and saw Jake still at the outside door, his gaze riveted on her. Her hair. Could he tell that this nut-brown wasn't her natural color? That it was a dye made from walnut leaves and husks?

It hit her then that her hair was down, plaited into a braid that lay over her shoulder and against her breast. That all she had on was her night rail and wrapper. That all he had on were…denims. His trousers were unbuttoned enough that she could tell the skin below his waistband was lighter than his chest, like the color of an acorn.

The night pulsed around them and Emma realized she was staring, too. She wrapped her arms around her waist. A muscle clenched in Jake's jaw and he jerkily barred the door then moved past her, heading toward the dining room. The scent of man and soap and the outdoors teased her.

"There's no telling what they wanted." He turned in the doorway. "All the livestock we put up in the barn were there and I didn't hear any cattle bawling like they would be if someone had stirred them up."

She heard his words, tried to pay attention to what he said. But what she was thinking was what beautiful eyes he had and how, in the softer light, his mouth didn't seem harsh at all.

"Could've just been someone passing through, but I doubt it," he said gruffly. "I'll take another look in the morning when it's light out."

She nodded, fighting the urge to bite her nails. There was a fluttery sensation in her stomach that she didn't understand. All because of him? She forced herself to look away from his chest, but she could feel his gaze traveling slowly down her body from her breasts to her bare toes peeking out from under her nightdress.

He cleared his throat. "What are you doing up? Is everything okay?"

"Oh, yes. I'm making onion tea." She eagerly latched on to the question. "The baby's been fussy and I think she has a stomachache. My mother used to make onion tea for that."

At the mention of her mother, unexpected tears burned Emma's throat and she swallowed hard.

Something unreadable and raw flared in Jake's dark eyes

and she was swept with the sudden ridiculous urge to go to him.

He seemed to sense her upset or perhaps he could see it on her face. "You're gonna give a baby tea made from an onion?"

The look of distaste on his face had her smiling. "I'll add sugar. She'll think it tastes good."

"Will it really settle her stomach?"

She nodded. "Sometimes it's also used to help babies with their sleeping schedule so they aren't awake while everyone else is trying to sleep."

"Sounds like you know your stuff." He backed up a step. "No one's out there so you don't need to worry. But, if you need to use the privy in the middle of the night, you should take the rifle. It's—"

"Behind the door, I know." She smiled in an effort to reassure him, to get him to leave.

But he didn't. Instead, his gaze dropped to her mouth and lingered. "Yeah, behind the door," he repeated in a raspy voice.

Something passed between them, something Emma had never felt for a man and it scared her. Hands shaking, she turned away and reached above the counter for a cup sitting on the shelf.

"Good night, then."

"Good night." She felt him leave, listened hard for the near-silent pad of his feet across the floor of the front room, then the slight creak of the stairs as he went up.

A breath shuddered out of her. She told herself she was shaking because someone had been outside. Someone who might've come for her, but Emma knew that wasn't it at all.

It was because of Jake Ross. Oh, lands.

Stubbornly, she focused on adding a couple of teaspoons of sugar to the onion liquid. She was being fanciful. He'd startled her, first with his presence then by saying someone had been outside.

That was what it was. That was *all* it was. Still, she decided it would probably be wise to keep out of his way.

The next morning, Emma managed to stay clear of Jake Ross before and during breakfast, and finally he left with the other men for the day. On the back porch, Molly played with a doll Emma had fashioned from a piece of old linen. Emma gathered yesterday's laundry from the clothesline a few feet away. It was strung between the porch and the henhouse. A roller wringer that squeezed water from clothes sat at the corner of the porch.

Georgia sat in a rocking chair, also keeping an eye on the baby as she shelled peas with one hand. Emma was amazed how much the other woman could do with just one hand and how well she did it. The climate was arid here, just like back in Kansas, although hotter. The breeze came too infrequently, but she wasn't nearly as hot today as she had been yesterday while doing the wash.

Pushing her spectacles up for the tenth time, she gathered clothes, folding them and putting them into the basket Bram had fetched for her yesterday. Emma's thoughts seemed stuck on Jake Ross. Just because she hadn't spoken to him this morning didn't mean she was unaware of him.

After seeing him half-dressed last night, Emma didn't think she would ever be unaware of him. Just the memory of his hard, bare chest was enough to make her stomach dip. She hadn't been able to look at him while serving breakfast and, thankfully, he hadn't seemed inclined to look at her, although she felt a carefulness in his manner that made her think he remembered last night, too.

The look he'd given her, almost reluctantly it seemed, had

been heated and hungry. Her skin had gone tight. No man had ever affected her that way. Emma might not have much experience with men or flirting, but she knew what happened between men and women. Her mother had told her during those weeks her stepfather had pressed her to marry Albert Crocker.

Albert had tried to kiss her once and she had pulled away. He'd been angry enough to raise his hand to her, though he hadn't hit her. She'd refused the railroad baron's son, not because she feared sharing his bed, but because Albert seemed to be as cruel as her stepfather. And her refusal had earned the burn scars on her back, one of the few times her mother had been unable to shield her from Orson Douglas's wrath.

Jake Ross was a big man, with big hands, like her stepfather. Maybe it was those things that made her nervous rather than some annoying awareness of him. Emma reached the end of the clothesline and pulled down the last sheet. After giving it a snap, she folded it.

As she bent down to place the linen on top of the other laundry, she got the sense she had missed something. She hadn't been paying strict attention to her task so she wasn't sure. She knelt and dug through the pile of clothes that would need to be ironed. She couldn't find her corset. Even though she knew she'd taken everything from the clothesline, she looked over her shoulder.

It wasn't there. She was positive she'd washed it and hung it out to dry because she didn't have it on beneath her gray work dress. And it was the only one she'd brought. Four days of hard riding to Baxter Springs to catch the train through Indian Territory into Texas had required that she and Molly travel light.

Getting a funny feeling in her stomach, Emma looked

through the basket again, but didn't find it. She stood, walking the length of the clothesline. Maybe it had blown away? But, if so, why hadn't anything else? There were several things lighter than her stays and they had all managed to remain on the line.

"Emma, I'm taking in these peas," Georgia called as she rose from the rocking chair. "Would you like me to get you anything?"

"No, thank you." She thought about asking Georgia if she'd taken the corset, but why on earth would the other woman take it? Why would *anyone?* Besides, she and the other woman were nowhere close in size.

Emma was the one who'd been out here with the wash, yesterday and today. She was the one who should know whether or not she had everything. Last night, her employer had heard a noise. Could it have been a thief? A thief who'd stolen a corset? That was ridiculous. Emma couldn't even fathom it.

A quick glance showed that Molly was still playing happily on her blanket, so Emma turned and walked the length of the clothesline again. She went into the henhouse, thinking that perhaps the undergarment had fallen and one of the birds had taken it. To use for a nest maybe? But, aside from straw, feathers and the eye-watering smell of ammonia, she found nothing.

Growing more perplexed and a little irritated, she came out, latching the door behind her. Keeping the baby in sight, Emma searched the side of the house, under the porch, shaded her eyes to look out over the knee-high golden-green prairie grass. She saw nothing. She had to find it. It was the only one she had. She couldn't go around without a corset. It was improper, immodest. Brazen.

Reaching the porch, she grabbed the basket and set it in

the rocking chair to dig through the pile of laundry again. Her search yielded nothing. Maybe a wild animal had taken off with it. Knowing that she might not find it made her suddenly, uncomfortably aware of her skin against the soft cotton of her chemise, the unbound freedom of her breasts. And that brought back the reminder of how Jake Ross had seen her in nothing but her nightclothes. How he'd looked at her. Oh, goodness. She *had* to find her corset.

She stepped off the porch, intent on searching every inch of ground. She circled the henhouse, made a wide sweep through the prairie grass behind it, but found nothing.

Muttering under her breath, she spun toward the house and came to a complete stop. Jake Ross stood at the corner of the porch with his head tilted and a quizzical look on his face. His holster hung low on his hips. How long had he been there? Good lands, he was a quiet-moving man. Heat flamed her cheeks. "You startled me."

"Sorry. My horse threw a shoe so I came back for another one. Thought I heard someone back here. Is everything all right, Miz York?"

"Yes, certainly." She adjusted her glasses.

His black eyes narrowed slightly. "You sure? You seem bothered."

It would bother her more if she had to tell him. She didn't want to tell him. She didn't have to, did she? Nothing of his had been taken.

"You lose something?"

"No." That wasn't a lie. She knew exactly where she'd put it. It just wasn't there.

He took a few steps toward her, his cowboy hat shading his eyes. "Is something missing?"

Why did he have to be back, anyway? she thought grumpily. Yesterday, he'd stayed gone until after dark.

He frowned. "Seeing as how I heard a noise out here last night, I'm starting to get concerned."

And her not answering his questions was only making him more determined. "Did... Did you take anything off the clothesline last night or this morning?"

"Did someone make off with the laundry? If any of my property's gone, Miz York, you'd best tell me."

She shifted from one foot to the other. If she had another corset, she wouldn't say anything about it. But she didn't have another one. And she felt half-naked right now standing here talking to him without it.

"Listen, lady." He took a step toward her, his gaze leveling into hers. "We had some outlaws making merry around Whirlwind not a year ago. They were known to steal clothes off lines—"

"Something's gone, yes, but it isn't yours."

"Then whose? Yours?"

Embarrassment seared every inch of her, but she nodded.

"What's gone?" Before she could answer, a slow awareness lit his eyes and his gaze slowly lowered to her breasts before returning to her face. His compelling features cautious, he cleared his throat, gesturing in her general direction. "Is it your...um, an undergarment?"

Before she could stop herself, her surprised gaze flew to his then away. How had he guessed that? She didn't know what she would wear until she got another corset, but she would have to figure out something. She certainly had no money to buy one right now. Georgia might be willing to lend her one, but it would be too big. Even laced as tight as it would go.

Face burning, she started for the porch. His long legs covered the distance between them in two steps and he blocked her way. She stopped abruptly, stiffening.

"Miz York, I know it vexes you to talk about this. It sure

as hell isn't what I want to talk about, but you need to tell me."

"I—I can't." She kept her gaze on his dusty boots.

For a moment, he didn't speak, then he said in a gruff voice, "I sometimes serve as a deputy for the sheriff in Whirlwind."

Emma's stomach plummeted. *A deputy?* She thought she'd been so careful to avoid the law and now she was living with a sometime-lawman. What had she done?

This wasn't the place for Molly. No, Emma corrected, quickly calming herself. It wasn't the place for *her,* but it might be good for her sister. Mr. Ross's being a lawman would be perfect for Molly.

"Over the last few months, there's been a rash of thefts," he said. "Farm equipment, jewelry, tools. And, lately, some things have been stolen off clotheslines. Women's…things. Corsets."

The word sounded rough on his tongue and a shiver rippled up her spine. Could he tell she wasn't wearing one? She couldn't bear the thought.

"Several women have had their…those stolen. I don't know if the thefts are being committed by the same person, but you need to tell the sheriff."

"Oh, no!" Her gaze flew to his. "I couldn't! I can't."

It wasn't just the humiliation of telling another man that her corset had been stolen. It was also that she needed to stay as far from Whirlwind's sheriff as possible. If her stepfather or one of his men showed up looking for her, the sheriff would be their first stop.

Jake Ross studied the ground then glanced up. "I know it's embarrassing for you, but we need to tell Davis Lee." At her frown, he added, "Sheriff Holt."

She could see he wasn't going to let this go.

"He needs to know there's been another theft."

And now that Jake Ross knew, Emma would suffer anxiety every time she saw him.

She couldn't believe she was discussing undergarments with a man. A man she'd just met. To whom she'd been lying since setting foot on his doorstep.

"Davis Lee's discreet. You won't need to worry about anyone finding out."

That was slightly reassuring. "Has this happened before?"

"Not out here!"

"Are you going to tell—"

"I won't say anything," he said quickly. "To anyone."

She believed him. "Thank you."

After a moment, he said, "We should probably go today."

We? "I'm sure I can manage the trip. I rode out here alone, after all."

His eyes flashed hotly. "You're not going alone. I don't know where that thief is or if he'll do something besides steal a woman's—" He shifted uncomfortably as if his boots were too small. "I'm not sure if he'd do something more dangerous than steal."

"But—"

"I'll have the wagon ready after lunch."

She nodded, knowing she couldn't protest further. He'd certainly start to wonder why she was hesitant to face the sheriff. Drat it all!

He moved aside so she could step onto the porch. She bent to pick up the baby, aware that behind her he headed toward the clothesline.

As if it weren't nerve-racking enough to talk to the sheriff, now she'd have to spend the rest of the day with Jake Ross.

Chapter Three

⦿⦿⦿⦿⦿⦿

They reached town a couple of hours after lunch. Being without her corset made Emma uneasy enough, but the possibility that Whirlwind's sheriff might have already gotten information on her had her palms sweating and a hard lump wedging under her ribs. Mr. Ross guided the wagon down Whirlwind's wide Main Street and reined to a stop in front of a weathered pine building. Several steps led up to a door with a sign hanging overhead that said Jail. She did not want to go in there.

Their ride had been mostly silent, broken occasionally by some polite, inconsequential talk that Emma felt both of them thought awkward. And, of course, none of it had been about the baby. Jake Ross appeared not to know Molly was even there.

The impression Emma had of the small West Texas town was that of a dusty, but neat community. The jail sat between the Pearl Restaurant, which Mr. Ross had told her about yesterday, and the blacksmithy. A hammer struck metal and Emma glanced over to see a large black man inside a frame shop working over an anvil. He nodded politely, and she nodded back.

The low rumble of people's voices was broken by the clop of horses' hooves. She managed to get down out of the wagon and pick up the baby from the seat before Mr. Ross rounded the horse. Across the street behind her, she noted Haskell's General Store, a livery and a saloon.

She mounted the steps with her employer, pushing the glasses up her nose and tightening her hold on Molly. Despite the late August heat, Emma had worn a light shawl in an effort to make it less noticeable that she wasn't wearing a corset.

Mr. Ross opened the door then followed her inside. The smells of pine and soap mixed with the clean male scent of the man who'd insisted she come. A handsome dark-haired man wearing a badge rose from behind a wide oak desk. A glass-front cabinet behind him held four shotguns. The lawman gave her a friendly smile, his blue eyes twinkling. "Howdy, ma'am. Jake."

"Davis Lee Holt." Mr. Ross took off his hat, gesturing toward Emma. "This is Miz York. She's the lady we hired to care for the baby."

"Miz York." The sheriff smiled at Molly, who turned her head shyly into Emma's neck.

The man seemed friendly and not the least suspicious, but that didn't ease the tightness across Emma's chest. Or keep her from mentally checking the derringer in her skirt pocket. On the wall behind him hung two Wanted posters and a notice about a circuit judge. Nothing about a runaway or kidnapped daughter. Which didn't mean the sheriff was ignorant about her, just that there was nothing on that wall. Being on her guard, almost paranoid, was becoming second nature.

"Little Molly looks good."

Emma wondered how the sheriff knew the child's name, then recalled that Jake Ross had stopped by the jail the day he and his uncle had brought Molly to town to post flyers advertising for the position of baby nurse.

The rancher stepped up beside Emma, his big body surrounding her like a wall, close enough that she could feel the sun's heat from his shirt. She wished this were over, wished she'd never had to come. If Mr. Ross hadn't found her searching for her corset, she wouldn't have mentioned a thing about it.

"What brings you two to town today?" The sheriff, who was two or three inches taller than the other man, eased down on the corner of his desk.

Mr. Ross glanced at Emma and said in a low voice, "If you'd rather speak to the sheriff alone, I can wait outside."

"No," she said quickly. The thought of him leaving her alone in the jail tied her stomach in a knot. Which just went to show how nervous she was about being face-to-face with the sheriff if she felt safer with Mr. Ross staying in here.

The baby grabbed at Emma's glasses, yanking them across her nose. She pulled her half sister's hand away, trying to decide how to delicately report what had been stolen.

Mr. Ross didn't wait on her. "There was a theft at my ranch last night. One of *those* thefts."

The sheriff politely kept his gaze on the rancher, but Emma was aware that the lawman's attention sharpened. "Same piece as what was taken a week or so ago?"

"Yes."

Heat flushed Emma's cheeks and she held Molly tighter to her breasts, feeling practically naked.

Behind her, the door flew open and a feminine voice exclaimed, "Davis Lee, there's been another one! Oh."

A broad grin spread across the sheriff's face. "Hello, wife."

Emma looked over her shoulder to see a petite brunette

move into the room beaming at Sheriff Holt. She tore her gaze from him to look at Mr. Ross. "Hello, Jake."

"Miz Josie."

Her warm green gaze lit on Emma and she stuck out a hand. "I don't believe we've met. I'm Josie Holt."

"Emma York." She shook hands, thinking she would probably like the sheriff's wife if given a chance to know her.

"Oh, I should've been quicker with an introduction," Mr. Ross apologized.

"It's all right." The other woman smiled then looked at her husband. "I'm sorry. I can see I've interrupted."

He nodded, an indulgent and amused look on his handsome features. As his wife reached out to touch Molly's blond hair, a look of painful longing flitted across her pretty features. "What a darling baby. This is the little girl someone left at your house, Jake?"

"Yes, ma'am," he said stiffly.

It didn't escape Emma's notice that his voice had changed the instant the baby was mentioned. Nor did she miss the fleeting glances that both the sheriff and his wife gave the man, looks that appeared to be compassion. Emma turned her head to prevent the baby from grabbing her spectacles. If anyone should get their compassion, it should be Molly, especially if the man who'd taken her in didn't want her.

"Hi there, little one." Josie Holt bent, looking into the baby's eyes as she stroked her cheek. "Would you let me hold you?"

Emma didn't think her half sister would go, but, when the sheriff's wife opened her arms, Molly studied her soberly then went. Without her sibling's tiny body covering her chest, Emma felt it was obvious that she wasn't wearing a corset. She drew the light shawl tighter around herself and made herself very still, the way she did when her stepfather went into one of his tempers.

"Aren't you a beauty?" Josie murmured, fingering Molly's fine blond curls. Her voice cracked. "Isn't she pretty, Davis Lee?"

"Yes." His gaze touched briefly on the child, then riveted on his wife, and the tender look on his face had Emma's heart clenching.

Molly grasped a button on Mrs. Holt's blue gingham bodice and the woman touched the baby's nose. "You did just fine by finding yourself at Jake's, little one."

Emma wondered if the woman would still think so if she knew how quickly the rancher had removed himself from the baby yesterday morning. The sheriff's wife brushed a light kiss against Molly's temple before returning her to Emma. From the corner of her eye, Emma could tell that Jake Ross was looking away.

Josie walked over to her husband and said in a low voice, "When you're finished, would you come to the shop? There's been another one."

Beside Emma, her employer snapped to attention. "Beggin' your pardon, Miz Josie, but do you mean another theft? Of…you know?"

"Yes, exactly."

Emma caught the look Mr. Ross shared with Sheriff Holt, who reached out and took his wife's hand. "I'll come as soon as I've finished talking to Miz York."

It was a bit of a relief to know that Mrs. Holt had also been a victim of the embarrassing theft. And, if Josie Holt stayed, maybe Emma wouldn't have to say much.

"You may as well stay, Mrs. Holt," she offered tentatively. "That's why I'm here, too."

"No!" Josie's gaze shot to Emma and she whispered, "A…corset?"

The sheriff chuckled. "Honey, we can hear you."

Smiling, she swatted at him, looking to Emma for an answer.

"Yes, ma'am."

"Last night?"

Emma nodded, adjusting her spectacles.

"Oh, my stars." Josie clutched at her husband's hand. "Davis Lee, you've got to do something. This can't go on."

"I'm doing the best I can, Josie. There are those other thefts I have to worry about, too."

"I thought the only garments being stolen were ones I'd made, but this most recent theft—the two most recent thefts—those pieces weren't made by me. You have to do something."

The lawman looked at Emma. "When did you first notice it was gone?"

"A few hours ago." So, Mrs. Holt was a seamstress. The sheriff's blue gaze was steady and probing, making Emma feel he might know she didn't need these glasses, that her eyesight was just fine.

The possibility that he might find out who she was, why she was in Whirlwind had her skin prickling. "I did the wash yesterday and left everything on the line to dry overnight."

Mr. Ross's deep voice rumbled out, "Late last night, I heard a noise outside, but when I looked around, I couldn't find any sign of anyone. Didn't realize then that Miz York's cors—" A dull flush colored his neck. "That anything had been taken off the line."

"What time was that?"

"I'd say just after midnight."

"Was it one of your finer garments?" Josie asked Emma, her gaze lingering on the baby.

"Yes."

Jake Ross didn't look at Emma or do anything that might

indicate he was thinking about their meeting half-dressed in the kitchen after midnight. But she felt a tension stretch between them and she knew he was thinking about it. Because she was.

Josie Holt nodded. "Pearl said hers was taken after dark last night. She discovered it when she went to the clothesline before bed."

"Pearl Anderson owns the Pearl Restaurant," Mr. Ross reminded Emma.

"Did she hear anything?" the sheriff asked his wife.

"She said no."

Sheriff Holt rose and moved behind his desk, opening a drawer in the middle and pulling out a leather-covered book. He flipped through a couple of pages then glanced at his sometime-deputy. "You made note when the last theft like this was reported."

"Yeah. It was Susannah's." Jake stepped around Emma to confer with the lawman. "If I recollect, it was just a little over a week ago."

As the men discussed dates of the other thefts, Josie eased up to Emma and said quietly, "Susannah is married to Davis Lee's brother."

Emma nodded.

"If you need another dress corset, I want you to come by my shop and get one."

Emma needed a corset, period. But she didn't have the money to buy one.

The seamstress seemed to sense why she hesitated and said kindly, "I want to give it to you. This is no kind of welcome to a new town."

Touched, Emma was speechless for a moment. The woman didn't even know her. "I can't, but thank you. Really."

"You can put it on account."

Emma couldn't do that, either. What if she and Molly had to run in the middle of the night? Emma wouldn't be able to pay on the account for a long while and that would be a reminder of her to these people. A reminder she couldn't afford if her stepfather or his man came looking for her. "I can come in after I get my first wages."

Josie looked as if she might insist, then smiled warmly. "All right then."

Behind them, the door opened. Emma turned to see a tall, red-haired girl who looked to be a few years younger than her.

"Mrs. Holt," the newcomer said. "I locked up the shop and I'm taking lunch to Zeke, if that's all right."

"Of course, Zoe. Thanks for letting me know."

"I won't be long."

"All right." Josie smiled. As the other woman backed out of the office and closed the door, Josie's attention came back to Emma. "That's Zoe Keeler. She works for me. Zeke is her younger brother."

Emma nodded.

Closing the book, the sheriff said to the other man, "I'm gonna come out to the Circle R later on and look around."

"I figured you would."

Emma's heartbeat sped up.

"Can you think of anything else that might be helpful?"

"No." Her boss looked at Emma with the same question in his eyes.

"I don't think so," she said. She hoped the sheriff wouldn't ask for a description of the garment.

"All right then." Davis Lee looked thoughtful. "This is the first time this thief has struck twice in one night. I wonder why."

"I wish he or she would quit it!" his wife burst out. "People are going to stop buying clothing from me."

"Honey, they know it isn't your fault."

"Oh, fiddle, people don't give a fig about whose fault it is." She paced in front of her husband, her skirts swooshing against the wood floor. "They just know that things I make are being stolen and they won't buy anything because they're afraid it'll be stolen, too."

He chuckled, catching her hand and stilling her.

"I hope you're wrong, Miz Josie," Jake said. "Because that's just plain silly."

"Thank you."

He smiled as he turned to open the door. "We'll be on our way, then. See you later, Davis Lee."

"Yeah."

Emma said goodbye then preceded Mr. Ross out the door, noticing how the baby watched him. Emma glanced back before starting down the steps and saw the sheriff pull his wife into his lap. Taken by the sight, Emma paused.

Josie put her arms around her husband's neck and laid her head on his shoulder. Davis Lee Holt was every bit as broad as Jake Ross and taller, but Josie Holt didn't act one bit afraid of him. Emma wondered what it would be like to be that at ease with a man. Just one.

About halfway down the steps, Mr. Ross stopped. "I forgot to tell Davis Lee something. I'll be right back."

"All right."

As she waited, she talked to Molly, pointing out the livery across the way then a hotel just beyond that looked almost finished. A sign across the front of the two-story stone building said New Owners. Construction to Resume Soon.

So far, the sheriff didn't appear to have any information about a senator's missing stepdaughter and daughter. The relief that moved through Emma was so strong it made her light-headed, as if she'd been out in the sun too long.

The heavy thud of boots sounded on the steps behind her and Jake Ross joined her. As they stepped into the dusty street, she started for the wagon, but he halted.

"Miz York, would you like something to drink before we head back?"

She hesitated, wondering if he realized the baby would have to come, too.

"Do you like lemonade? Pearl makes a good one."

"Lemonade?" she asked in surprise. She loved lemonade, thought longingly of her mother's. "Yes, I like it."

"I'm thirsty and you probably are, too. Let's have us a glass before we head back to the ranch."

She supposed she could refuse and wait for him in the wagon, but lemonade… "All right."

He gave a sharp nod and gestured to the right.

As they walked to the Pearl Restaurant, Emma wondered what his feelings toward the baby really were. She didn't think she'd misread him, but she needed to be sure. She was no good at coaxing information out of people, but she wanted—needed—to know if Jake Ross was the one who should raise Molly.

As they stepped up on the plank walk in front of the restaurant, he stopped abruptly, calling out to a sturdy, red-haired man walking toward them. "Hoot!"

Emma halted beside Jake, keeping her head bent toward the baby. The fewer people who got a good look at her, the better.

The man stopped several inches away. "Jake. Ma'am." He extended his hand. "Hoot Eckert."

"This is Miz York, the baby's nurse."

"Hello," she murmured, shaking his hand.

Eckert's face was as round as his body and the red mustache and long sideburns gave him a jovial look. He peered at Molly. "So, this is the little girl you found."

"Yeah," Jake said. "I was wondering if you'd had any replies to that ad yet."

Emma's spine went to steel. This man ran the newspaper and Jake Ross was asking if a family had been found for Molly. Anger hummed through her.

"No, not yet. If I hear anything, I'll come out to the Circle R or send Chesterene."

"I'd appreciate it." Jake shook hands with the man, who tipped his hat to her and walked on.

Emma didn't know who Chesterene was and she didn't care. All she cared about was the disappointment in Jake Ross's taut voice that he was still responsible for Molly. Emma had to keep her mouth shut—the baby was supposed to be only a job to her.

The lanky rancher held open the door to the Pearl, his expression neutral until she passed in front of him with the baby. Then his face closed up like a coffin.

His reaction to the little girl was so obvious that Emma was unable to stop a flare of temper. "If you hadn't found someone for the job, would you have sent Molly to that orphanage?"

Surprise flashed through his eyes before they went hard. Emma braced herself. He couldn't—wouldn't—do anything in front of these people. And, if he tried, she had her derringer in her skirt pocket.

Jaw clenched tight, he stood in the doorway of the restaurant, looking away. "I would've figured something out."

What did that mean? Emma was afraid she knew. As much as she wanted to stay out of Jake Ross's way, she had to find out if this was the place for her to leave her half sister. She had to learn as much about him as she could. Without giving away anything about herself.

If you hadn't found someone for the job, would you have sent Molly to that orphanage? Damn if it was any of her business.

They'd left Whirlwind about an hour ago and that question had been sawing at Jake ever since. He wouldn't have been able to send the kid there. Still, he didn't like Emma York asking questions like that. She worked for him. She didn't need to know any more than that.

But there was something about her. He couldn't stop staring at her, though he'd managed to keep from it in Davis Lee's office. The Pearl had been another matter. He'd ordered their lemonade and been surprised by Miz York's reaction. She didn't just like the sweet drink; she loved it. The first true smile he'd seen from her spread across her face and chased away the shadows in her eyes. And, just like that, Jake was staring again.

She wore a pink calico dress that hung a little loosely on her slender frame. Her long, dark hair was up today, not down as he'd seen it last night. As the wagon rocked along the hard-packed road toward the ranch, his mind seemed stuck on their meeting in the kitchen. The lamplight had gilded her hair with amber. He had wanted to touch the silky thickness. Because he still did, he tightened his grip on the reins.

Still, thinking about Emma York was a sight better than thinking about his brother-in-law, whom he'd glimpsed as they'd left town. Quentin hadn't seen Jake and Jake hadn't stopped to remedy that. He didn't want to think about his brother-in-law so he turned his thoughts to the visit he'd paid to the sheriff.

He'd been planning to let Miz York go in alone to see Davis Lee, but she'd been trembling. There had been as much apprehension on her face as there had been embarrassment. As difficult as it had been for her to tell Jake about the theft of her corset, it had to be at least that hard to tell another man. No one at the ranch knew why he and the baby nurse had gone to Whirlwind. He didn't see any reason to deepen her embarrassment by telling his family, who couldn't do anything about it, anyway.

Knowing her corset had been stolen and observing how tightly she wrapped that shawl around herself had Jake figuring she didn't have on a corset. Just as she hadn't last night.

Coming upon her in the kitchen had torched something inside him, something he hadn't felt in a lot of years. Bathed in the soft amber light, Emma York had looked like an angel. He hadn't been able to see anything bare save her dainty feet, although that hadn't stopped him wishing he had.

"The sheriff and his wife are good friends of yours?"

He sliced a look at her. She hadn't said a word since they'd left town. Or, well, since they'd stopped a half mile back to make a pallet in the wagon bed for the baby, who'd fallen asleep. Miz York had held the child all day.

"Yeah, I've known Davis Lee my whole life. He and his brother, Riley. Miz Josie moved here only last fall. She's a real nice lady."

"Did she come here to marry the sheriff?"

Jake chuckled. "No. Those two danced around each other for a while on account of Miz Josie coming here to kill one of Davis Lee's prisoners."

"What?" The nurse's jaw dropped.

Jake wasn't much of a storyteller, but he seemed to hold her attention as he told her about Ian McDougal, the outlaw who had murdered Josie's parents and fiancé. "He was part of a gang of brothers. They also killed a man from Whirlwind and nearly did in a Ranger when they murdered his partner. When Ian was finally caught, he was put in Whirlwind's jail to wait for his trial."

"Goodness," she breathed. "So did he have a trial? What happened? Did Mrs. Holt kill him?"

"Not in the end, but she had a chance to. He hit me upside the head and escaped from the jail."

Miz York frowned as she glanced at him. "How badly were you hurt?"

"Just had a big knot on my head. And my pride stung a little. Miz Josie and the sheriff both took off after McDougal, but she wound up letting him escape so she could bring Davis Lee back here because he got shot. The McDougals also killed our stage driver. That man's brother-in-law ended up being the one to bring in the outlaw. Ian McDougal was tried and hanged not long after. Which he should've been, but Loren Barnes had to suffer for his part in it."

"Why?"

"He made an attempt on McDougal's life while the man was in jail here. Loren went to prison, but a lot of people, including the sheriff, didn't think that was right. Davis Lee and his cousin, Jericho Blue, a Texas Ranger, were able to convince the judge to reduce the sentence to nine months. Loren's supposed to get out next month. His sister, Cora, still lives here so I figure he'll be coming back."

"Aren't people afraid?"

"Of Loren? Naw." If they had to talk, Jake would much rather talk about this than anything about himself. He hadn't spoken this long at a stretch since his school days when he'd been required to read aloud from *McGuffey's Reader* every single day. "He was only trying to get justice for his widowed sister."

"Whirlwind seems like such a quiet place."

"It generally is." He glanced over, catching a whiff of her soft scent and the flowers that grew in wild patches across the prairie. "What about where you're from?"

"What do you mean?"

She looked as if he'd caught her sneaking around in the dark. "You come from a big town in Illinois?"

"A little bigger than Whirlwind," she said quietly.

"You got people back there?"

She looked over her shoulder to check on the baby, but Jake got the impression she did it to avoid giving him her full attention. "Like who?"

"Your husband's family or yours, I guess."

"My mother and father are both there. Do you have any family besides the people at the ranch?"

Even now, five years later, it hurt like blue blazes to think about the wife and child he'd lost. "That's it."

"Georgia said Mr. Bram hasn't been here all that long."

Why was Miz York so all-fired interested in his family? Or was it only Bram? "He's a drover."

"Drives cattle?"

He nodded, dark thoughts creeping in. Of his resentment over Delia leaving him the way she had, of her brother, whom Jake didn't want to feel responsible for anymore. "A lot of ranchers are sending their cattle to market and slaughter by train so work on the cattle drives is drying up. Bram came home about five months ago to work with me and Uncle Ike."

"How long have your uncle and Georgia lived with you?"

"Always." His jaw tightened. His whole family lived at the ranch and Jake liked it. Being cast off by their own mother, it was the only home he and Bram had ever known.

For a few short years after marrying, Jake had had all he'd ever wanted except a child with Delia. He'd wanted that more than anything and that desire had killed his wife. Now she was gone and so was his hope of having a family. Pretty much his interest in having one, too.

Jake hoped Miz York would shut up now. He was talked out. She sure did ask a lot of questions for someone who wasn't all that free with information about herself. He didn't mind answering some questions, but when she ventured into territory that made him think about his wife, he'd had enough.

They were less than a mile from the Circle R when a slow shrieking noise split the air. At the same instant Jake realized what it meant, a sharp crack sounded. The wagon hit the ground hard on Miz York's side, the right front wheel splintering.

Before he could grab her, she pitched out of the wagon into the tall grass. She cried out, her skirts flying up to reveal the hem of a petticoat and a flash of white stockings. The crash jolted the baby and she screamed then began to sob. The horse drew up abruptly.

With a sick feeling in his gut, Jake half slid, half scrambled out of the wagon to check the little girl. Though he didn't want to, he moved his hands over her. She was carrying on as if her tail were on fire, but she didn't appear to be hurt. No blood, no scratches, no immediately visible broken bones.

He turned, looking for the baby nurse. Where was she? There, yards away, her pink calico dress almost hidden by the tall grass. He strode toward her. "Miz York!"

He told himself to remain calm, but as he moved, a black rage began to build. Knowing that wheel was weak, he'd told Waylon two days ago to fix it after he and Uncle Ike had returned from Whirlwind. Now Miz York might be hurt. The baby could've been, too.

Jake reached the slight woman just as she pushed herself to a sitting position. Her glasses were gone, tendrils of brown hair escaping from her chignon.

"Are you all right?" He knelt, but she got quickly to her feet, swaying slightly then steadying herself.

"The baby! Where's the baby?"

"She's still in the wagon." He stood.

The nurse rushed past him.

"She's okay. Are you?" A glitter in the grass caught his eye and he picked up her spectacles just before stepping on them. They were scratched, but not broken.

"Did you just leave her there?" Her voice trembled with anger. "Did you check on her at all?"

"Of course I did!" he snapped as he followed her to the wagon. What did she think he was, a coldhearted SOB? "She wasn't bleeding, she wasn't scratched, she didn't appear to be hurt, but I wasn't so sure about you. I'm still not. Did you bust anything?"

"I think I'm fine." Reaching over the side of the wagon, she gathered the sobbing infant to her, cuddling her close and murmuring to her.

He sure couldn't fault her care or concern for that child. As she turned toward him, Jake saw a cut over her left eyebrow and a scratch along the line of her jaw. Fury exploded inside him. His fist closed, nearly crushing her glasses. He ripped off his hat and started toward her.

Her eyes went wide and she backed up so fast she hit the side of the wagon. Her arm came up as if to ward off a blow. "Stay away! Stay back."

"What?" Jake frowned, his gaze skipping over her, looking for further injuries. Maybe she'd taken a hit to the head. Waylon was going to answer for this.

"Stop! Don't come any closer." Holding the baby with one arm, she fumbled at her skirt pocket.

It registered then, how her voice shook, how the color had drained from her face. And Jake understood. She thought he was coming after her. She thought he was going to hit her!

That stopped him cold in his tracks a few feet away from her, cooling the rage pumping through his blood. A deep pain sliced at him. "You think I would hurt you? I would never—"

"Please, please stop." She kept her hand in her pocket.

He realized he had taken another step toward her. He halted, reeling with disbelief and realization. Someone had hit her before. That made Jake angry all over again, but he struggled to keep it from showing.

"I'll back up," he said as he did it. The woman was terrified, her green eyes huge in her pale face. The distrust on her face twisted his gut. "I'm not coming closer, see? I'll stay right here."

After long seconds, she nodded, her pretty eyes full of turmoil.

Crushing his hat in his fist, he said quietly, "I'm sorry. I didn't mean to frighten you."

The wariness in her eyes was so deep, so dark that he wanted to gather her to him and soothe her until she knew there was no need to fear him. But that would probably scare her spitless. "Can you tell me if you're hurt?"

"I'm fine," she said tautly, her arms wrapped so tightly around the baby that the little girl protested with a loud noise.

"You have a cut above your eye. Your left one."

She reached up to touch it, looking surprised at the blood on her fingers. "I'm all right."

She was as frightened and defensive as a wounded animal. He could see she wasn't going to let him get any closer and they needed to get home before dark. "I'll tell you what. I'm gonna unhitch the mare. I'll walk and you and the…baby can ride back to the ranch."

She looked at the horse, then the damaged wagon. "I'll walk, instead," she said quickly.

He started to insist she ride then realized he would have to help her mount. She didn't want him putting his hands on her.

Agreeing to let her walk went against everything his uncle

had taught him about how to treat a lady, but Ike hadn't seen the pure-dee terror in Emma York's face when she'd thought Jake was going to hit her. "Are you sure you won't ride—"

"I'm sure."

The unsteadiness of her voice told him she was still afraid. He didn't blame her. She didn't know him well enough to know that she didn't need to fear him. "If you're in pain or hurt anywhere else," he said gruffly, "I can carry her."

"*I'll* do it."

He knew the relief was plain on his face when her mouth tightened. After placing her glasses carefully on the corner of the lopsided wagon, he walked around the mare's head to the other side. Letting Emma York know she had plenty of room.

Jake jammed his hat on his head. After making sure the mare was uninjured, he unhitched her and looped the wagon reins into one hand. Letting his nurse walk to the ranch, especially carrying the baby, grated hard on him. "You tell me if you need to stop or if something starts hurting."

"I will."

With one last look back at her, he started walking. But she didn't. After a long moment, he finally caught her movement out of the corner of his eye.

Someone—some *man*—had obviously hit her before. Who? When? Was that why she was here? Was she running from someone?

Jake didn't want any trouble, didn't need to get involved in someone else's trouble. He was involved in plenty of his own.

But he couldn't forget the paralyzing fear he'd seen in her face, her eyes. Jake cursed under his breath. He could shine it up any way he wanted, but he was involved.

Chapter Four

⟨⟨⟨⟨⟨⟨⟨⟨⟨⟨∞⟩⟩⟩⟩⟩⟩⟩⟩⟩

Well after dark that night, Emma's nerves were still jumping and it wasn't so much from the wagon accident as it was from the man who now believed she was afraid of him.

The incredulous look in Jake's dark eyes when she'd cowered from him was burned in her brain. He'd quickly masked it, but he had been wounded by her reaction.

She was in the kitchen, where she'd stayed as much as possible since Sheriff Holt's arrival shortly after supper. He and Jake had remained outside until the sun had set.

Georgia had offered to help Emma clean up, but she'd waved off the older woman's assistance. So, Georgia had kept Ike and Molly company in the front room until the older two had brought Emma the baby and gone up to bed a few moments ago. Jake's uncle and cousin seemed to really like the little girl. Everyone did, except Jake.

Emma sang softly to Molly as she swayed back and forth, putting the little girl to sleep. The buttery scent of corn bread and savory meat still lingered in the room. She waited until she could no longer hear the retreating hoofbeats of the sheriff's horse before she stepped out of the kitchen. With

Molly asleep on her shoulder, she scanned the spacious living area for any sign of Jake or his brother.

She caught a movement out of the corner of her eye and glanced over, toward her room. Jake stood in the doorway, his wide shoulders filling the space.

Emma started in surprise. She hadn't heard him come in, let alone make his way to her room.

He looked startled, too, as if *he* were surprised to see *her*.

"Oh. There you are," he said gruffly as he moved to the dining table, staying on the opposite side. "I just wanted to let you know that Davis Lee didn't find anything to help us with that thief, but we'll keep looking. Not just for your, uh—" His gaze skipped away. "You know."

She realized he was trying not to look at her chest. Her corsetless chest. Oh, lands.

"Okay," she said in a half whisper, her own gaze dropping. Heat moved up her neck and into her cheeks. She needed to think of a way to make do until she could get another corset. Maybe two chemises? That sounded miserable in this hot weather.

Hugging the baby close, she moved over to the bearskin rug in front of the fireplace and gently laid down the little girl. The mingled scents of man and horse and outdoors drifted from her boss. When Emma straightened, she saw Jake's big hands curl over the back of a heavy dining-room chair, his knuckles white against the dark bronze of his hands. As if he was trying to keep himself from moving.

And he was, she realized. He was trying to keep some space between them. Again, regret rolled through her. She wanted to apologize for reacting the way she had after the accident, but it was better this way, wasn't it? The less comfortable she became with him—with his family—the easier it would be when she had to leave.

"I don't know if we'll be able to get your clothes back," he said tautly.

She nodded, returning to the table as she adjusted her spectacles. They'd gotten scratched when she'd flown out of the wagon and Jake had picked them up. Which was good, because Emma had forgotten she was supposed to wear them.

Releasing the chair, he stepped away as he gestured at her. "How are you feeling?"

"Fine," she said quietly. Her jaw was sore and scratched and the cut above her left eyebrow stung, but it could've been worse. The baby could've been hurt, too. Georgia had tended Emma, saying the wound wasn't deep enough to require stitches. Thank goodness.

"I'm glad you're all right." The lantern light behind him stretched his shadow across the ceiling and far wall. His dark gaze burned into hers, causing a quiver in her belly. "It never should've happened."

She managed a small smile, her body humming with a low vibration she didn't understand. And a heightened awareness that she and Jake were the only two down here.

The front door opened and they both turned toward the sound. Bram came in, pulling off his dirty cowboy hat and hanging it on the rack behind the door. Red dust floated from his dark hair and rugged work clothes to the floor as he backed into the wall, toeing off one boot then the other.

Jake took a step toward the other man. "Any luck?"

Bram nodded, his gaze going to Emma. "Hi, Miz York."

"Hello. I was just fixing a plate for you. I'll get it."

"Thanks." His voice was gritty with fatigue. "I'm so hungry I could eat my saddle blanket."

She walked the few steps into the kitchen, able to hear their low murmurs and catch a few words. She appreciated that they were keeping their voices down so as not to wake the baby.

Jake had told her earlier that Bram had gone out today with a group of ranchers, all riding fence to check on their cattle. In the last two weeks, the Circle R had lost four prime steers to a rustler. Jake had mentioned that a neighboring spread, the Rocking H, and the nearby Triple B ranch had also lost some prime beef. The Rocking H belonged to Sheriff Holt's brother, Riley, but Emma couldn't remember the name of the other owner. She knew they were both friends of the Ross family.

"We found an old camp and three ash piles." Bram's voice was scratchy with fatigue. "Riley and I figure it's from the fire they used to heat their own brands and change ours."

"A running iron?"

"Yeah."

"They're modifying our brand, Holt's, the Baldwins."

"Yeah, and right now we don't know what mark they're using. Could be a bar, a circle. We just don't know."

"You got a brand book?" Jake asked.

"The last one issued by the livestock association and a copy of *The Prairie Caller* for double-checkin'. There may be some new brands in the paper's latest edition."

Emma knew *The Prairie Caller* was the newspaper in Whirlwind. The newspaper in which Jake had run an ad hoping to get a family for Molly.

"At least the book will show us what's legitimate," Jake said. "Maybe help us figure out the brands that aren't."

The men's voices dropped so low that Emma couldn't hear any more. She uncovered the plate of corn bread and ham she'd put aside for Bram. After removing a cloth from the earthen pitcher of buttermilk, she filled a real glass, then carried it with the plate to the dining-room table. She set down the food, glancing toward the brothers.

Jake's gaze flickered over her, his jaw locking, his eyes

flashing. Apprehension had her going still. Why was he looking at her like that? What were they talking about?

"Well?" Bram leveled a look at his brother.

Jake turned away and started for the stairs. Over his shoulder, he said, "Good night, Miz York."

"Good night."

Bram gave a derisive snort and came to the table. Emma looked from him to Jake, who was already halfway up the stairs. What was going on?

Bram slid into his chair. "This looks really good, ma'am. You're a good cook."

"Thank you, Mr. Ross."

"You'd better call me Bram." His blue eyes twinkled. "You'll talk yourself dizzy calling all three of us Mr. Ross."

"All right." She turned for the kitchen. "I'll be in here, finishing up. If you need anything, let me know."

He nodded, already digging in. Giving one last look to make sure Molly still slept, Emma went back into the kitchen and pumped water into the deep sink. Back in Topeka, her mother's house had boasted an indoor pump and a bathing tub. Emma had been pleasantly surprised to find those conveniences here, too. There was even an oblong bathing tub in her room. Jake Ross and his family must do very well with their ranch.

She washed the bread pans, the griddle, the egg beater and the good china Georgia said had been her mother's, setting everything on the wide counter to the side to hand-dry when she finished rinsing.

As she worked, her mind went again to the wagon accident. Once they'd arrived home, Jake had gotten her and Molly into the house. His jaw had been set, his features cold and intimidating, but he hadn't yelled or punched or threatened the way Emma's stepfather did when he was angry. He had simply said, in a voice vibrating with quiet fury, that he was going back for that busted wheel then would be in the barn fixing it.

Georgia had told her a ranch hand named Waylon was the one who had neglected to fix the wheel when Jake had told him to do so, and he'd been fired. There were enough dangers on a ranch without making their own by being remiss.

"That hit the spot, Miz York," Bram said as he walked into the kitchen.

Jerked out of her thoughts, she smiled over her shoulder at him. "I'm glad you liked it."

"The baby's sleeping real good. I just checked."

"Thank you." She turned and took his plate, their fingers brushing. Emma thought back to when her fingers had touched Jake's yesterday morning at breakfast. His touch had sent heat streaking up her arm and into other places of her body. But she felt nothing like that at his brother's touch.

Bram moved to her other side, snagging a clean dish towel from the rack on the wall beside the sink. "I'll help you dry."

"Oh, no! That's not—"

"Do I smell too much like dirt and cattle?"

He did smell of those things, but Emma didn't find it un-pleasant. She was more worried that someone—Jake—might think she wasn't doing her job if everyone kept helping her all the time. With the back of her hand, she pushed her eye-glasses up. "You look worn out."

"No offense, but so do you. If we work together, we can both turn in sooner."

"Wouldn't you rather eat the last of the apple pie?"

He gave her a sheepish grin. "I thought I might sneak that upstairs."

She laughed as he picked up the skillet and began drying. He glanced over at her. "Jake told me there was a wagon ac-cident today."

She tensed, wondering if his brother had told him why they'd been in the wagon to start with. It was bad enough that Jake knew she wasn't wearing a corset; she would be mortified if he'd told his brother about the theft.

But the other man acted as if he had no idea about her missing undergarment. "It's good the baby's okay, but Jake said you got banged up a bit."

"Just a scrape or two."

"I'm glad it wasn't worse."

"Me, too."

"A busted wheel can be dangerous. Sorry."

"Yes. And loud." She smiled at him, relieved to think that Jake had told his brother only about the wagon accident.

"Did he see anyone in town besides Hoot—"

He broke off abruptly and her gaze swung to his. So, he knew Jake had asked the newspaper man, Mr. Eckert, about the ad regarding Molly.

Bram chewed the inside of his cheek, looking as if he wished he hadn't said that. After a long pause, he continued, "Did he talk to anyone named Quentin?"

"No, only the man from the newspaper." The thought made her mad all over again and she couldn't keep her voice from shaking. She rinsed the coffeepot and began drying. "He just *had* to know if anyone had responded to his ad about a family for Molly."

This time, it was Bram's gaze slicing to her and Emma winced inwardly. She had to watch what she said. Comments like that could anger these men. Any time she had expressed her opinion at home had certainly made her stepfather angry.

But, when Bram spoke, he sounded thoughtful, reassuring. "I don't look for him to find a family. Not one that's suitable, anyway. He won't let her go with anyone if he isn't a hundred percent sure."

Emma didn't see why Jake had to try and give Molly away, at all. She put the clean coffeepot back on the stove, asking softly, "Do you want to give her away, too?"

"No, but I haven't been through what he's—"

Emma glanced up, waiting.

Bram peered hard at the skillet he dried. "He'll come around. He's a tough nut to crack sometimes."

She wanted to believe Bram; he certainly knew his brother better than she did. But what had he meant about Jake? What had he been through?

Before she could ponder too long, the big man beside her stacked the now-clean pans and placed them up on the long shelf that ran the length of the wall behind the sink. He hung the damp towel on the rack.

"Thanks for your help." She dried her hands on her apron.

"You're welcome. You should get some shut-eye. You've had a rough day."

She doused the lantern, then followed him out of the kitchen.

He took care of the lantern at the foot of the stairs then started up, his piece of pie wrapped in a cloth. Pale yellow light washed down the stairs from a hall lamp by the bedrooms. "Good night."

"Good night." She bent and picked up Molly, soothing the little girl when she stirred. In the few steps it took to reach their room, the baby was again deeply asleep.

Emma moved to the bed, noticing a plain brown wrapped package at the foot of the mattress.

Last night, in the middle of the night, the little girl had climbed out and toddled over to Emma. She'd wanted to play and, when Emma had finally gotten Molly back to sleep, she'd kept the baby in bed with her. She couldn't have her sister wandering about at night.

She settled the little girl into the fat mattress, where she would sleep until her bed arrived. Emma folded the blanket to the foot of the bed and left only the top sheet. The nights were too hot for more than one layer. She picked up the package and walked to the washstand against the far wall to turn up the lamp a bit. Amber light flickered on the floor as she sank down into the rocking chair that sat near the window. Tired and sore, Emma took off her glasses and placed them on the washstand. She closed her eyes for a second before unknotting the twine around the package and opening it. She gaped.

A corset!

As her fingers skimmed over the pale colored sateen-weave cotton and cream lace trim at the top, she wavered between embarrassment and pleasure. But, when she touched the satin ribbon threaded through the lace, the embarrassment faded. Jake had gotten her a corset. It had to have been him; no one else knew. How had he done it? When?

The package hadn't been in the wagon; it would've flown out during the accident and Emma would've seen it. She lifted the undergarment, taking note of the fine whalebone, the steel busk at the center front where it hooked together. It was a "spoon busk," curved in at the waist and widened into a pear shape at the bottom. That was what gave it smooth, slim lines, what every fashionable woman wore.

The garment was much finer than Emma's stolen one. She held it up by the side seams to check the width. It would fit. It looked perfect. Her throat tightened.

Jake Ross had gotten her a corset.

She stared in amazement. She had to thank him.

It wouldn't suit to ignore the gesture, regardless of the gift being so intimate. She pushed out of the rocking chair, clasping the undergarment tight as she hurried out of her room. She stopped outside of the door.

Everyone was asleep. Jake probably wouldn't be coming back down here tonight and Emma certainly couldn't go up there. Slowly, she turned and went back into her room, so overwhelmed she felt as if her chest might burst.

Believing her to be afraid, he had kept a marked distance from her ever since they'd reached the ranch. The smart thing to do would be to keep her distance, as well. It was best for her and Molly's safety. But Emma couldn't ignore the gift. She just couldn't. The first time they had a moment alone, she would thank him.

Emma had been wearing her new corset for the last two days and she knew Jake was aware. Three times she had caught his heated gaze on her. But she still hadn't had a single opportunity to thank him alone.

She wanted it done. Maybe then she could stop thinking about him in her room, touching her corset.

It was midafternoon and Georgia had gone into town for a Saturday meeting with the library committee. The men were out stringing fence. Emma had heard more talk last night as they'd tried to decide how to set a trap for the cattle rustlers.

About a half hour ago, Emma had put the baby down for her nap then swept and dusted the rooms upstairs. Now she surveyed the freshly scrubbed kitchen floor and fanned herself with one hand. Perspiration trickled between her breasts and down her spine, and she plucked the light cotton dress away from her skin. Pushing back the hair that had come loose from her braid, she undid the top two buttons on her bodice.

Since it appeared she wasn't ever going to be able to talk to Jake alone, she would write him a thank-you note. She walked across the room to the big oak desk that sat in a space off the living area. A quill pen and ink well rested on the far corner, but Emma saw no paper.

She doubted anyone would mind if she borrowed the pen and ink. Just as she reached for it, the front door slammed open.

She whirled around as Jake stalked to the dining table, his boot heels thudding heavily on the wood floor. The door swung shut, a wave of hot air rolling inside. What was he doing home in the middle of the day?

He lowered himself into the nearest chair, cursing under his breath. Worn leather gloves came off then hit the table's surface as he twisted, trying to see his left side.

"What happened?"

His gaze jerked to her, plainly surprised at her presence. As she drew even with the chair, she saw his side. And the way his pale blue shirt stuck to him. Blood! She gasped. "You're hurt!"

His shirt was ripped from just below his ribs and around to his back. "Damn—danged barbed wire came loose and caught me."

Beneath the torn fabric, Emma caught a glimpse of whitish pink ragged skin. She swallowed hard. "It looks bad."

"Get Georgia. She'll be able to tell—" He broke off with a hiss. "I forgot she's gone."

"I can help you." She pulled her gaze from the wound. "Just tell me what to do."

"Are you sure?" His chiseled features were pulled tight, his eyes narrowed to slits. He pulled off his cowboy hat and dropped it on the table over his gloves, glancing up. "You look wobbly."

She'd treated only burns and bruises and less serious cuts, but she could do this. "What do you need?"

"Water and soap, carbolic acid." His voice was thin.

"That's in the brown bottle, in the space between the kitchen's sink and the wall."

She hurried to get the things and returned with them as well as the scissors and a few clean cloths. He had his shirt pulled up to the middle of his torso, straining to look under his arm and see the wound. His chest was leanly muscled and tanned, his stomach hard sinew. A moderate dusting of black hair covered his chest. The sight of him set her pulse to pounding until she saw the smear of blood at his waist.

That shook some sense into her. She went to him, setting the bottle of antiseptic on the table along with the bowl of water and the soap. "Hold up your arms and I'll slide off your shirt. I'll be as gentle as I can."

He gingerly lifted his arms over his head and she reached down to grasp the hem and pull the garment off. He smelled of heat and man and sunshine. And his skin was hot, she realized as her hands skimmed up his arms along with the shirtsleeves.

He barely felt her touch before his shirt was gone. She was quick, which Jake appreciated. But it was her fault he'd had the accident in the first place. Her fault that his side was torn up and pain skewering him like a pike.

And why? Because he'd been thinking about the first time she'd worn that damn corset and how she'd turned a pretty shade of pink every time she had looked at him during breakfast. On account of that, he hadn't been paying full attention to the fence and a tack had popped loose before he had noticed it wasn't hammered in solidly. The barbed wire had snapped back before he could move.

She placed his bloody shirt on the table, hesitating over her next move.

"You need to look at it and tell me if you think it needs stitches. I can't see back there well enough to tell."

"All right." She took a deep breath and moved to his side.

As she studied the wound with a tiny frown, the color leached out of her face. "I can't tell. I need to clean it, first."

He grunted, giving a sharp nod. The gash hurt like hellfire and he tried to level out his breathing.

"I don't want to hurt you."

"You just gotta do it, Emma," he said in a guttural voice. "'Cuz I can't."

"All right." She opened the bottle of carbolic acid and dampened a clean cloth; then, looking apprehensive, she touched it to his skin.

Gripping the table's edge to keep from jerking away, he couldn't hold back a groan. Sweat broke out on his face. It burned like a son of a bitch!

She drew in a sharp breath as she probed around the wound. Though she was gentle, Jake wished for a piece of wood to bite because he was about to holler like a branded calf.

She knelt on the floor beside his chair, her head barely reaching his shoulder. "I don't think you need stitches and I think I cleaned it well."

"Good. That's good," he panted, blowing air as hard as a winded horse in an effort to control the pain.

She cut a strip of cloth and folded it until she had a thick pad. Still on her knees, she laid the bandage the length of the wound and held it there, then began wrapping the longer piece of cloth around him.

"I can hold it," he offered roughly.

"All right."

He put his hand over hers, noticing the blood on her fingers and his as she slid her hand from under his. Light glanced off her gold wedding band.

Her hair tickled his chin as she leaned forward under his arm to run the cloth across his torso and bring it fully around his body. The delicate scent of woman drifted to him and he glanced down. Her bodice was unbuttoned just enough to show the hollow of her throat and the dampness of her skin, but it was the sudden wash of her breath against his bare belly that had him sucking in a deep breath.

"I'm sorry," she murmured, obviously thinking she'd hurt him.

Hellfire. He tried to keep his thoughts away from her, but he couldn't ignore her. He wanted to touch her dewy skin just once. Wanted to *taste* her.

"Do you have something to dull the pain? Should I get it?"

"No, that's all right." He would've liked a bottle of whiskey right now to help dull his awareness of *her,* but something held him back. "If you were sewing me up, I might reconsider."

As she started a second layer around his waist, her breasts brushed against him. Biting off a curse, he closed his eyes, trying to squeeze out the images of her without that corset, the ache that went clear to his gut.

As Emma bandaged his wound, she knew she had to take this chance to thank him for replacing her corset. She reached around and grasped the end of the bandage with her free hand, trying to gather her courage.

Just say it. She'd already said the word *corset* around him more times than she'd said it in her whole life, but she still hesitated. Rolling the strip of cloth across his back, she finally managed to say, "Thank you for the corset."

His eyes flew open. Deep rose flushed her cheeks, but she held his gaze. "That was so kind. I didn't— I wasn't sure—"

He could tell it was difficult for her to address the subject and he was hit with an unexpected urge to stroke her cheek. Which had him clenching his jaw in irritation.

"I'd like to pay you for it."

"No. Your property was stolen off my land. It's only fitting that I get you another one."

After a long moment, she said quietly, "No one's ever done anything like that for me before. I won't forget it."

"You're welcome." The softness in her green eyes pulled hard at his gut and his words came out more gruffly than he'd intended.

"How did you know what size?" She adjusted her glasses then leaned forward, smoothing another layer of cloth across his torso. "And how did you get it here without me seeing it?"

"Josie, the sheriff's wife, did everything. All I did was ask her to pick one out for you at the general store. She could've made you one, but I figured you'd want it sooner rather than later."

Truth be told, Jake had cussed himself twice today for buying it. He had liked knowing there was only soft woman and a thin chemise beneath her bodice. And he liked knowing that he was the only one privy to that information.

Whoa. It was exactly those thoughts that had stirred his blood so much the last couple of days that he'd had to stay out of the house as much as possible. Those thoughts that had gotten his side ripped up. He had no business thinking about being with Emma York, especially when he had no intention of going down that trail with her.

"The package couldn't have been in the wagon," she mused, easing back to look at her handiwork. "It would've flown out when we did."

She gave him a careful smile. She did a lot of things carefully, Jake realized. As if she was wary of people's reactions. "Uh, Davis Lee brought it when he came out that evening."

Her eyes widened in horror and he hurried to add, "He didn't know what was in it."

"Good," she breathed, relief plain on her delicate features.

Her scrapes from the wagon accident appeared to be healing. She tied off the bandage and rose, eyeing her work.

Jake looked down at the neat binding and its single dangling end. "That's a fine job, Miz York."

He reached for the scissors at the same time she did and their fingers brushed. They both went still. Sensation shot up Jake's arm. He told himself to pull away, but, instead, he turned his palm up and let his fingertips rest lightly against hers.

She trembled, but didn't move her hand. She stared down with a wary kind of amazement.

"Miz York, after the wagon accident—" He broke off, cleared his throat. No woman had ever looked at him with fear in her eyes and he hadn't liked it. The memory had eaten on him the last two days. "I don't know who hurt you, but you don't have to worry about that here. Not ever."

She looked stricken and, for a long moment, her gaze stayed locked on their fingers. When she finally regarded him, her eyes were suspiciously bright behind her lenses. "I'm sorry for thinking such a thing of you. I...shouldn't have assumed the worst."

"No need to apologize. I figure you have your reasons. All I want is to put your mind at ease."

She had intended to avoid the subject. She wished he had. But what had her nerves wound tight was the fact that she was touching him. Practically holding his big hand. And she didn't want to pull away. Stunned at the realization, she nearly missed his next words.

"You don't know me well enough yet, but you'll come to see that I won't ever hurt you. Nobody here will."

His gaze roved over her face, pausing on her mouth. She held her breath. She told herself to close her eyes, to stop looking at him, but she couldn't. His eyes were so black, so hot and, when his gaze met hers again, sensation shot through her clear to her toes.

Jake leaned toward her, barely moving a muscle. She stilled, looking at his mouth. His fingers curled against hers, bringing her a tiny bit closer.

The loud thud of boots had them jumping apart. They dropped their hold just as the front door opened.

Blushing deeply, Emma gathered the water, soap and antiseptic as Jake caught sight of his uncle. After getting cut up with that fence wire, Jake had fired a single rifle shot, the signal they'd agreed on to mean one of them was hurt.

"I heard your gunshot, but it took me a while to make it back." Ike's gaze went to Emma. "Oh, good, Miz York's here."

"Yeah," Jake said in a gravelly voice, astounded at what he'd almost done. What *they'd* almost done. Gesturing to his wound, he told his uncle what had happened.

The older man grimaced, pushing his dusty hat back on his head and giving Emma a grateful smile. "Thanks for tending him, Miz York."

"Certainly. If you'll excuse me, I'll clean up."

Jake grabbed the scissors and trimmed the bandage. He didn't miss her subdued tone of voice or the way she kept her eyes averted. He wasn't sure why she wouldn't look at him, but he knew why he couldn't look at her.

Because he wanted to get his hands on her. He wanted to peel off that damn corset and—

He reeled with the realization that if his uncle hadn't come in, he might have kissed her.

Hell, he *would* have. And he thought she might have let him.

As much as he didn't like it, he felt something for her. He told himself it was responsibility. After all, she was under his protection now. But responsibility didn't have one blamed thing to do with wanting to kiss her. Or see her naked.

If Ike hadn't interrupted, what would've happened? Nothing, Jake ruthlessly told himself. Not one thing. Because he just wouldn't let it.

Chapter Five

He should've kissed her. Eight hours later, the want still hammered at him. After Emma had bandaged him that afternoon, Jake had gone to the barn until supper. His body had been tight all over and he'd known he should be glad his uncle had walked in on them. But glad wasn't what Jake had felt.

Because of his injury, he couldn't return to work on the fence today so he'd decided to finish repairs on a saddle and some tack. He'd thought he had the desire under control, but seeing her at supper had wound him up all over again.

As if no time had passed, he could still feel the soft stroke of her hands, her breath on his belly. And he kept picturing her pretty mouth on other parts of his body. So here he was, back in the barn, repairing a worn cinch. A job that should've taken a couple of hours had stretched into twice that. Because of her.

She was in his head. And he was damn good and ready to get rid of her.

Ever since she had fixed him up, a hollow ache had bored a hole through him. Everyone had gone to bed long ago. Jake had thought he would be ready to do the same by now, but as restless, as edgy as he felt, sleep wasn't coming any time soon.

Frustrated, he flipped the unfinished cinch over the saddle seat and laid down his stitching awl. He walked from the saw-horse over to the ladder then climbed up to the loft. Moon-light streamed through the open loft door. A staggered stack of hay bales angled toward the opening, which allowed them to lower what they needed from the upper barn floor with-out carrying it down the ladder. Jake eased down against the bales, hay scratching his shoulders and back through his shirt.

Reaching behind him and between two bales, he pulled out a bottle. Brand new, full. The glass winked in the play of shadow and light, the amber liquid sloshing as he opened the bottle.

Bending his knees, he laid his head back and tried to blank his mind. He stared out at the fat white moon and the stars twinkling on the night sky as he took a long pull of whiskey. It burned going down, a tingle, numbness then warmth. Touched the cold dead place inside him that had been there since Delia and the baby had gone. He took another long swallow. Then another. And another.

Sometime later, he got to his feet, swaying a bit. He wasn't sure how long he'd been out here. Bleary-eyed, he squinted at the bottle in his hand and saw that it was more than three-quarters gone.

From the loft, he could see the front of the house. It was dark. Everyone was in bed. *Emma* was in bed.

No, don't think about her. Gripping the liquor bottle, Jake slowly made his way down the ladder, getting his bearings when his feet hit dirt.

Dust stirred around his boots as he wove his way to the house. After two attempts, he managed to get inside. He carefully shut the door behind him. The room swam and he leaned against the wall until it stopped.

Unsteady on his feet, he started toward the sofa, his boots crashing against the floor like thunder. Loud, too loud. Had to get those off. He changed direction and went to the dining table, setting down the whiskey. With both hands curled over the table's edge, he managed to toe off his right boot. He slid it onto the table and started working on the other one.

A hoarse cry shattered the quiet and Jake started violently. His wound pulled hard, pain arrowing through him. The noise had come from Emma's room. Hadn't it?

He heard another sound, this one muffled and more prolonged. Yeah, definitely Emma's room.

Keeping his balance with one hand on the table, Jake eased up its length and took the two steps to her door. Hit with a sudden dizziness, he rested his forehead against the door and braced his left arm on the frame. More muffled sounds came from inside.

"Emma?" he whispered.

No answer. Jake whispered louder, "Emma? Emma, c'mout."

The door opened slightly, and he saved himself from stumbling by gripping the door frame. She peeked out at him without her spectacles, her dark silky hair loose around her shoulders.

He peered hard at her. "Are you okay? I heard a noise."

"I'm fine," she said in a low voice.

"Lemme see." When she didn't move, he clumsily motioned her out, raising his voice. "Lemme."

Frowning, she glanced over her shoulder, then pulled the door wider to step into the opening. Pale light streamed through the window across the room, shifting on the floor behind her, silhouetting her slender curves. Her wrapper was belted loosely, as if she'd donned it hurriedly. The light cotton of her night rail showed in the robe's vee lapels and he thought he could see the valley between her breasts.

Following his gaze, she stiffly pulled the edges of her wrapper together. "Are you all right? Do you need me to look at your bandage?"

He shook his head, bending close to squint at her. "Were you crying?"

"No," she answered breathlessly. Upon opening the door, she'd caught the scent of liquor. How much had he drunk?

"You cried out."

"Did I?" She pressed her spine against the opposite jamb. Her chest was tight and she couldn't catch her breath. She didn't know if it was due to the nightmare that had yanked her awake or the big man taking up far more of her space than she liked. "I...just couldn't sleep."

"Me, neither." His gaze roamed over her hair and lingered where the weight of it hung over her left shoulder and lay on her breast. He waggled a finger toward the dining table. "Want some whiskey?"

"No." Despite the poor light, she could see the heat in his gaze and sensation rippled up her spine. "Thank you."

"It doesn't work, anyway. You're still in my head. You been there all damn day."

Before she knew what he was about, he dipped his head, his whisker-roughened cheek touching her soft one. A rumble sounded in his chest.

The husky pleasure in his voice nearly buckled her knees. He nuzzled her hair and her heart kicked hard in her chest. The surprise of his actions held her in place.

"You smell good, like soap."

Probably because she'd bathed then sat in the tub with the dark rinse on her hair.

He must be very drunk. She stayed motionless, reassured by the fact that she could reach into her pocket for her derringer if she had to, but something told her Jake wouldn't hurt her.

His breath tickled her ear and she started to tremble. Her hand rose involuntarily to his chest to steady herself. Beneath her touch was hard, hot muscle; the tuft of dark hair at the top of his unbuttoned shirt placket tickled the tips of her fingers. Sensation tugged deep in her belly. Mercy.

He pulled back slightly, warm breath washing against her temple. "You're not wearing your spectacles."

He said it in the same tone he might've said, "You're not wearing any clothes."

Rattled by the way her body went soft, she retorted, "Well, I don't sleep in them."

Evidently, her mind had softened, too, because she had an overwhelming urge to bury her face in his chest, breathe in the scents of leather and the outdoors and an earthy darkness that was all Jake's.

He slouched against the door frame, his gaze heavy-lidded and slumberous. "I think you've got the prettiest eyes I've ever seen."

Her spine stiffened. "Mr. Ross, I don't think—"

"You're some woman, Emma. Is there anything you can't do? If there is, I sure haven't seen it."

To her dismay, tears stung her eyes. No one had ever said such a thing to her before.

"You take care of that kid, this house, my family. Me. You take real good care of me," he murmured.

Oh, my. Emma knew he was drunk, but she was affected anyway. The deep bass of his voice stroked over her like a touch. She should go back into her room, but she didn't want to move. She'd never felt anything like this. Fascinated and curious and…a little wicked. "Mr. Ross, it's late. You should probably turn in."

"Okay." He straightened as if to leave, then gazed earnestly down at her. "I wouldn't have kissed you today."

She blinked, her hands clutching at the rough wood jamb behind her. "Wh-what?"

"I mean, not because I didn't want to. Because I did. Real bad. But because I shouldn't. Kiss you, I mean."

Her head was spinning. Heat traveled through her body, tingling in her fingertips. "All right."

"Kissing's not a good idea, because you work for me."

Dazed, she could only nod.

"I'm sorry."

He hadn't kissed her. He'd barely touched her. She struggled to catch up. "For what?"

"For not kissing you."

Who would have thought her quiet, serious boss could make her smile? "Mr. Ross, I really think you should go."

"Yeah." He looked toward the living area, narrowing his eyes before he began to move cautiously in that direction.

Holding the edges of her wrapper together, Emma watched. He made it as far as the long sofa then eased down, looking as if he couldn't remember why he was there. After a moment, he stretched out on his back, one boot dangling off the end of the couch.

Emma waited a long moment. When he didn't move, she crept toward him. Taking his boot and the whiskey bottle from the table, she placed them on the floor near his head. She turned and gathered up a quilt Georgia had draped over one of the large chairs, rolled it into a makeshift pillow and gingerly lifted his head to slide it underneath.

He didn't stir, didn't blink. His chest rose and fell evenly, but her heart still raced from their exchange.

She didn't know what to think about the things he'd said. The way just his breath had struck sparks inside her. Emma told herself to go back to her room, but her feet wouldn't move. He was so big. His hands could easily span her waist. Her neck. He could've done much more than nuzzle her earlier. He could've done whatever he wanted, but she hadn't felt threatened by him.

Instead, she'd felt the same hot flutter in her stomach that she had the night she'd encountered him in the kitchen, the night her corset had been stolen. Excitement, she identified. And anticipation.

His features were roughly sculpted. Just like his body. Wide shoulders, lean waist, strong muscular thighs. His wearing one boot and one sock made him less intimidating. Every part of him was iron hard and powerful, except his lush dark eyelashes. And his mouth. Both kept his features from being too harsh.

She studied his lips for a long moment, unable to stop wondering what it would have felt like if he'd kissed her.

Suddenly she was aware that she'd reached out to touch his hair. She wanted to sink her hands into all of its thick softness. Jerking back, she stepped away.

Heat flushed her whole body as she remembered the feel of his cheek against hers, the intimate tone in his voice. Annoyed, she shook her head. She should've gone back inside the minute he'd bent down to her. She should never have opened the door to him. But she had and she wished he'd kissed her even though it was a bad idea for a lot of reasons. Feelings like this were dangerous, whittled away the guard she worked so hard to maintain. That she *had* to maintain.

Why did he have to affect her this way? Why him? Why now? Her body still quivered and it wasn't because of her frequent nightmare.

It was because of the charming man she'd glimpsed beneath Jake's usual toughness.

If there was a hole in hell, he was in it. Even Jake's eyeballs throbbed and it took a few seconds before he could pry his lids open. The sun gleaming through the window beyond the dining table still held a tint of early-morning gray, but it burned his eyes just as sharply as the noontime sun.

He squinted at the ceiling, gathering the fuzzy edges of his mind together. He was on the sofa, his sofa. Good. He had dreamed…he was with Emma. Not good.

He levered himself up to a sitting position and groaned, grabbing his head. With sluggish movements, he got his feet to the floor then braced his elbows on his knees, still clutching his skull. Hell, his head hurt so bad he'd have to be dead for two days before it stopped.

The whiskey was punishing him now and he resented it since the liquor hadn't even helped last night. At least not as much as he'd needed. He'd still thought about Emma. The wound in his side burned and the warm stickiness beneath his bandage probably meant it was bleeding.

As some of the fog cleared from his mind, he realized he wore only one boot. He caught sight of the other one set neatly to his right, alongside his Old Farm whiskey. He hadn't put either of those things there. Something gnawed at him. Something about last night.

It hadn't been Georgia who'd arranged the items. It had been Emma. That realization sparked an image of her green eyes wide with shock. Jake's gut twisted up like rusted wire.

He'd seen her after coming in from the barn. He remembered that. His mouth felt thick and dirt-dry. Trying to drag the memory of last night from his whiskey-soaked brain had his head pounding like a hammer on an anvil. Sliding a look over to her room, Jake recalled him and Emma standing in the darkened doorway of her bedroom.

He tried to think around the agony searing his brain. What had happened? He'd offered her whiskey and…

He groaned, which only sharpened the pain in his skull. He had to get out of here. Gritting his teeth in agony, he pulled on his right boot and stood. Though wobbly, he headed for the door and the outside pump.

The thud of footsteps upstairs told him everyone was awake and getting dressed for church. He hadn't seen Emma and he planned to get outside before he did.

Rounding the sofa, he headed for the front door just as she stepped out of the kitchen with a plate of biscuits. She saw him and faltered, blushing three shades of red.

Oh, hell and back. Setting the food hastily on the table, she turned in a swirl of skirts and ducked back into the kitchen. If possible, Jake's head pounded harder. He needed to talk to her, but he wasn't up for it yet. Clearing out fast, he made for the pump beside the barn.

After two quick pulls on the handle, he stuck his head under the gush of cold water. The immediate shock against his warm skin sent an arrow of pain through his skull, then it started to ease. He washed out his mouth, then gulped a handful of water. Maybe he should keep his head under here for a while. Until he drowned.

As his thoughts gradually cleared, he realized he'd been in this same condition last Sunday. Which meant he'd gotten drunk two Saturdays in a row. Hanging his head between his arms, he let water run from his hair and face into the tin trough. The neck and shoulders of his shirt were wet.

Emma couldn't even look at him, which meant whatever he'd done was bad. *Jackass.*

She'd cried out, he recalled, and that was why he'd gone to her door. And then…a series of impressions. The scent of sweet woman. Soft skin against his face, silky hair in his fingers. He froze. He'd touched her. Nuzzled her cheek with his.

Grabbing the pump handle, Jake stuck his head back under the hard stream of water. What if he'd tried to kiss her? That had been all he could think about yesterday. The reason he'd downed that bottle of liquor. Was that it? Was that *all?*

Why had she blushed like fire when she'd seen him? His thoughts were muddled. He wasn't sure what was real and what he had dreamed, but he knew what he had to do about it. Apologize.

Ten minutes later, he was seated at the dining table with the rest of the family. Biscuits and ham and eggs were mounded high on platters in the center of the table. Places were set, steam rising from the coffee cups. No sign of Emma or the baby. He realized he hadn't seen Molly with Emma earlier, either.

Everyone was talking about their plans for after church. Bram and Uncle Ike wanted to speak with Riley Holt and the Baldwin brothers about their missing cattle. Georgia had arranged to trade quilt squares with Cora Wilkes. Jake murmured in the appropriate places, but his brain was working double time to try and remember everything that had gone on last night between him and the baby nurse.

She appeared, leaving another plate of eggs then refilling their coffee. Bram spoke to her; she responded with a smile. Ike told her something the baby had done; she laughed. Georgia asked about Molly's whereabouts and Emma said the baby was in the kitchen with her. Then she slipped away like smoke. She never looked at him. Not once.

The minutes crawled by until, finally, breakfast was over. Once everyone finished their last-minute grooming, they started outside for the wagon.

When the rest of his family was out of the house, Jake paced back and forth between the sofa and the dining table. Emma wasn't coming out to clear the dishes. That probably meant she was waiting on him to leave. He'd sure like to, but he couldn't. Not yet.

He sucked in a deep breath, as nervous as a crippled fly in a spiderweb. His feet were cold; his neck was hot. He'd hoped to recollect a few more details, but this couldn't be put off any longer. He went to the kitchen and stepped inside.

She stood with her back to him, holding the baby on one hip and reaching into the dry sink with the other.

"Miz York?" he said hoarsely.

Her spine went as stiff as a wagon axle, but she didn't turn around. She didn't move at all. The baby did, though, staring at him as she squirmed in Emma's arms and flapped her little hand in his direction.

The air in here was suddenly stifling, suffocating, but Jake knew he had to plow on. "I want to apologize for last night."

She remained silent and motionless.

He didn't know whether he was concerned or impatient. Both. "Miz York, are you all right?"

Molly blinked her wide eyes at him, but Emma didn't move, didn't speak. He couldn't even tell if she was breathing. Damn.

Jake ground his teeth. He hated this. Even on his best day, his conversation was awkward. Being with her just made it worse. Words jammed in his throat like wood and his chest squeezed tight. He shoved a hand through his damp hair. "Miz York—Emma. Please look at me."

Finally, *finally* she turned toward him, though she managed to keep her face mostly obscured by the infant.

"I know I shouldn't have come to your room last night."

Around the baby's chubby body, Jake could see a deep flush rise on Emma's neck and work its way to her cheeks.

"All right." She wouldn't meet his eyes.

All right. Not sure where to start, he fumbled through his thoughts. "I'm not exactly sure what all I did, I mean, what all we talked about last night."

A quick flash of hurt darkened her eyes then was gone. She didn't offer to refresh his memory.

He rubbed his nape, now clammy with nerves. "Did I… hurt you?"

She opened her mouth, then made a low sound of distress. Before he could ask what was wrong, she thrust the baby at him. What the hell!

She lunged to the side and Jake saw that the soup pot was boiling over. His hold tightened reflexively on the little girl to keep from dropping her. Emma wrapped the edges of her apron around her hands and quickly moved the pot from the stove to the counter behind her.

Jake stood there like a lifeless lump, staring into the kid's innocent gray-green eyes. Her hand patted his mouth and she planted a wet kiss on his chin. His heart thudded hard and panic streaked through him. Gruffly, he said, "I don't know what I'm supposed to do with her."

"Just hold her."

He looked at the kid. The kid looked at him.

Emma opened the stove door and picked up the nearby poker to distribute the embers more evenly, her movements efficient and competent. Molly gurgled and clumsily grabbed at his face. A sharp pain razored straight through him.

Agonizing and, at the same time, amazing. The weight of her tiny body reminded him of the baby he had never gotten to hold. Would this have been the way he felt about his own child? This terrifying, exhilarating sense that his heart could crack open any minute.

Emma wiped her hands on her apron then turned and slid

the baby from his hold. The look on his face drew her up short. He stared at the child as if he wasn't sure she was real.

The man vexed her. And confused her. Emma didn't quite know how to act. She'd thought—hoped—that seeing him once this morning would've lessened her embarrassment, but it hadn't. If anything, she was more aware of him. Beneath the scents of fresh air and clean man was a hint of whiskey. She knew the rough velvet feel of his face against hers, the granite-hard brawn of his chest.

Trying to calm her racing heartbeat, she looked away. She'd had suitors, but, if they hadn't met Orson's expectations, he'd gotten rid of them. She'd never been involved with any of them long enough to become comfortable. And none of the ones she'd preferred had ever wanted her badly enough to try again.

What had happened last night was the closest Emma had been to a man who attracted her and she had no idea what to do. She knew Jake wasn't courting her. And, if he was, she couldn't allow it. But that didn't stop her from wishing things were different.

He grimaced. "I touched you, didn't I?"

Was the thought so distasteful to him? She realized then. "You don't remember," she said in flat disbelief.

He'd said he couldn't drink her out of his head. She'd been beside herself all night and he didn't even recollect! What had happened between them, slight as it was, had kept her tossing until morning with no thoughts of anyone but Jake.

"You can't even look at me." His jaw tightened. "Did I take liberties? Did I do anything to frighten you?"

She *should've* been frightened, but instead she'd been intrigued. She had wanted to know more about him. Why had he been drinking? How often did he do that? Last night had sparked interest in her, but, to him, it had been forgettable.

It was just as well she'd decided to avoid him. Which she'd been doing just fine until he ruined it by coming in here.

His dark gaze leveled on hers, earnest and piercing. "Emma, please, will you accept my apology?"

She was glad she hadn't completely lost her wits and confided in him about her mother and her horrid stepfather. "But you don't know why you're offering one. Maybe you don't need to."

"Why don't you tell me so I'll know?"

She should, she supposed. But it pricked her pride that he couldn't recall it on his own. She should be glad he didn't remember. That would make it easier for *her* to forget. It wasn't as if those few secret moments would lead to anything, anyway. Even if she could stay—which she couldn't—she wasn't who he thought she was and she couldn't tell him the truth about that. It was too dangerous. Better to leave it all in the past.

"Emma?"

"Let's just forget anything ever happened. Or, well, I'll forget like you did."

The calm tone of her voice belied the tight set of her mouth. She was insulted, Jake realized in amazement. It wasn't as if he'd meant to forget. Hell, he'd never meant for it to *happen*. Whatever *it* was.

Whatever he'd done with her—*to her*—last night didn't seem to bother her nearly as much as the fact that he couldn't recall it. This woman could drive him crazy. He wanted to kiss her, give her something they'd both remember, which made him feel about as smart as a rock.

"I'm sorry for whatever I did." Jaw tight, he strode across the kitchen to the outside door. "And whatever else I might do."

The door banged shut behind him. There, he'd apologized. Now all he had to do was stay the hell away from her.

Chapter Six

All week, Jake had wanted Emma just as badly as he wanted whiskey. All week, his nerves had wound tighter and tighter. He would never have *her*, but as soon as he finished his bi-weekly visit with Quentin, Jake was headed for a bottle. As he rode through Whirlwind and to his brother-in-law's house, his thoughts were irritatingly fixed on the woman he should consider only an employee.

She was nothing like his vivacious, chatty wife had been. He didn't feel anything for Emma like what he'd felt for Delia, so why couldn't he stop thinking about the bespectacled nurse who worked for him? Yeah, he wanted her, but that didn't mean he had feelings for her.

Staying away from her wasn't the problem. It was the hold she had on his thoughts. He had kept his distance this past week, even after he'd finally recalled most of what had happened the night he'd gone to her room. Especially then.

Apologizing for not kissing her? Telling her she was some kind of woman?

Jake remembered it all, but he saw no reason to mention it. He'd bumbled his apology badly enough; he didn't need another go at it. After telling her that she didn't need to fear anyone at the Circle R, what had he done? Gone to her room, drunk.

As he reached the Prescott house on the northwest end of Whirlwind, the usual dread and reluctance burrowed in. Being inside the house where his wife and her brother had grown up brought everything about Delia sweeping back. The guilt, the anger, the emptiness. And now, somehow, Emma was all tangled up in that.

Jake rubbed a hand down his face, aching for a drink, ready to crawl out of his skin. He dismounted in front of the modest white house distinguished by a fancy arched window over the door and a steep roof. After shifting his holster, he looped his reins over the porch railing. He left his rifle in the scabbard on the saddle.

May Haskell, whom Jake paid to cook and clean and wash for Quentin, didn't stop by on Saturdays so Quentin would be here alone. Glancing over his shoulder, Jake's gaze honed in on the back side of Pete Carter's saloon. The sooner Jake was done, the sooner he could get that drink.

As Jake stepped up on the wide porch that stretched the width of the house, a crash sounded inside. Then a curse. He reached the door in one stride and pounded hard, opening it as he did. His brother-in-law lay on his side, trying to push himself up with one hand while bracing the other against the wood floor. The thin, wasted man cursed viciously enough that Jake winced.

The wheelchair had also toppled over and Quentin reached for the closest arm, pulling it toward him. Then he saw Jake, leveled a slit-eyed stare at him. The man who'd once treated Jake like a brother now hated his guts and Jake couldn't rightly blame him.

He knew better than to lend Quentin a hand without being

asked, so Jake righted the chair, then looked questioningly at his brother-in-law. There was nothing to support the man's weight. The dining table was across the room and Quentin couldn't reach high enough to grab the edge of the solidly built cupboard behind him.

Jake gestured to the wheelchair. "Will you let me help you?"

"Who better to do it?" the man snapped, sweat slicking his dark hair to his forehead. "Since you're the one who put me in it to start with."

Jake ignored the cutting remark. It wasn't the first time he'd heard it. Five years ago, the day Delia and the baby had died, Quentin had ambushed him in a barrage of bullets. At first, Jake had refused to shoot, but, when one of Quentin's shots had skimmed Jake's scalp, instinct had kicked in and he'd fired.

Quentin had gone down. And Jake had been paying for it ever since he'd learned that his bullet had hit Quentin's spine and he would never walk again. Jake had shot in self-defense, but that didn't make it any easier to swallow.

He shrugged against the cold sweat that prickled his nape. Curling his forearms under Quentin's arms, Jake lifted the man as Quentin gripped the chair beneath him.

He sank down, immediately rolling away then swinging back to face Jake. Quentin's string-thin mustache accented his sharp features and cold eyes.

Jake pulled off his hat and thumbed sweat from his forehead. "I checked your wood bin when I came in. I'll fill that up before I leave so you can use your cookstove. And there's a plank on your porch that needs to be replaced."

Quentin nodded.

"Anything else you need?"

"No."

Jake figured part of the tension in his brother-in-law's voice was on account of Jake's walking in on Quentin's fall. "I'll get over to Haskell's and pick up the lumber to fix your porch, then I'll stop by Pearl's and bring you back a pecan pie."

"I'll get the pie myself." Hazel eyes, the same color as Delia's, glittered like shards of glass. "I can still do some things."

Jake nodded. He'd learned a long time ago to let Quentin do for himself as much as he was able. Just as Jake turned for the door, a knock sounded.

"You can get it," Quentin ordered.

Jake opened the door to find Davis Lee. The two men exchanged greetings as the sheriff walked inside. Jake told the lawman he was headed to Haskell's General Store and started to leave.

Davis Lee shook hands with Quentin. "Got your message that you needed to see me."

"Yeah. My new handsaw files and my bucksaw are missing. Last night, they were outside with my other tools and today they're gone."

His brother-in-law's words had Jake pivoting slowly. A simmer started in his blood. Why hadn't Quentin told him about the stolen tools? As a part-time deputy, Jake was working with Davis Lee on the recurring thefts. Quentin knew that, as well as he'd known that Jake would be by today, but he'd sent for Davis Lee. Jake's jaw clamped tight.

Studying Quentin, Davis Lee raised an eyebrow and hitched his thumb toward Jake. "You know, Jake is helping me with these thefts?"

"I figured."

An impatient look flashed across the sheriff's face and he braced his hands on his hips. Just like everyone else in town, he knew how antagonistic Quentin was toward Jake. "You could've saved me some time by telling Jake, since he was already here. He would've reported it to me."

The other man didn't miss a beat. "I wanted to tell the real law."

Trying to rein in his anger, Jake shifted his gaze to the glass-front cabinet where the few pieces of Delia's family china were displayed. After her death, Jake had returned them to her brother. He hadn't been able to look at the pieces day after day, facing the reminder that she was gone. Now, when he came to this house, he could see her in the front room at his ranch, carefully unpacking them. Some days he even caught a whiff of her rosewater scent.

His throat tightened. They'd been married almost as long as she'd been gone. The room closed in on him and he shifted his shoulders against the sense of being trapped like a calf in a pen.

The sheriff asked a few more questions, then had Quentin show him where he stored his tools. Outside, by the back door, Davis Lee took a careful look around as did Jake.

Jake pointed to a spot in the dirt next to the single step. "There's a footprint here, but it's too sloppy to tell much."

Davis Lee nodded, walked around a bit more then all the men went back inside. "I'm keeping track of these things, Quentin. I'll add your tools to the list of stolen items."

"Thanks."

He nodded. "Oh, before I forget, Hoot wanted me to tell you to set this announcement for *The Prairie Caller.*"

He slid a piece of paper out of his front trouser pocket and passed it to Quentin. Jake's brother-in-law did typesetting for Hoot Eckert and the newspaper. It was a far cry from his previous job of laying track for the railroad, and he'd been bitter about it for a couple of years. But he seemed to have finally accepted it and somewhat enjoy the less physical work.

Quentin skimmed the note, glancing up at Davis Lee. "Russ Baldwin is the new owner of the Fontaine?"

Jake had learned from Russ last Sunday about his friend's purchase. When finished, Whirlwind's newest hotel would be darn near as fancy as the Texas Crown in Abilene.

Davis Lee's gaze included Jake in the conversation. "The primary investor, from somewhere in Kentucky, died. So Russ bought half ownership."

"Who bought the other half?" With ink-stained fingers, Quentin reached into his trouser pocket and withdrew a pencil.

"Some woman," Jake answered, his jaw setting when he caught the irritation on Quentin's face that he had dared to speak.

"Russ isn't sure when she'll arrive," Davis Lee put in. "But he wants to get the inside finished as quickly as possible so they can open for business."

"What's the problem?" Quentin scratched a note on the scrap of paper he held. "The outside has been finished for a while."

"First, some legal snafus slowed things down," Jake responded just because he knew it would annoy the hell out of his brother-in-law. "And now, with all the construction in Abilene, Russ is having trouble getting some of the materials."

Davis Lee adjusted his cowboy hat. "Guess I'll get back to the jail and make a note about the missing tools."

"Anything new on the other thefts?" Jake asked.

"No, but one good thing is that nothing else has been reported this week, until now. How are things working out with that baby?"

Jake had been friends with the tall, dark-haired lawman since they'd worn short pants, but he didn't want to go into a lot of detail with Quentin present. Holding that baby in the kitchen last week had shaken him up. He'd felt as if his chest was being pried open, and his guilt over how his wife had died trying to give him a child had flooded him like a black, bitter tide. "I think she's settling in."

"And the nurse?"

A little hum started in Jake's blood at the mention of Emma. He cleared his throat. "She's real good."

There must've been something in Jake's tone or on his face because his friend grinned like a possum eating persimmons. "She's pretty."

"I suppose," Jake muttered, giving Davis Lee a warning look. He'd had a devil of a time getting her out of his head today and he didn't want to talk about her, certainly not around Quentin.

Davis Lee chuckled and clapped Jake on the shoulder as he walked out the door and strode toward the alley between the saloon and the livery.

Jake set his jaw, determined to get what Quentin needed from Haskell's General Store, make his repairs and leave. He stepped out onto the porch. "I'll be back."

"I heard about your baby nurse."

The rancor in his brother-in-law's voice had Jake stiffening. "Yeah."

It stood to reason that Quentin knew about the handbill Jake had printed up advertising for help. The man had probably set the type himself.

"Young, is she?"

There was a heap of resentment beneath the words, but Jake refused to be baited. He looked over his shoulder. "The kid seems to like her."

"Now that my sister's gone, I guess you finally got that baby you wanted so bad."

Jake pivoted and took two aggressive steps forward, stopping when he realized what he was doing. Smoldering anger urged him to ignore the fact that Quentin was in a wheelchair and plow his fist through his brother-in-law's face. Instead, he said harshly, "I wish to hell Delia had told me what the doctor said. I could've made sure she didn't conceive."

Quentin went on as if he didn't hear. He narrowed his eyes. "You getting cozy with that woman? Making the family my sister died trying to give you?"

"It's not like that," Jake gritted out. He hadn't thought about setting up house with Emma, but he suddenly felt as guilty as if he had.

And, even if there was something going on with him and the baby nurse, it was none of Quentin's business. The son of a bitch made it sound as if Jake had wanted Delia to die five years ago. That he'd gotten her pregnant despite the doctor's warning that it could kill her.

But Jake hadn't known she was at risk, hadn't known she'd been warned repeatedly by the doctor not to conceive. His wife had kept that from him and she'd gotten pregnant. The next six months had been some of the happiest Jake could remember. Until Delia had begun to hemorrhage and had lost the baby. Until Jake had put them both in the ground.

"You as good as killed her yourself."

It didn't matter how long ago Quentin had screamed those words at Jake. He figured he'd never stop hearing them. Or half believing them.

Dealing with his own anger over Delia's keeping secrets, he'd tried to explain to Quentin that he hadn't known anything about the doctor's orders. But Quentin had been blind with rage, had kept shooting and shooting and shooting.

The walls pressed in; Jake's throat closed up. Stepping

outside, he asked hoarsely, "Need anything else from Haskell's store?"

"Horehound drops."

Jake agreed to get the candy, pulling the door shut behind him and dragging in a lungful of dry, hot air. Even now, there were times when the pain over Delia cut him in half.

For the most part, he'd learned how to live around the emptiness, the loss, but he couldn't ignore what his desire for a family had done to his wife. That fact pinned him like iron bars.

If he ever forgot how it felt to lose the woman he loved, a visit with Quentin always brought back the agony in stark, searing waves.

Emma had pushed that to the back of Jake's mind for a while, but that hollow, gut-twisting pain was back now. Even if he wanted to—and he didn't—he couldn't go through another loss like that. Not with Emma. Not with anyone.

The next Sunday morning, Emma left Molly in Georgia's lap, then slipped out of her seat on the Ross family pew in church and went outside to get Molly's doll from the wagon. The restless little girl needed something to help keep her quiet. As Emma had walked behind the family, she had been careful not to look at Jake.

This past week she had avoided him as much as possible. He still didn't appear to remember what he'd said to her that night at her room and it smarted, in part because *she* couldn't seem to forget. Maybe she should start drinking. That seemed to be his secret. The only thing pushing him out of her mind was the nightmare, which she'd had three times this week. It was the reason she'd been up last night at midnight when he'd come in drunk.

This morning, she'd seen Jake and his uncle outside arguing. Both had looked like thunderclouds. Behind her, Georgia had wondered aloud what was bothering Jake, saying she hadn't seen him drink like this since right after his wife had died.

He'd been married! Emma had thought about that all the way to Whirlwind. What had happened to his wife? How long had they been married before she'd died? Long enough to have children?

This curiosity was risky and foolish. She shouldn't be thinking of him at all, certainly not in the wanton way she'd been doing. There were more important things to consider. In the last several days, Emma had started to feel comfortable, too comfortable. She needed to see if there was any word about the search for her and her half sister. That was one reason she'd come to church with the Rosses. The other was that they had intended to bring the baby and, at least for now, Emma wanted to spend as much time with Molly as she could.

The wagon was south of the church, parked a few yards away. Two other wagons sat under the one lone tree on this side of the building, so the Ross wagon was in the blazing sun. As she leaned over the hardwood side, she caught a movement from the corner of her eye and looked down Main Street. Past the gunsmith's shop and a lawyer's office to the mercantile. A giant of a man stood beside a dust-coated bay, searching through his saddlebag.

He glanced quickly over each shoulder then continued what he was doing. The glimpse she had of his profile was too quick for her to recognize him, even if she'd known many people in town.

Emma's ever-present wariness kicked in and she turned for the church, doll in hand. She patted the derringer in her pocket. A glance back showed that the man she'd seen going through his saddlebag was gone. Scanning the planked walkway of businesses on both sides, she saw no sign of him. Where had he gone?

She hurried inside and back to her seat at the far end of the family's pew, catching Molly as her sister lunged into her arms from Georgia's lap.

She spent the next half hour trying to listen to the sermon and wrangle an increasingly restless baby. Jake glanced at her a few times, his unreadable black gaze sending a flash of heat across her skin. Molly's soft coos turned to a high-pitched squeal, prompting Emma to take the baby outside. Before long, the service was over and people streamed out of the building.

Jake headed toward her while the rest of the family lingered behind. He ran a hand through his thick black hair before putting on his light gray hat. It shaded his eyes from the sun's glare, but his mouth was pulled tight as if he was in pain. A result of last night, no doubt.

"Everything okay?"

She pushed her spectacles up her nose. "Yes."

"Good." His gaze slid over her, causing her nerves to jump. Tension coiled in his large body.

Not once did he look at the baby. He and his wife probably hadn't had any children because he didn't like them, Emma thought uncharitably.

Hearing his name, Jake half turned to look behind him. Davis Lee and Josie Holt walked over, holding hands. The lanky man's black trousers and white shirt were similar to what Jake wore. Josie was dressed in a smart navy-and-white striped silk and a flat-brimmed straw hat accented with a navy ribbon. Her husband greeted Emma then stepped over to shake Jake's hand.

How Josie managed to look cool in this hot weather was

a mystery. The one good frock Emma had allowed herself to bring, a pale pink silk with dark pink trim on the short sleeves and at the hem, was rumpled and limp next to Josie's fine visiting dress.

Thinking of the wardrobe she'd had to leave behind when she'd escaped Topeka, Emma asked wistfully, "Did you make your dress, Mrs. Holt?"

"Please call me Josie." Her green eyes sparkled. "And yes."

"You're very talented." Emma had liked the other woman the moment she'd met her. It would've been nice to become better friends, but there was no point since she would be leaving. The thought brought a quick swell of loneliness.

Her hold tightened on Molly as the little girl squirmed around to see Josie's face.

"May I hold her?"

Emma wasn't completely comfortable handing over her sister, but she had no good reason to refuse. Besides, Josie Holt seemed to adore the baby and Emma was there to make sure nothing happened. She didn't expect trouble, but, then, she hadn't expected her mother to be murdered, either. The only place she didn't feel paranoid lately was at the ranch. So far, the sheriff didn't act suspicious of her; she couldn't tell that anyone was.

As she passed the little girl to the petite brunette, Molly grabbed for Josie's hat. The woman laughed and managed to evade the chubby little hand.

Sheriff Holt tipped his fawn-colored hat, smiling at the baby, then at Emma. "Miz York, how are you today?"

"Fine, thank you." She touched her glasses to make sure they were in place.

Smoothing Molly's blond curls, Josie asked Emma, "How are things going out at the Circle R?"

"Very well, thank you." There had been no more late-night visits from her employer, although that hadn't stopped Emma from thinking about it.

Josie bounced the baby on her shoulder and Emma moved closer so that she wouldn't be overheard. "Thank you for getting the corset. That was very generous. I haven't had anything so nice in a while."

"You're welcome. I hope I had your size right."

"It fits perfectly."

The petite woman shot a look past Emma, then lowered her voice. "Jake was so cute when he came in and asked me to replace the one that was taken."

Cute? Emma didn't think of him as cute so much as she thought he was handsome enough to make a girl stop thinking about doing right and doing…other things.

Taken aback at her thoughts, she felt a blush heating her cheeks.

"He couldn't look at me," the other woman continued with obvious delight. "And he couldn't say *corset* to save his life. He said, 'Can you get Miz York one of those things she had stolen?'" Josie laughed, dodging another wild grab from Molly by catching the baby's small hand and kissing it. "Y'all have to come for supper soon."

Emma's eyes widened. Did the other woman mean Emma and Molly? Or her and Jake? She wasn't about to ask.

Watching the brunette with her sister, Emma knew she could do worse than to let Molly grow up in Whirlwind, around people like Josie Holt and her husband.

The sheriff's low-pitched words to Jake reached Emma. "Did you stay long at Quentin's after I left yesterday?"

"No." He dragged a hand across his nape. "Fixed some things up for him and went on my way."

Who was Quentin? she wondered.

"It's been what," Davis Lee asked, "five years?"

"Just about."

"He's never going to let it go, is he?"

"Sure doesn't seem like it." Jake's voice was scratchy.

What were they talking about? *Who* were they talking about?

Josie leaned close and said softly, "They're talking about Quentin Prescott. He's Jake's brother-in-law. Or used to be, when his sister was alive and married to Jake."

Emma was dying to know more, but she didn't think she should ask questions. She touched the underside of the gold band on her ring finger. Jake Ross was truly a widower, unlike her.

"I wrote down the tools Quentin said were stolen from him."

Emma perked up at the sheriff's words. Something else had been stolen and this time it hadn't been a corset.

Davis Lee stroked his chin thoughtfully. "Did you get any more information after I left?"

Jake gave a bitter laugh. "You know better than that. Quentin wouldn't even tell me to go to hell if it meant he had to talk to me."

"True."

So Jake had been at his brother-in-law's when the man had reported some items stolen? From the conversation, it sounded as if his visit was nothing out of the ordinary. Emma wondered if it had anything to do with his being drunk last night.

Then again, it might have nothing to do with his being intoxicated. He'd been drunk last Saturday night, too, and he hadn't been to town that day.

Emma didn't realize she was staring at Jake until his gaze locked on hers. Sensation fluttered in her stomach as she froze, unable to drag her eyes from his blunt, sun-weathered features.

He was first to look away, shifting his attention to a group of people who made their way over and introduced themselves to Emma. Her head swam with all the names. She remembered Davis Lee's brother, Riley, and his wife, Susannah. And the Holts' cousin, Jericho Blue, and his wife, Catherine. An older man strode toward them from the crowd gathered around the church steps.

The gentleman, robust and solidly built, removed his cowboy hat as he came abreast of them, revealing thick gray hair. "Ladies."

"Hello, J.T." Josie gently bounced Molly on her shoulder and gestured to Emma. "This is Emma York. She's the baby nurse Jake hired."

A wide smile split his leathery features, crinkling his blue eyes at the corners. "J. T. Baldwin, ma'am. And this is my son, Russ." He indicated the dark-haired man on his right, who had a mustache.

Russ Baldwin looked as big as the stranger she'd seen when she'd come out earlier. His blue gaze skated warmly over her, darkening with interest.

He swept off his hat and shook her hand. His plainly admiring stare made her feel self-conscious as she pulled her hand from the callused warmth of his.

Josie laughed. "Emma, I have a feeling you'll probably start seeing this gentleman at the Circle R quite a bit."

"To welcome you to Whirlwind, proper like." Russ's dimples deepened.

Adjusting her spectacles, she gave a small smile, frustratingly aware of Jake staring hard at them. Baldwin. Emma recalled Jake saying some of their cattle had also been stolen.

J.T. settled his hat back on his head. "Excuse me, ladies, while I talk some business with Davis Lee."

"Of course," Josie said.

As he moved a few steps away, he grinned at Emma. "Nice to have you in town, Miz York."

"Thank you."

Russ stayed with her and Josie, asking Emma questions about where she was from, how long she'd been in Whirlwind, if she liked her job. She answered, trying to relax the tension in her shoulders. She couldn't help but overhear J.T.'s next words.

"Davis Lee, got a theft to report."

"Something of yours?" the sheriff asked.

"Yes." The rancher rubbed his whisker-stubbled chin, looking sheepish. "I had a mirror in my saddlebag, and it's gone."

"A mirror?" Jake looked puzzled.

"A fancy handheld job," the man mumbled.

"A woman's mirror?" Russ turned toward his father, his expression as confused as Jake's.

"Yes." His gruff answer challenged anyone to question him further.

Emma frowned. Why did everyone seem so surprised, so curious?

Josie leaned close and whispered, "His wife passed a long time ago. He must be courting someone. Ooh, I wish I knew who. It's not like anything can stay a secret for long in Whirlwind."

Emma hoped some things could, like her situation. "Maybe it's someone in Abilene?"

"That could be. I wonder why he doesn't want anyone to know. It appears even Russ doesn't know."

Jake's deep voice drew Emma's attention back to him. "That makes two thefts in the last twenty-four hours."

"Right here in town." Davis Lee inclined his head in the

direction J.T. had pointed. "The thief is getting mighty cocky, stealing in broad daylight."

Jake glanced over his shoulder. "Is that your bay hitched in front of Haskell's?"

"Yeah."

"Taking something in plain sight like that is bold."

"Or dumb," Davis Lee said.

Emma followed their gazes to Mr. Baldwin's horse and her heart thumped hard. She recognized the animal from earlier. That bay belonged to Mr. Baldwin, not the man Emma had seen looking through the saddlebags. Was he the thief? Had he been stealing right under her nose?

She drew in a sharp breath, aware of it only when Jake's gaze swerved to her. Josie looked at her curiously.

"Anything else taken, J.T.?" Davis Lee asked.

"No, just the mirror."

"So, we've had tools stolen, clothes and now a bauble."

"Dang it, we don't even know what this person looks like," Jake said.

Emma was afraid she did. The more she thought about it, the more she was certain she'd witnessed the theft of the mirror. She hadn't gotten a good look at the man's face, but she knew his size and hair color.

She didn't want to say anything. From all appearances, no one suspected anything about her and, if her stepfather was looking near here for her, she had no doubt the sheriff at least would've mentioned it. What she knew probably wouldn't be very helpful, she reasoned. But how could she keep it to herself? This person was likely the same one who was making off with the corsets.

The sheriff frowned at the elder Baldwin. "Did you see anyone hanging around when you came out of church?"

"No. And I wouldn't have even checked my saddlebag if

I weren't going to see my—uh, if I hadn't wanted to make sure the mirror wasn't broken."

Davis Lee and Jake looked bemused as the man tripped over his words.

Russ looked completely flabbergasted and left the women to walk over to his father. "Pa, what's going on?"

"Something was stolen from my saddlebag," the man blustered. "That's all."

"I'll go take a look around your horse, although any tracks are probably gone by now," Davis Lee said.

Looking vexed with his father, Russ thumbed his hat back on his head. "Maybe somebody saw something."

"Everybody was in church," J.T. pointed out.

Not everyone, Emma thought.

"Up until now, all the thefts have been at night," Davis Lee mused. "Or the ones reported, anyway."

"If we just had some idea about who's doing this," Jake said. "Anything."

Giving in to her conscience, Emma eased over next to Jake. Inhaling the pleasant scent of man and leather, she touched his arm, feeling the warmth of his skin through his sleeve. "Mr. Ross?"

He looked down, his gaze flaring hotly.

"I think I may have seen the thief."

"What?" Davis Lee and the Baldwins burst out in unison and rushed toward her.

The three huge men bearing down on Emma had her shrinking back, reaching automatically for the pocket where she kept her derringer. To her surprise, Jake shifted so that his big body partially blocked her.

The men halted. Davis Lee's gaze flicked curiously over his sometime-deputy then back to Emma.

After a moment, Jake looked at her, his voice calm and

steady. "You think you might've seen something when you came out to get the doll?"

"Yes." With Josie listening in, Emma told the men what she'd witnessed, apologizing when she finished. "I didn't know the person who was with that horse wasn't the owner. I thought he was going through his own things or I would've told someone."

"You did just fine," Davis Lee said. "At least we have somewhere to start."

"What did he look like?" Jake asked.

"I only saw him from the back," she said. "He was wearing brown trousers and a white shirt."

Jake encouraged Emma. "Go on."

"His hair is brownish red, in need of a trim. And he's big."

"How big?" Sheriff Holt asked. "Taller than me?"

Emma thought for a moment. "I don't think so, but he was much broader. All over. And he had big hands. I could tell that."

The men fell silent, digesting this information.

"I'm sorry. I wish I knew more." In truth, she wished she didn't know this much.

"It's more than we've learned so far." Jake's slow smile sent a jolt of heat through her.

Her breath caught and sensation pooled low in her belly. Oh. That was how he'd smiled that night at her room. Don't look at him, she ordered.

"Thank you, Miz York," Davis Lee said. "You've been a big help, although I'm racking my brain for a name to go with that likeness. I'm not getting one."

"Neither am I," J.T. said. The other men murmured agreement.

"But now we have a description." The sheriff smiled and some of her uncertainty faded.

"Maybe the thief doesn't live in Whirlwind," Russ suggested.

"I thought about that," Jake replied. "But why ride here to steal things? There are bigger, more well-to-do towns in every direction."

"True."

"We'll just have to keep an eye out," Jake said.

"Yeah." Davis Lee chewed his cheek for a moment, then his eyes lit up. "Miz York, do you think you'd know the man again if you saw him?"

"I...think so."

"Would you be willing to sit with me later tonight in town and watch people come and go? Maybe we'll get a glimpse of him."

No, she wasn't willing! Spending time with a lawman seemed as reckless as announcing her real name and the reason she was here. "Well, I...I have the baby to care for."

"Georgia can watch her for a couple of hours," Jake said. "Or Ike can."

"Or I will," Josie offered. "If you need to bring her."

Her employer turned to Davis Lee. "Yeah, she can do it. I'll bring her to your office just before dark."

Jake Ross did not speak for her! Biting back the words, Emma curled her hands into fists. She knew she couldn't refuse to help the sheriff, but she didn't like it.

"That will help a lot, Miz York." The lawman grinned. "You may have found our thief."

And she might also have just made things more difficult for her and Molly. She gave the sheriff a weak smile.

After Emma made arrangements to meet later with Davis Lee, she took the baby and followed Jake to the wagon where the rest of his family waited. After helping her into the wagon bed, he mounted his dun mare.

As the wagon lurched into motion, Jake told the others about the latest theft and what Emma had seen. Hanging on to her squirming sister, Emma sat quietly.

She wouldn't have been able to live with herself if she'd stayed quiet and things kept disappearing. But why, oh, why, did she have to be the one to have witnessed that theft?

With a sideways look over her shoulder at the big man who rode beside the wagon, she sighed inwardly. Most likely, Jake would be the one to bring her back to Whirlwind. After managing to avoid him for the better part of a week, spending so much time with him in one day whittled at her nerves. At least she wouldn't be alone with him after they arrived at the sheriff's office.

Chapter Seven

❧❦❧

The hard yellow of the sun had begun to soften to gold as Jake and Emma headed toward Whirlwind late that evening. There was enough daylight to reach town and the jail before dark. Then she could spend the rest of her time with someone other than Jake. Away from his clean earthy scent, the heat of his body.

The ranch house faded from view. Spoke-high grass swished against the wagon, spreading out in front of them like a golden-brown blanket. Emma felt Jake studying her face and looked over.

"Looks like you're all healed up from the wagon accident."

"Yes." When he looked at her so intently, she couldn't think for a moment. "What about you?"

"My run-in with the fence?" he asked ruefully.

She nodded. She hadn't bandaged him since that first time, but she knew someone had to have been.

"It might leave a scar," he said. "But it's healed up."

"Good." She smiled, looking out across the prairie and the pinkening edges of the golden sunset.

"We'll spend the night in town," Jake said.

Spend the night? Her pulse jumped, but she didn't know if it was due to apprehension or anticipation. Either way, the idea made her skittish. "I don't mind driving back tonight."

"It could be real late before you and Davis Lee finish."

"What about Molly?"

"Georgia has Ike and Bram if she needs help."

The thought of staying in town overnight had Emma's palms clammy. She mentally calculated the change in her skirt pocket. She didn't think she had enough for a room at the Whirlwind Hotel, but more worrisome was the amount of time she was spending in town. And with Jake.

"I can bed down at the jail and there's a real nice lady friend of mine who's agreed to let you stay with her."

"A lady friend?" Emma's spine stiffened. He wanted her to stay with his...his *lady friend?* Absolutely not! "The hotel will be fine."

"There's no need for that. Cora's more than happy to have you."

Hit with a sharp emotion she didn't recognize, Emma tried to keep her voice level. "I'd be more comfortable at the hotel. Your...friend would probably prefer I stay there, anyway."

Jake snapped the reins against the horse's rump. "Cora likes company."

I just bet she does, Emma thought hotly. "Still, I don't want to intrude on any plans you might have."

"Plans?" Jake frowned, then comprehension swept across his features. "Oh. You think Cora's my—"

"It's none of my business," Emma said stiffly.

"Well, I think it might—"

"Please, Mr. Ross." She barely restrained a wail, feeling her cheeks grow hot with embarrassment. "You shouldn't tell me these things."

"You don't need to worry about her. She's been my—"

"Mr. Ross." Her throat was dry, her voice paper-thin. Were all men so obstinate? She squeezed her eyes shut. "Please, please stop."

What was wrong with the man? He never strung together this many words and now she couldn't get him to hush. Lands.

"All right, then."

She heard amusement in his voice, no doubt at her expense, and turned her body slightly away from him on the wagon seat. They bounced along the uneven grass-covered prairie. She could see him out of the corner of her eye and she thought he was smiling. Drat the man!

Stay with his mistress? Emma couldn't believe the man's nerve! It took several long minutes for the blush to cool from her cheeks. Neither of them said much else the rest of the way.

Emma wished she could turn off this awareness of him as effectively as she'd finally managed to stop the conversation. Why did she have to be so aware of his big callused hands on the reins? As rough and dark as they looked, she knew they could be gentle.

The wagon hit a rut and Emma bounced hard on the seat, grabbing the side to steady herself. As she resettled herself, she glanced at him, then shifted her gaze straight ahead. His hat shaded the smooth planes of his cheekbones, but not his strong whisker-stubbled jaw. The ends of his black hair curled slightly against his nape.

She could not believe she had been harboring carnal thoughts about a man who had taken up with a harlot.

She clasped her hands, conscious of the sweat on her palms. She told herself it was due to the heat, but she knew it was really because of the man beside her.

By the time they drove into Whirlwind, the sunset had shifted from shadowy pink to gray. They passed the new hotel sitting dark at the west of town, then the blacksmith's shop where a lantern burned inside.

Jake reined up at the jail, then came around to help Emma from the wagon. He managed to get there before she could get her foot on the step. When his hands closed around her waist to lift her down, a funny sensation streaked through her. She pulled away as soon as her feet touched the ground.

Light from the sheriff's office illuminated the steps as she and Jake walked up together. Just before they reached the top, he said, "I'll be here when you and Davis Lee are finished."

"All right." Between now and then, she'd think of a way to convince him she was not going to his...*lady friend's* house. Because she wasn't.

He opened the door with one hand while palming off his hat with the other. She walked inside, with him close behind her. Very close. His heat reached her through the light silk of the pale pink dress she'd worn to church.

The kerosene lamp on the sheriff's desk was turned up high, the light weaving through Emma's shadow. Davis Lee and his wife stood in a doorway across the office. Beyond them was a jail cell. The lawman and his wife greeted Emma and Jake warmly, still not appearing suspicious of her. She glanced at the wall behind the sheriff's desk, relieved to see there were no new notices there.

The Holts exchanged a look then Josie moved toward Emma and Jake. What was Josie doing here? Emma smiled as the woman walked over with a soft-looking yellow fabric draped over her arm.

"Josie," Jake murmured, his gaze going across the room to Davis Lee, who still stood in the open doorway. "Davis Lee."

"Hello, Jake." Josie breezed past him and tugged Emma toward the lamp on the sheriff's big oak desk. "I want to show you what I made for Molly."

Emma saw Davis Lee motion Jake over then turned her attention from the sound of his boots on the wooden floor to look at what the seamstress held. It was a small yellow dress embroidered with a sprinkle of pink flowers and a matching bonnet.

Tears tightened Emma's throat. "You did this for Molly?"

Josie nodded.

"You're too kind."

"Oh, nonsense." The other woman squeezed Emma's hand, then held up the clothes. "Won't she look cute?"

"Yes." Emma bent over the dress as Josie showed her she'd have plenty of seam to let out the garment for a while as Molly grew.

Emma smiled at the other woman. "You really love children. Are you planning to have some of your own?"

"Yes, it just seems to be taking us longer than most." Sadness flitted across Josie's face. "A lot longer."

Emma squeezed her friend's hand. "It will happen."

"That's what Davis Lee says, too." She smiled, the shadows disappearing from her green eyes.

Jake's voice carried in a low rumble across the room. "You want me to do *what?*"

Emma glanced up, her gaze going over Josie's shoulder to the two men. Davis Lee stood with his arms folded, the light winking off his tin star. The authority of his office was plain on his face.

Josie touched Emma's arm. "If the bonnet doesn't fit, let me know."

She nodded, as aware of the other conversation as she was this one.

"But I thought you were going to do this," Jake said.

"Something came up and I don't want to put off this thing with Emma. What if this man she saw leaves town?"

"What if he's not even still here?" Jake asked gruffly.

"This way, we can find out."

Jake turned his back to Emma and whispered something she couldn't make out. Davis Lee responded in a low voice. There was a fast exchange of words, then her employer shifted to her direction, looking at her then back to the sheriff. Davis Lee grinned like a fool while Jake looked as if he'd just been taken to the wood shed.

Davis Lee walked toward her and his wife. After a slight hesitation, Jake followed. Dread curled in Emma's stomach. She didn't know what was coming, but she knew she wasn't going to like it.

Josie turned, curling her arm through her husband's when he stopped beside her.

His blue eyes crinkled at the corners as he smiled at Emma. "Something's come up for me, Miz York, so Jake will be with you tonight."

Jake! No! Emma barely kept from groaning. The stone-hard look on his face made it plain that he wasn't pleased about this, either. But what could she do? Refuse to watch the town with him, after these people had been so kind? Besides, it sounded as if Jake had already protested. If that hadn't changed the sheriff's mind, nothing she said would, either.

Jake leveled a steely stare at his friend. "If you're going to be gone, then I should stay here."

"Since we have no prisoners, I'll just lock up. That way, you can go with Emma. I'll take care of my business and whoever gets back first can unlock." He looked expectantly at Emma. "All right, Miz York?"

A muscle flexed in Jake's jaw, making his feelings clear. Well, Emma didn't like it, either!

"All right." Unable to look at Jake, she kept her attention on the lanky man in front of her. She pushed up her glasses, hoping she appeared calm because inside her nerves were jumping.

Sweat prickled on her neck and chest.

She'd had enough trouble keeping her mind off Jake all week. She didn't want to sit with him. Alone. In the dark. That flutter in her stomach was *not* excitement. It wasn't. Oh, why had she ever opened her big mouth?

Jake and Emma walked silently from the wagon to the Fontaine Hotel, where Davis Lee had decided was the best vantage point for Emma's "observing." Jake wondered if she suspected the same thing he did. He didn't like where his thoughts were taking him, but he would bet his boots that he and Emma had just been conned. Davis Lee and Josie had pulled off a matchmakin' scheme as slick as a couple of husband-hunting mamas.

Small puffs of dust swirled around their feet as they walked. The rise and fall of voices behind them and across the street had Jake reluctantly agreeing with Davis Lee's insistence that there would, indeed, be enough people in town that Emma had a chance of spotting the thief. He glanced at the small woman at his elbow, his jaw clenched tightly enough to break teeth. She hadn't looked at him once since she'd been pawned off on him.

Noting that she had to take two steps to every one of his, he slowed down. It wasn't her fault they were here together. She drew even with him, holding the lap robe he'd taken from the wagon after she had declined his offer to get a chair. They passed in front of the new three-story hotel with its arched doorways on the second and third stories. The fifteen-foot-high balcony was set off by a railing of black swirly ironwork.

His baby nurse sure did smell good. Like peaches and starch and that bar of Ivory soap Georgia had given her. As they reached the corner of the hotel, lanterns from the nearby livery and saloon put off enough light to see down the long outside wall of the hotel. And the staircase leading up its side to the balcony.

The steps were made of the same pale sandstone as the rest of the hotel, but the stairway wasn't quite wide enough to accommodate both him and Emma. Jake stayed a step behind, his gaze sliding over the thick braid hanging between her shoulder blades, the slender length of her back, the nip of her waist.

Without warning, she stopped and spun to face him. "We don't have to— Oh!"

Losing her balance, she pitched forward, narrowly missing his chin with her head.

He grabbed the iron railing with one hand and curled his other around her waist, steadying them both. "Whoa!"

She caught herself with a palm in the middle of his chest, gasping. "Oh, I'm sorry!"

"I'm fine. Are you?" He looked her up and down. "Did you twist your ankle or anything?"

"No, I'm not hurt." She blinked those big eyes at him and lowered her hand from his chest. "I didn't realize you were so close."

"No harm done." His hand flexed on her taut waist. In the moonlight, her skin looked as soft as down and he wanted to touch her. Stroke her slender neck, run his fingers down the row of buttons that held her bodice together. Hell.

Though he figured she didn't want to be up here with him any more than he wanted it, he released her with reluctance.

The night pulsed around them, teasing him with her fresh scent, her nearness. Jake's body went tight, the way it did more and more often around her. Only inches separated them, making him aware that he smelled like leather and horses and sweat next to her.

In a breathless voice, she said, "Before I nearly tumbled us down the stairs, I was going to say we don't have to do this tonight. I bet the sheriff would let me do it the next time he's available."

"It doesn't matter when you do it," Jake muttered, deciding they better move before he did something stupid like pull her even closer. "Davis Lee isn't going to be available."

She frowned. "Why not?"

Jake cupped her elbow and guided her up the remaining steps, steering her ahead into the darkest corner of the balcony. He set down his canteen and the harness he planned to repair while they watched for the thief.

Taking the lap robe from her, Jake folded it in half and arranged it on the hard stone floor. "No matter when you agree to do it, he'll send you with me."

"But why?"

The back of Jake's neck heated. As silly as this sounded, as fiddle-footed as he felt saying it, he knew he was right. "I think Davis Lee did this on purpose."

"Well, yes." She gave him a perplexed smile. "The sheriff said something came up. You heard him."

"The *something* was that he and his wife wanted to pair us up."

The confusion on her face was quickly replaced by horrified realization. "The sheriff is playing matchmaker!"

"He wouldn't think of it on his own." Jake offered his hand, helping her lower herself to the blanket.

She shifted to one hip and curled her feet to the side, arranging her skirts in a billow of pink fabric.

Jake eased down beside her, shifting his holster. "But *Josie* would think of it and Davis Lee would go along."

"Oh."

The silence settled awkwardly between them. Emma wouldn't meet his gaze and, even in this dim light, Jake could tell she was blushing.

"Oh!" She sounded as if she'd solved a puzzle.

He scooted up to the edge of the balcony, dangling a leg on either side of a wrought iron spindle. "What?"

She flicked him an uncertain look. "Today, after church, Josie said she wanted to have *us* over for dinner."

Jake's gaze cut to her. "Yeah?"

"At the time, I didn't know if she meant Molly and I. Or you and…I."

"I think we know now," he said dryly.

"But why would they want to pair us up? I work for you."

"You lost your husband, I lost my wife."

A strange expression crossed her face. She looked away. "Don't they know about your…lady friend?"

"Yes." He liked teasing her, but he should probably come clean about Cora. "She's not what you think, Emma."

"I don't think anything," she said primly. "It's certainly none of my business."

Yeah, he knew he should feel that way, too. But he didn't. He cared what she thought and he didn't want her thinking he was involved with someone when he wasn't. For a lot of years, he hadn't even considered that he might want to get tangled up with another woman, but ever since that night at Emma's room, the thought weighed on him more and more.

"Cora's a widow, like us."

"I'm not asking, really."

"I've known her for a long time."

"Mr. Ross, please." Shaking her head, she covered her face with her hands.

Seeing her flustered was a change from her usual calm and quiet. He liked it. He wondered if she'd get flustered if he kissed her. He could warm up to that idea. "She's my uncle's age. Even if she'd have me, there's too many years between us."

Emma spread her fingers, peeking out at him. Despite the darkness, she could see the amusement in his eyes. "So, she's not your—"

"No."

Emma dropped her hands. "I'm sorry."

He couldn't resist. "You're sorry that she's *not* my lady friend?"

"No!" Her gaze flew to his. The smile playing at his lips was rare. "You let me think she was a…your…you know."

He chuckled. "Hey, I tried to explain on the way into town, but you didn't want to hear it."

"You were teasing me."

"I was."

"That's just ornery!" The words were out before she could stop them.

She froze. If she'd said anything like that at home, Orson would have hit her. Or tried to, while her mother stepped between them and took the blows. But, instead of anger on Jake's face, she saw a grin.

"Yes'm. I've been called on that before."

Thanks to Orson's controlling strictness, no man had ever teased her or flirted with her after she'd come of age, but Jake had. She liked it. After a minute, she relaxed.

"Anyway, I apologize for my friends."

"I'm sure they meant well."

He grunted. "They jumped the gun. You might not be ready to step out with anyone. They don't know how long you've been a widow."

Neither did he, Jake realized. And he wanted to know. "I hope you didn't take offense."

"I didn't."

He waited, not surprised when she didn't offer further information. Drawing up one knee, he rested his elbow there, wondering if he should ask about her husband. He really wanted to know about the man because…well, because he did.

Taken with the way the moonlight glided over her delicate cheekbones, he murmured, "Is it still fresh for you?"

She stiffened, sitting close enough that he could feel her fingers tangling in her skirts. "Probably no more so than for you," she said quietly.

"My…Delia's been gone about five years. How long for you?"

Again, that subtle tensing of her body. "It seems like forever. Were you married very long?"

"About the same amount of time she's been gone. And you?"

"Nowhere near that long."

"Was your husband from Illinois, too?"

"No."

Jake wanted to ask what had happened to the man, but it was apparent she didn't want to talk about it. And he didn't much feel like spitting out more details about his wife and how she'd died trying to give him a child. He hadn't discussed it with anyone since he'd talked to Bram on the night Quentin had come gunning for him.

He and Emma stared down at the street, silent. Still.

Hidden in the darkness high above Whirlwind, they had a good view of both sides of town through the iron railing. Jake gestured toward the jail. "I see Davis Lee is still gone, taking care of whatever mysterious thing he had to do."

Emma leaned slightly forward and pointed to two men who'd stepped out of the blacksmith's shop. "Who's that?" she whispered.

The smithy's smeltering fire glowed orange behind two broad silhouettes. "The big black man is Ef Gerard. He's the blacksmith. Real fine at it, too, and a good man to have at your back. The other one is Russ Baldwin."

"Oh, yes, I met him at church. He's the one who owns this hotel?"

"Yeah."

"Neither Mr. Gerard nor Mr. Baldwin are the men I saw today."

"Didn't figure they were." He watched as Russ and Ef finished their conversation, then shook hands.

The rancher strolled up the street past the jail, laughing when Ef called out something. Just as Russ reached the Pearl Restaurant, its door opened and a tall, straight-spined woman stepped out. Jake grinned. "See that lady there?"

"Yes."

"That's Cora. Cora Wilkes."

She studied the older woman then flicked a look at Jake. "She doesn't look like she'd let herself be anyone's kept woman."

"No." The thought of such a thing made him chuckle. "No, she surely wouldn't."

"You really told a whopper."

"She was widowed about two years ago. That outlaw gang I told you about before? The McDougals? They murdered her husband, Ollie." From the corner of his eye, he could see Emma gnawing on her thumbnail. What had her tail in a knot? "The two of them helped me a lot after Delia passed."

"Do you still miss her? Delia?" The baby nurse held herself completely motionless, as if wary of provoking a violent reaction in him.

"Sometimes," he admitted hoarsely. Although, except for yesterday's visit with Quentin, the pain lately hadn't been as deep or as frequent. Undoubtedly due in some part to his whiskey. "Do you still miss— What was your husband's name?"

Emma bowed her head so that her profile was eclipsed by the shadows. "Mr. Ross—"

"Jake." Why wouldn't she call him by his first name? She did everyone else.

After a long pause, she said in a half whisper, "Jake. I think I should tell you something."

"All right." He waited as seconds dragged by, wondering what she had to say that made her so hesitant.

Finally, she blurted, "I'm not a widow."

Surprise held him still for a moment. Several explanations for her lie ran through his mind, but one stood out. Her husband was still alive, he'd hurt her and she was running from the bastard. That explained Emma's wariness around men, her skittishness. Like the day of the wagon accident and again this morning when Davis Lee, Russ and J.T. had started toward her at the same time.

"Your husband isn't dead," Jake said roughly, taken aback at the cold, black fury moving through him.

"No, he isn't." Even behind her spectacles, the apprehension in her eyes was easy to see. "I mean, I've never been married."

Relieved that his first assumption had been wrong, he recovered a mite quicker from her second admission. "Then why say you were?"

"I'm traveling alone." She lifted her left hand, touching the gold band on her third finger. "It's safer if people think I'm married."

"And saying you're a widow?"

"That stops a lot of questions and makes me appear more experienced."

She was making do by herself. He admired that. For all her softness and quiet, she was strong. "So, you've never been married, huh?"

"No."

"Why tell me your secret?"

She curled her hands in her skirts, then uncurled them. Curled them. "It seems wrong to pretend I've suffered the same pain you have."

The rigid bracing of her body told Jake that she expected him to be angry. But he wasn't. "That's pretty smart, Emma."

Her eyes widened. "Really?"

"Yeah. I know how it is for a woman on her own, especially out here."

She licked her lips, the sight of her tongue causing a tug of sensation in his belly. Relief shone in her eyes. "I'm so glad you understand. I wouldn't want you to think less of me or my ability to care for Molly."

To his way of thinking, her secret had no bearing on her ability. He shifted toward her, catching a whiff of her fresh skin-warmed scent. The edge of her blanket rubbed against his thigh. "Do you have *any* family?"

"Not anymore." Her voice cracked and she linked her fingers together. "My father passed away about five years ago, like your wife. And my mother—more recently."

The quiver in her voice warned him, but, when Jake saw a tear slide down her cheek, he froze for a moment then reached over and covered her hands with one of his.

She stilled, but, instead of pulling away as he expected, she stared at their joined hands in her lap.

Though she hadn't flinched or shied away as she had after the wagon accident, Jake still felt compelled to ask, "Is this okay? Am I spooking you?"

"No." Then on a quivery breath, she added, "It's nice."

When she raised her gaze to his, the combination of gratitude and loss in her green eyes sent a sharp longing through him. And a stab of memory. He knew that deep searing emptiness. He wanted to wipe away the pain. He wanted...to pull her into his lap and kiss her.

Her gaze dropped to his mouth then skittered away. She wanted it, too, he realized in amazement as his hand tightened on hers. He had barely registered the thought when she tried to tug her hands from beneath his. He withdrew immediately.

She didn't move away, just sat quietly for a few minutes. Then she pointed toward Haskell's General Store. "Who's that?"

A sturdy young woman strode across Main Street and disappeared into the alley between the Pearl Restaurant and the telegraph office. Jake recognized the purposeful walk, the unruly hair curling from beneath a soft cap.

"That's Zoe Keeler. She and her brother live in that line of houses just behind the jail. She has an older sister who's deaf."

"She works for Josie," Emma said. "I saw her that day we came to town to tell the sheriff about my...corset."

He nodded. "She does all the jobs she can find so she can keep her sister at a special school back east and take care of their younger brother. Zeke's old enough to work, but he's simple. Just a little slow, although people don't seem to want to let him do as much as he's able. Still, he's cheerful about it."

"Oh."

As windows and doors began to darken, Jake quietly gave her information on the people making their way home. He pointed out Tony Santos and his nephew, Miguel, when the telegraph operator and the young boy locked up the telegraph office. And Penn and Esther Wavers as they left the Pearl to return to their rooms at the Whirlwind Hotel, which they owned and managed.

Finally, all the lights in town had been doused, leaving the place bathed in white moonlight. No one stirred below. The only sounds around were the chirping of insects and the occasional snort of a horse at the livery.

Jake checked his pocketwatch and saw it was eleven-thirty. He got to his feet and offered his hand to help Emma stand. She took it and rose, quickly releasing him.

He gathered the canteen and his worn harness, only then realizing he hadn't worked a lick on the tack; she folded the blanket.

He glanced at her. "Are you okay about staying at Cora's?"

Her smile was a mite timid. "Yes. As long as she doesn't mind."

"She won't. She likes the company." Jake placed a hand in the small of her back as they walked across the balcony. "I'm glad you don't mind staying overnight. Now I'll be able to have a few words with Davis Lee."

She pushed up her glasses. "About my not seeing the thief?"

He nodded. They reached the steps and he motioned for her to precede him.

"And your having to take his place tonight?"

"That, too."

"He certainly put you out by foisting me off on you," she ventured softly.

Was that hurt beneath her words? Jake wanted to see her face. He touched her shoulder, turning her slightly toward him as he moved to the step below hers.

"I guess I acted like that at the beginning, but I've reconsidered. Sitting up here with you wasn't a chore at all. I liked it."

That teased a smile out of her and, when her lips curved, all Jake could think about was doing what he'd wanted to do earlier.

He bent his head, keeping his gaze on hers, his intent plain. If she had winced or stiffened or even looked away, he would've stopped. But, instead, she stared at him with a hopeful anticipation that went straight to his head.

She seemed to be holding her breath. His lips brushed her lightly and she trembled. He felt the sensation go through her entire body, and then his as she eased closer and pressed her mouth to his.

Her kiss was unpracticed, but willing, accepting, and had him operating on pure sensation. He wanted more of the heated honey of her mouth, her wine-dark taste, the feel of her breasts against him.

He slid his free arm around her waist and brought her into him from chest to toe, letting her feel the evidence of his desire. When he touched her lips with his tongue, she let him in, one of her hands lifting to grip his upper arm.

Suddenly she pulled away, drawing in a deep breath and burying her face in his chest. "Oh, lands." Her words were muffled against his shirt. "I don't think we should've done that."

It was an effort to level out his breathing, to let his arm slide from her waist. She hadn't slapped him or run away or said she didn't like it. She still had her forehead butted up to his chest. He could feel the rapid beating of her heart beneath her bodice. Her breath came in short little pants.

"You make me forget myself," she murmured.

A surge of primitive male satisfaction surprised him. No woman had ever reacted like this to him. He didn't know what to do. With a shaking hand, he stroked her hair. "Are you okay?"

"Yes." She drew back, unsteady on her feet, but gathering that stillness inside herself until all the dreaminess left her eyes, until she stood stiffly in his arms. "I'm sorry."

"Well, I'm not," he said huskily. "I liked kissing you. I've wanted to do it for a long time."

She blinked up at him.

"I'd like to do it again, but that's up to you. I'm not going to push or try to make you do something you don't want."

"Thank you." She looked dazed.

"When you decide you're ready, and I hope you will, I'll be here."

After a long moment, she asked in a small, disbelieving voice, "You're leaving it up to me?"

"Yes." Jake wished he could kiss her again and dissolve all her doubts, make her admit she wanted him, too. *Now.* But he wasn't smooth and practiced like the Baldwin brothers.

Even so, he knew what he wanted. He wanted Emma and he was going to have her. Someday.

Chapter Eight

Emma had liked kissing Jake and wanted to do it again. Which must mean she didn't have a lick of sense where he was concerned.

Before the hot, wicked slide of Jake's mouth on hers, she'd had one kiss from a suitor. It had been quick and dry and tight. *Nothing* like Jake's.

Jake hadn't been forceful, but he'd been insistent and persuasive. Lordy, had he. She'd thought her knees might give out. He'd held her fully against him, almost sheltering her and she'd felt the hard angles of his body from her breasts to her knees. His firm hold around her waist, the power of his brawny chest against her were so at odds with the softness of his lips, his clean male scent. Her initial surprise had lasted less than a heartbeat and then she'd simply felt. Excited and giddy and a melting warmth.

Here it was, five days later, and she couldn't figure out how to stop the ache that grew deeper and sharper each time she caught him looking at her with those hot eyes.

And she'd caught him more than once since Sunday night. His frank male interest set off a ticklish flutter in her stomach.

True to his word, he hadn't pushed, hadn't tried to kiss her again or even hold her hand. Even though she was disappointed, she told herself that was best. There could never be anything between them.

She couldn't stay. And, if she didn't slow things way down right now, it was going to hurt as badly to leave him as it was to leave Molly. *If* Emma was able to leave her sister at the Circle R. Jake hadn't said anything about changing his mind and keeping the little girl. That should've irritated Emma enough to forget that kiss, so why didn't it?

Because, she admitted, aside from wanting Jake, she liked him. More than once, she'd found herself smiling when she thought of his teasing her about Cora Wilkes. Emma had enjoyed the time she'd spent with Cora. After meeting the independent, no-nonsense woman, she understood why Jake had thought his little joke so funny.

But she felt more than like for him. His understanding about why she'd lied about being a widow, then sharing the loss of his wife had comforted Emma. And made her realize Jake was the first man she'd trusted since her daddy had died.

She trusted him so much that she'd caught herself daydreaming about telling him the whole truth, of staying here with him and Molly. But she couldn't think about herself. She was here to find a safe and loving home for her sister. Doing that didn't require getting further involved with Jake. It certainly shouldn't involve kissing him.

If nothing else, his being her employer should've been enough to keep her head from being turned by him, but it wasn't. She had to remember her place here. And her purpose. No matter how lonely or worried she became, she couldn't get any closer to him. But, as she drifted off to sleep on Friday night, her last thought was wishing she could tell Jake about her mama's murder and her attempt to escape the man responsible.

* * *

"Emma! Emma!"

"I'm coming!" Uncertain of where she was, Emma ran and ran, looking for Mama. Her breathing was labored; her side ached. The darkness was deep and endless. Why wasn't there a lamp or a candle? Or moonlight?

"Emma!"

She pushed herself to go faster, straining to see in the black night. Her legs pumped harder and her lungs burned.

Heavy footsteps rushed behind her. He was gaining ground.

"Emma, help me!" The cry was faint now.

Panicking, she flew, her feet barely touching the ground. Her heart beat so frantically that she felt as if her chest might burst. Not even a pinprick of light pierced the heavy shadows. Why couldn't she see anything? She was lost. Suddenly someone loomed in front of her and hard hands gripped her arms.

"Mama!" Emma screamed, snapping straight up in bed.

Breathing hard, whimpering, she stared blankly at the moonlight sliding across the sheet as she slowly came to her senses. Tears wet her cheeks. Quaking, she shoved her hair back out of her face with both hands. She struggled to drag in air, get a full breath. Beside her, Molly slept on.

She'd screamed only in her nightmare, Emma realized thankfully. Sweat had her light lawn night rail clinging to her body. Gasping, fighting to keep her heavy sobs inside, she felt as if she were suffocating.

She stumbled out of bed. She somehow had the presence of mind to pile up her pillow and the rolled-up quilt along Molly's side, safeguarding the baby between the bedding and the wall.

Instead of dreaming the usual awful scene where she'd walked in on Orson standing over her lifeless mother, Emma had been running. Trying to find Mama, trying to save her and escape the senator. A scream built in Emma's throat, tearing at her like a wild thing.

Moving on wobbly legs, she snatched open the bedroom door and rushed around the wall into the alcove where the laundry basket was stored. Tears blurred her vision as she opened the wooden door that led out to the root cellar. She left the screened door latched, letting in the light September breeze. Slumping forward against the jamb, she covered her mouth, her chest heaving.

Her initial panic lessened, leaving a chilling emptiness inside her. She had to be quiet. She didn't want to wake Molly or anyone else. She ordered herself to stop crying, but she couldn't.

Violent shuddering breaths racked her body, the sound roaring in her ears. As though from a distance, she thought she heard a voice before a big hand cupped her shoulder.

Struggling to collect her emotions, she let herself be turned around. She registered that it was Jake and didn't resist when he tugged her to him. Fresh tears trickled down her cheeks.

"Emma? Are you all right? Are you hurt?"

She was appalled for him to see her like this. She was practically coming unhinged.

Jake shook her gently. "Did someone try to hurt you?"

She felt him shift, knew he was looking over her head to search the darkness beyond the door.

"N-no, I'm not hurt," she managed to choke out.

His muttered response was lost beneath her sobs. She'd had nightmares since finding Mama dead, but they'd never frightened her this badly. It was more than fear. Emma cried for having to run away from her home, for losing both her parents, for having to leave her sister. Emma realized then that someone other than her was crying and she lifted her head. Hitched in the crook of Jake's arm, Molly wailed.

The lanky rancher winced and the helplessness on his face mirrored what Emma felt. A fresh burst of tears had her burying her face in his chest again, wetting his white work shirt.

"Easy now. Easy," he soothed, jiggling the baby lightly.

Emma didn't know if Jake was talking to her or her sister, but Molly quieted. Emma was finally able to draw a shallow breath, then another.

Jake eased back until his broad shoulders were braced against the wall, Emma in one arm and Molly in the other. He didn't fidget or seem in any hurry to move; he just held them.

Tucked against his broad chest, Emma's sobs lessened. She realized both her arms were wrapped around his waist. He was so steady, so solid. She didn't want to let go.

Hearing a wet smacking sound, Emma looked up through tear-blurred eyes to see her sister sucking her thumb. She wiped at her tears as Molly's eyes fluttered drowsily.

Jake exhaled, his breath stirring the fine hairs at Emma's temple. His heart beat rapidly beneath her ear. "Hell, y'all scared me to death."

His heart was pumping like a steam engine. Assailed on both sides by bawling females, all Jake knew to do was handle them the same way he would a spooked horse. In a low, calm voice, he murmured soothing words that made absolutely no sense. Emma finally quieted with only the occasional hiccup of a cry. Molly snuggled into his neck, her hot baby breath puffing against his skin. Her eyes grew heavier.

"I'm sorry," Emma said shakily. "I didn't mean to wake you."

"You didn't. I was in the kitchen, washing up after I checked on Nugget." Jake's prize palomino was due to foal twins any day. She was one of two mares who hadn't foaled back in the spring. "I heard a noise and saw your door was open, so I went to check."

"Molly was still sleeping when I left. I was only gone for a second. I wouldn't have left her if—"

"It's okay, Emma. No harm done." For the first time, he noticed she wasn't wearing her spectacles. Or shoes. Or a wrapper.

She sniffled, brushing at the dampness on her face. "Was she crying when you looked in?"

"Not at first." Jake wasn't about to admit that the kid hadn't started squalling until she'd seen him. He had stared at the baby, silently willing her to shut up. After a few seconds, it had occurred to him that *he* would have to be the one to do something with her or she'd wake the whole ranch.

When he'd reached for her, he'd expected the child to scoot away, but, instead, she'd held up her chubby arms. Despite the big tears rolling down her face, the little girl had looked at him with complete trust. As he'd lifted her, something cold and scary had shoved under Jake's ribs and he'd fought the urge to drop her on the bed and run straight for a bottle of whiskey.

"She likes you," Emma said softly, wiping at her cheeks.

Jake hoped not. "I don't know about that."

Over the past week, he'd found himself listening for the baby, watching for her, but he hadn't held her. Hadn't wanted to. He'd hardly picked himself up from losing one child. He wasn't getting attached to another one. Now, Emma, she was a different story.

"What happened, Em?"

"Nothing. I'm fine, really."

The hell she was. She had simmered down some, but only minutes ago, she'd been huddled against the screen door, sobbing her heart out.

She felt so soft and tempting against him. Her delicate scent—body-warmed soap—teased him, her thick dark hair draping over his arm like heavy silk. Beneath his palm, he felt the warmth of her skin through the fabric of her gown. No wrapper, no undergarments. The fullness of her unbound breasts against him had his body going hard. He wanted to lay her down on that bearskin rug behind him. The urge to run his hands over her and peel off her clothes tied Jake's gut in knots, but he willed it back.

He intended to keep his word about not pushing her, but want cut through him like a straight edge. This was the worst time for the heavy throb in his blood, the ache gathering in his lower body. It was torture to feel her like this and do nothing, but Jake didn't want to release her.

There was no ignoring the fierce swell of protectiveness inside him. He tightened his arm around her and she looked up, her dark lashes spiky, her eyes a wet deep green.

"The baby's asleep," he said in a half whisper, forcing back his desire. "After I put her back to bed, we're going to talk."

Alarm flashed across Emma's fine-boned features. "There's no need. I'm fine."

He admonished her by squeezing her waist. "You're scared out of your wits and you're gonna tell me why."

When she straightened and pulled back, he let her go, but only to guide her the few feet from the alcove to the dining table with a hand at the small of her back. Aided by the sweep of moonlight through the window, Jake pulled out a chair and gently urged her down into the seat. One-handed, he struck a match against the wooden surface and lit the lamp in the center of the table. Whatever had spooked Emma might seem less threatening if she had some light.

Hoping the baby wouldn't wake up, he carefully put her

back to bed. After double-checking the barrier Emma had erected from a pillow and a quilt, he walked out and left the door slightly ajar. Emma sat at the table, still swiping at her eyes, her sable hair falling over her right shoulder, revealing her nape and the tender skin behind her ear.

He wanted to pull her into him, kiss that patch of flesh. Instead, he went into the kitchen and took a clean cloth from the cupboard beside the sink. After wetting it, he came back to the table, pressing the rag into Emma's hand as he pulled out the chair beside her and sat down.

With one hand, she held the wet cloth to her face and, with the other, she plucked at the dampened bodice of her gown. The lightweight material clung to her breasts and the concave dip of her stomach. Jake swallowed hard and tore his gaze away. She needed reassurance and his jumping on her like a starved animal wouldn't do it.

He angled his chair to face her. "What happened, Em?"

"It was just a dream. I was…startled," she said in a small voice as she fiddled with the corner of the damp cloth.

"You'll feel better if you tell me." Jake took the linen from her and put it on the table then folded both of her trembling hands in his. "You're still shaking."

She sat silently, wanting to tell him, knowing she shouldn't.

"Does it have anything to do with why you're skittish around men sometimes?"

She didn't want to lie to him, but she couldn't tell him anything about Orson. And she knew she *shouldn't* tell him anything more about herself.

He waited, his gaze patient. The dark stubble along his jaw softened the rough angles of his face. His hands were strong and steady on hers. And hot. She felt so alone. Maybe if she told him about the dream, it would stop torturing her. She wouldn't share everything, but a little couldn't hurt, could it?

Those dark eyes invited her to trust him, to confide in him. "Since my mother died," she began haltingly, "I've had dreams. Nightmares."

"About her dying?"

"Yes." She took a deep breath. "Tonight, the dream was different. She called out for me and I ran and ran, but I couldn't find her. It was pitch black. Finally I couldn't hear her anymore. I couldn't help her."

His thumbs stroked the center of her palms. "How did she die?"

Emma shook her head, sliding her hands from his. "I can't talk about it."

"All right."

Why did he have to be so kind? He didn't reach for her again, but he stayed close. His big hands rested on his knees, close enough that she could see the individual hairs on his forearm. She wanted to climb into his lap, let him chase away the fear that chewed at her composure. She absolutely could not do that.

Dragging her gaze from his, she stood. "I don't know why I was so upset. It was just a dream."

"One that scared you silly." Jake rose, too, smoothing his hands over her shoulders. "Is this the same dream that upset you the night I came to your room?"

"I wasn't—"

"Em, I know you were crying." He stroked a hand down her hair.

She bowed her head. "It wasn't exactly the same dream, but, yes, it was about Mama's death."

"How many of these dreams have you had?"

She hesitated. "A few."

Sliding a knuckle under her chin, he tipped her face up to his. "Emma."

"Almost every night when I first came, but not so often now." Her dreams were as likely to be about him as they were about what had happened to her mother. "It hasn't affected my job. I would never let that happen."

"I'm not thinkin' anything like that, honey."

"I'm glad. It helps to talk to you," she admitted shyly.

"Good."

When he tugged her close, she went with no thought of resisting. "Jake?"

"Hmm?"

"What happened to your mother?"

"She lit out when Bram and I were small. About twelve years ago, we got word she'd died in San Francisco."

"You lost your father, too?"

"A few months before Ma left. He died of pneumonia."

"I'm sorry." Despite the shrug he gave, she knew it had to be painful. "I shouldn't have brought it up."

"You can talk to me anytime you want." His breath wafted against the crown of her head. "About anything."

She wouldn't, but she nodded anyway as he folded her against him. The solid strength in those steel-hard arms sheltered her, settled her. His shirt button pressed against her cheek, his trouser button nudged her stomach. Along with something else.

Heat flushed her body as she felt the hard ridge of his manhood. The only thing separating their skin was her lawn night rail and his light cotton shirt. He could easily touch her anywhere. Everywhere. She should pull away and go to bed, but she wanted—needed—to stay here just a bit longer. She tentatively put her arms around him. He felt so good.

He brushed his lips across her hair and she squeezed her eyes shut. More than anything, she wanted to turn her face up to his and kiss him, but she didn't.

She shouldn't let things go further between her and Jake, but, when he wrapped her up in his arms, she felt as if she mattered and her common sense crumbled.

She trusted him. He was the first man to take care of her since Daddy's death, but it changed nothing. She couldn't stay. And she couldn't tell him the truth.

She felt foolish. All day, Emma had floated around with her head in the clouds, thinking about how wonderful Jake had been to her last night, believing he had finally started to soften toward Molly and would probably keep her. Then Emma had learned at supper four hours ago that he hadn't been working in the south pasture today as she'd believed. He'd been in Abilene, checking to see if anyone had answered his ad about a family for her sister.

Which was why Emma was in the barn so late on this Saturday night. Unwilling to chance Molly's waking and getting out of bed, Emma had brought the sleeping child with her. The baby nestled in the big laundry basket, which Emma had padded with a quilt. Glancing at Molly just inside the stall behind her, Emma's heart tripped painfully. It was her fault.

If she hadn't started crying over that nightmare, Jake never would have heard her and he never would've had to deal with a wailing Molly. Emma should've been able to control herself. She shouldn't have let Jake take care of her or the baby. At the very least, she should've relieved him of her sister. He probably thought she was a hysterical female.

He'd said from the beginning he didn't want Molly. Emma hadn't forgotten that, but she had let herself start to hope, believe what she wanted to about her sister belonging here. And, if she had done a better job of keeping the little girl away from Jake, he wouldn't have gone to Abilene looking to give the baby away the day after he'd acted as if he were starting to care for her.

If he found a family for Molly, Emma would have to go, too, whether it was to Abilene or somewhere else. She couldn't let her sister go off by herself, especially if it was to a busier town. It would be much easier for Orson Douglas to find them in a city like Abilene, closer to the railroad line. And, if he found them, Emma feared he would murder her as he'd murdered her mother.

Jake might have already given her sister away. Emma gnawed at her thumbnail. She wasn't sure how long she'd been waiting in the barn. At least a half an hour. The night air was almost cool, but sweat slicked her palms. How much longer? Surely he wasn't spending the night in Abilene. If he did, Emma wouldn't get a wink of sleep. She had to talk to him now. She had to convince him to let Molly stay.

Apprehension swept through her as she paced back and forth in front of her mare's stall. The dainty bay Emma had ridden out to the Circle R on her first day watched her with wide, unblinking eyes. The smell of horseflesh and hay scented the air. Emma's gray skirts trailed across the straw-littered dirt floor, stirring up small plumes of dust.

Her mare snorted, gently bumping her nose into the stall slat and alerting Emma to a noise. The sound of a horse cantering up to the barn. Jake, she hoped. After a quick scrub of her tear-stained face and eyes, she smoothed a hand over the kerchief that held back her hair. She adjusted her glasses and tried not to rush forward as a man stopped in the barn doorway and dismounted.

Yes, it was Jake. Relief mixed with determination and fear. He led his horse inside. The first ten feet inside the barn were cleared, the space left to accommodate a myriad of things, be it a sick animal or a busted wagon wheel. Tack and tools hung neatly on the walls above a plow and a hay baler on one side and sawhorses on the opposite one. Stalls on either side were separated by a space wide enough to drive in at least one wagon. Deep in the shadows, Emma stood at the corner of the first stall, near an unused sawhorse.

Behind her, Molly gave a soft snore, but slept on. Emma swallowed hard, stepping forward as Jake dismounted. She wouldn't cry. She wouldn't. Before she could make her presence known, he groaned and gripped the saddle, bowing his head to rest it against the seat.

She stilled. What was wrong with him?

After a long moment, he palmed off his cowboy hat and hooked it onto the horn. A quick tug of the saddle string released his canteen and he walked out of the barn. He hadn't seen her. The squeak of the pump handle reached Emma's ears then the gush of water.

After a few moments, Jake returned, taking a long swallow from the canteen. The sweep of moonlight glistened against his wet hair and face. A dark shadow on the neck and shoulders of his shirt showed that the garment was wet, too. He scowled as he ran a hand down his face. Then he saw her.

He blinked, took a step forward. "Emma?"

"Yes." Moving into the dim light, she tried to sound calm. She shoved her hands into the pockets of her old gray work dress to hide her ragged nails. Inside, she was a mass of nerves, so twitchy that she would jump if a moth so much as fluttered in her direction.

A crooked smile hitched up one corner of his mouth. "Hi." His voice was soft, welcoming as his gaze slid hotly over her.

She was astonished by a sudden urge to smack him, although that did make it easier not to be distracted by his smoldering look. Trying to decide how to start, she took a deep breath. There was no mistaking the tang of liquor on him. And she thought his eyes were glassy.

Suddenly concern flashed across his features. "Is everything okay? Are you all right? What's happened?"

You and your irksome ad! she wanted to scream. The risk of provoking him had her quaking inside, but she couldn't back down. She had to do this for Molly. Aware of the sleeping child behind her, she kept her voice low. "Your brother said you went to Abilene today."

He nodded, lifting the canteen to take another drink of water.

She pushed herself to follow through. "You went there to look for a family for Molly?"

After a slight hesitation, as if he'd only then realized she might not like his answer, he gave a jerky nod.

"Last night wasn't her fault. It was mine. I shouldn't have shirked my responsibility and expected you to take care of her."

He shook his head as if to clear it, sending droplets of water through the air. "What are you taking about? When you had the nightmare?"

"Yes. Shh." Emma glanced over her shoulder.

Jake's gaze went past her. "Why do we have to be quiet?"

"Molly's asleep."

"Out here!" he exclaimed. With a grimace, he said in a low voice, "Sorry."

"I wasn't going to risk her waking up while I was gone, especially after last night." Unable to stand still any longer, Emma paced the length of one stall and back. Her hair fell over one shoulder and she impatiently pushed it away. "She's a good little girl. She is."

After a slight pause, he said, "Yeah."

Emma could read nothing in his reply. "She's already started to think of this as her home. Don't make her leave."

"Trying to find her a family is nothing new," he said in a grainy voice. "What's got you so het up?"

"She shouldn't be held accountable for something that was my fault. If I'd done my job and kept her out of the way, you wouldn't feel the need to hand her off to someone else. She isn't any trouble. The problem is that I didn't do what I should have."

Closing his eyes for a brief second, Jake pinched the bridge of his nose. "It has nothing to do with you."

"You could hire someone else." If he did, it would tear Emma up. "The woman who was here when I arrived for my interview might still be available."

"I wouldn't have her raise a dog, much less a kid," he growled in a half whisper. Taking another sip of water, he winced as if he were in pain.

He had definitely been drinking. Maybe this wasn't the best time to talk to him, although he didn't seem incapacitated. Nothing like how he'd been the night he'd come to her room. "How will you know if you've chosen the right place for her? You can't let her go to someone who might not love her."

He looked insulted. "Do you think I'd give her to a family I didn't think wanted her?"

"Want isn't the same as love." Emma moved closer, her voice low and urgent. Beneath the smells of leather and horses, she caught Jake's own unique scent.

A stark silence fell between them. Regret etched his face and Jake looked away.

"She shouldn't be the one to go. It should be me."

"No," he said in a hard, low voice.

"Why not? She's settled in. Your family likes her. It would be easier for me to move on than it would be for her." She refrained from pointing out that he was the only Ross who didn't want the little girl. "There's really no reason to send her away."

"There are reasons," he said gruffly, walking over to his horse and loosening the cinch on the saddle.

Sliding it off, he slung it over his shoulder as if it weighed nothing and moved past her to the darkened space where he kept the sawhorses. Tilting back his head, he took a long drink from the canteen.

Even in the dim light, Emma could see his face closing up. He settled the saddle onto the sawhorse then retraced his steps to remove the horse blanket and bridle from his mount.

He muttered under his breath. "Maybe my reasons for finding her a family have nothing to do with you."

"Oh?" She waited expectantly, but he didn't continue. He didn't even look at her. "If she goes, I'll have to go with her."

At his startled "Why?" she knew she had to be careful not to reveal her true connection to the baby.

"She will have been uprooted from familiar surroundings twice in a short period of time. The least I can do is stay with her until she's settled, help ease her way."

Mouth tight, his gaze leveled into hers. "No one said anything about you leaving."

"If Molly's gone, no one will have need of me." Why couldn't he just say the baby could stay?

"We hired you to cook and take care of the house, too."

"You can easily find another cook or housekeeper."

"I don't want another one," he muttered, a muscle flexing in his jaw.

"Please consider hiring someone else for Molly. Someone who will do what you want. She's such a good little girl."

"No."

Emma's tightly held control slipped and she cried, "I don't understand!"

"Maybe it's that she deserves a better place." The words sounded forced out of him. "A better family."

The grim set of his face had Emma's heart clenching. "Why would you say such a thing?"

Jake remained silent. He wasn't going to answer Emma's question.

Tentatively, she touched his arm. "You told me last night I could talk to you about anything."

"I remember what I said." He tried to keep his voice emotionless, flat. The last thing he wanted was to tell Emma why he had a problem with the baby. But, thanks to his earlier stop at Delia's grave, the guilt and the anger were riding him too hard to dismiss.

His drinking in Abilene hadn't helped dull anything. Instead of drowning his thoughts, the whiskey only clouded them further.

Just get it over with, he told himself. He dreaded seeing the disdain in Emma's eyes when she learned the truth, but he couldn't let her continue to blame herself for something that wasn't her fault.

The canteen dangled from his right hand and his left braced against his gelding's neck for support. "I told you about my wife, but I didn't tell you what killed her."

Agony throbbed beneath his words and Emma sensed a raw vulnerability she'd never felt in him before. Suddenly she didn't want to know his reasons for not wanting to keep Molly. "It's all right," she said quickly. "You don't owe me any explanations. I forgot my place."

"No, you didn't. You have a right to know, to understand that my decision to give up the baby has nothing to do with you."

His shoulders were rigid with tension, his back bowed as if fighting off a blow. "Our baby died, too."

Oh, no. Emma's chest caved.

"Delia, my wife, was six months along when it happened."

Emma closed her eyes as emotion twisted her heart. She had thought perhaps Jake's wife had died before they could have children, but, instead, the woman had died while carrying their child. Now Emma recognized that the cold, hard glitter she'd seen in his eyes when he was near Molly wasn't resentment, but pain. And grief. "Jake, I'm so sorry."

"It was my fault. Delia never should've conceived." Still beside his horse, he shoved a hand through his hair, looking tortured.

Emma eased close enough that her shoulder grazed his shirtsleeve.

Jake's gut was already knotted up tighter than wet leather. Having her so near, feeling the heat of her body played havoc with his resolve to tell her everything. He didn't want her to look at him the way Quentin did.

"There was an accident or something?" she asked quietly. "What happened?"

"I happened," he grated out. Even beneath the smells of hay and dirt and animals, he caught her fresh soap scent. It made him feel dark and dirty against her sweetness. "From the time we married, all she heard was how much I wanted children. A big family," he said bitterly. "And finally she conceived."

Emma started to tremble, although she didn't know why.

"When she was six months along, she began to bleed." His voice cracked and he cleared his throat before continuing.

"There was so much blood. I couldn't stop it. Neither could Georgia or Ike. By the time we got to Whirlwind, Delia and the baby were gone."

Oh, Jake. Emma pressed a hand to her mouth, hating the helplessness that swamped her. She wished she knew what to say. There were no words that could comfort after such a loss. There certainly hadn't been any after the death of her mother.

"I couldn't figure out what went wrong. I blamed the doctor, my cousin, my uncle. Everyone but myself." The self-loathing in Jake's eyes made her want to go to him. "Until that night when Quentin found me. He accused me of killing her."

Shock and anger hit her at the same time. How could someone say that to another person?

"He was right. She'd been warned repeatedly by the doctor not to have children, but she didn't tell me."

"Why would she keep such a thing from you?"

"Because all she ever heard from me was how much I wanted a child."

"There's nothing wrong with wanting a family."

"There is if your wife thinks she has to risk her life to give you one."

Emma's anger grew at the guilt still eating at him. Jake's wife bore the responsibility for keeping the secret, but it wasn't Emma's place to say so. Especially since she was keeping secrets from him, too. "So, that's why it pains you to be around Molly? Why you want to give her away?"

He nodded.

The admission had Emma flattening a hand against her suddenly queasy stomach.

Lines carved deep grooves around his mouth. His eyes glittered like black ice in the pale light. "I don't want you worrying about the way you do your job. My problem with the baby doesn't have anything to do with you."

If he only knew how much Molly did have to do with her, Emma thought on a swell of regret. She nodded, wanting to smooth away the bleakness in his face. His wide shoulders appeared visibly weighted by guilt. Did he want to be alone? Even if he did, Emma couldn't leave him like this.

What he'd just told her had ramifications for Molly, but right now Emma couldn't think past the grief and guilt in his eyes. He'd lost so much. Following an impulse, she slipped her arm through his.

Plainly surprised, his gaze swerved to her.

"It isn't your fault," she said. The words sounded weak, but they were all she had.

Tension lashed his body and his large hand folded over her smaller one, holding her to him. She wished he could believe her, but he blamed himself, just as Quentin blamed him. To Emma's way of thinking, Jake's brother-in-law had no room to point fingers. If the man had known his sister had been warned not to have a baby, he would've also known that she hadn't shared that information with her husband. Why hadn't Quentin made sure Jake knew what Delia was keeping from him?

Jake wouldn't have risked his wife's life, no matter how badly he wanted a child. Emma knew that with everything in her.

Her heart ached for him, but as she stood silently beside him, she began to realize just how ill it boded for Molly. Jake might never overcome his aversion to the baby. Emma couldn't leave her sister here and risk Jake never being able to do more than tolerate her.

Forget convincing Jake to let Molly stay. Emma knew now that neither of them could.

BUSINESS REPLY MAIL
FIRST-CLASS MAIL   PERMIT NO. 717   BUFFALO, NY

POSTAGE WILL BE PAID BY ADDRESSEE

HARLEQUIN READER SERVICE
3010 WALDEN AVE
PO BOX 1867
BUFFALO NY 14240-9952

NO POSTAGE
NECESSARY
IF MAILED
IN THE
UNITED STATES

Chapter Nine

————

W hat had just happened? Jake felt as if he'd been poleaxed. He was glad he'd told Emma about Delia and the baby. Relieved actually. But it hadn't been relief that had grabbed him around the throat when Emma had said she would go if Molly did.

Emma leave? It had taken Jake a bit of time to comprehend what she'd told him. The lingering heaviness of liquor hindered his thinking, but even so, he'd been especially slow on the draw. By the time he'd figured out why she was worked up, so was he.

Last night, when he'd held that kid, he'd felt something disquieting. Intimidating. That was why he'd gone to Abilene. He'd found Molly the perfect family, but that news had gotten lost in the wake of Emma's upset and his memories. Probably for the best, he thought. He wasn't ready to tell her what had happened in Abilene. Hell, he couldn't even explain it to himself.

For the next few days, Emma blatantly avoided him and he saw the baby less than five times. The times when Emma couldn't avoid him, she acted as skittish as a cornered cat.

Jake tried not to let it bother him, but it did. He knew in his gut that she didn't blame him for what happened to Delia. However, Molly's fate was another story.

He had plenty to occupy his mind with the birth of Nugget's twins—both females—and his other chores, but Emma's skirting him chafed his pride like burrs in his long johns.

Three evenings after meeting up with her in the barn, Jake walked into the house for supper and found everyone in the front room frozen in place. Bathed in the softening light of day, Emma set food on the table. Ike stood at the back of the sofa with Bram several feet away to Jake's right. Georgia knelt on the floor, her good hand resting on Molly's shoulder. Their rapt stares were fixed on the child, anticipation thick in the air. The little girl stood between them and Jake.

Bram held up a staying hand and Jake halted in midstride. He glanced over at Emma. She kept her gaze on the baby.

Molly teetered then took a halting step away from Georgia. The older woman beamed.

Bram went to his haunches. "C'mon, Molly. Come to Uncle Bram."

"No!" she squealed. She wrinkled up her nose and took an unsteady step, then another. But, instead of moving to Bram, she pointed herself toward Jake.

"Hey!" his brother said indignantly. "I'm the one who's been helping you. Not him."

"No!" Arms flailing, Molly immediately plopped down on her bottom. Before Bram or Georgia could reach her, she got to her hands and knees, pushing herself back up. And once again headed for Jake.

An unfamiliar warmth welled up inside him. It filled every inch of his chest and kept him in place. Anticipation tightened his muscles as he silently willed the child not to fall.

One jerky step at a time, she made her way closer. When she wobbled to within about three feet of him, Emma started forward.

To pick up the little girl, Jake knew. He waved her off, wanting to see if Molly could make it to him.

She swayed, nearly falling and Jake realized he was holding his breath. After a second, she regained her balance and clomped toward him. She flashed her two teeth in a big grin. "No!"

"Why does she keep saying that?" he asked.

"It's her favorite word right now," Bram informed him dryly.

With lurching steps, she came closer, the rest of his family hovering behind. When she was a foot away, she suddenly launched herself through the air at Jake.

He barely caught her. With his heart in his throat, he automatically swung her up in his arms, praising, "Look what you did."

He felt the weight of his family's stares. Of Emma's. The room was hushed, as if everyone were holding their collective breath. Then Georgia, Ike and Bram moved closer, clapping and laughing.

Molly laughed, too, patting her hands together. She smiled up at Jake with a trust and innocence that split his heart wide-open.

"You did it, Molly!" Emma hurried over.

There was a smile on her face, but Jake saw the dark worry in her eyes and he knew the cause. She believed he had no desire to be near the child.

His family gathered around, making a to-do over the baby. Jake peeled her chubby hands off his blue work shirt and passed her to Emma.

He followed everyone to the table for supper. And, while

the rest of the family talked about this and that, including the most recent theft in town, Jake's thoughts stayed stuck on the baby. It took him until dessert to realize that the giant bubble of emotion in his chest was pride. In Molly.

He'd seen the shocked disbelief on his family's faces and the downright dismay on Emma's. For cryin' out loud, they acted as if he'd never held the kid when he certainly had. At least...twice. Was that all?

Emma appeared only to bring more food or drink, coffee for all of them except Bram, who had milk. She hardly spoke. Jake surreptitiously watched her during those times. She was pale, visibly nervous. Probably blaming herself for his picking up the baby, which meant he hadn't put Emma at ease about her job the other night.

When she started to clear the plates from the table, he shifted his attention to the baby, who had crawled out of the kitchen. Tangling a hand in the nurse's gray skirts, Molly hauled herself to her feet, swayed drunkenly then sank to her bottom. After a moment, she repeated the same pattern.

Bram scooted his chair away from the table and rose, moving behind Jake to scoop up the little girl. He tickled her until she squealed and giggled. "C'mon, punkin. I'll keep her out of your way, Emma."

The brunette nodded, disappearing into the kitchen, loaded down with plates.

Jake rose, too, contemplating the kitchen doorway. Every time he looked at Emma, her face grew more anxious. It had to be the situation with Molly that vexed her and the turmoil in her eyes had him looking for some space. He had enough work to do in the barn to stay busy for an hour or two.

As Jake passed Bram on his way to the front door, Molly lunged toward him. Reflex had him opening his arms to catch her. She landed with a grunt against his chest and he grinned.

"You're gonna be one of those kids who jumps off the roof to see if you can fly, aren't you?"

"No!"

He laughed along with the others, shifting her to his left arm. "Let's go to the barn. I'll show you the fillies."

"Good idea." His brother shared a look with their cousin and uncle before regarding Jake curiously. "I'll go with you and get an extra bucket of water for the supper dishes."

As they walked out, Bram goosed the little girl in the hollow where her neck met her shoulder. She shrieked, bucking in Jake's arms and diving for his opposite side in an attempt to escape his brother's pestering.

Jake chuckled. "I've got ya."

When the other man stopped at the pump, Molly waved fiercely. "Bye! Bye! Bye!"

"See ya in a bit," Bram said.

As Jake moved down the left row of stalls, the little girl patted his shoulder. "Yake. Yake."

Heart tripping, he looked down into her innocent gray-green eyes. Hesitantly, he touched his finger to her nose. "Molly."

Blond curls bouncing, she smacked a hand on her tummy, smiling broadly. "Ma-wee."

"Yes, you are." Jake's chest felt as if it were about to burst.

Her attention was already somewhere else. She grabbed one of the four buttons on his shirt placket as he continued on to the last stall. One of the fillies stuck its muzzle through the slat, bumping against the wood eagerly. The other one huddled against Nugget a few feet away.

When the mare saw Jake, she nickered and ambled to him, dipping her head over the stall to rub it up and down his arm. Her white tail and mane against her rich gold coloring made her one of the most beautiful palominos Jake had ever seen.

Molly said something he couldn't interpret, but he understood her reach toward the animal and the wonder on her face. He stepped up to the horse, smoothing his free hand down her velvety nose as he said to Molly, "Here, you pet her."

Instead, she leaned over and planted a big wet kiss between the horse's eyes. Nugget's ears pricked.

Jake chuckled at the animal's interest. Both fillies stood next to their mother now, pale blond tails twitching, their black eyes trained on Molly. The little girl dove for the closest one and Jake caught her, guiding her hand to the animal's forehead. "Go easy, now. Right there."

He smoothed her little fingers down the satiny nose. She mimicked his movement, sliding her hand down again and again.

The child didn't have a skittish bone in her body.

A fierce pride filled Jake, which was ridiculous because he didn't have one thing to do with her being comfortable around horses or anything else. He knew then that she belonged at the Circle R. Realizing that also explained the acceptance he'd felt toward her the other night. She had gotten under his skin. He couldn't let her go now. "You like 'em, huh?"

He scratched both fillies behind their fuzzy ears. They tolerated the petting for a minute, then one of them jumped back and head-butted the other one.

The pair nipped at each other then darted to the far side of the space. Molly laughed at their antics. Jake went around the stall's corner and to the rear, reaching between two slats to unlatch the door that opened out to the corral. The fillies took off in a skitter of hooves and dust.

Nugget blew out a hot, horsey breath, nibbling at Jake's shoulder. "Didn't bring anything for you, girl."

Molly lunged with both hands and he barely caught her before she poked a finger in the mare's eye.

Ears twitching, Nugget shook her head and stepped back out of the baby's reach. The swish of skirts had Jake's gaze going to the opposite end of the barn. Emma walked in with Bram, her steps hurried although she couldn't outpace his long strides.

Seeing the concern that pinched her face, Jake started toward them. She looked more nervous than she had a few minutes ago.

Sounding slightly breathless, she said, "I'm sorry. I thought Bram had her. I hope she didn't bother you."

"No." He wrapped his arm firmly around Molly's waist as she lunged over his shoulder to jabber something to the mare.

She didn't look at him, just took the baby and cuddled her close as she backed away. "Come on, Molly. Let's go inside now."

Her relief at having the child in her arms was so plain that Jake should have been insulted. Was she uneasy about the baby being with him? Worried that Jake would neglect her? If so, he needed to set Emma straight on that. "I was just showing her the horses."

"Jake has things to do." Emma brushed a kiss against the little girl's temple before looking at him. Or rather, at his chin. "I'll be more careful."

"It was no bother, was it, Jake?" Bram shot him a look and jerked his head toward Emma, clearly trying to get Jake to reassure the woman.

"No."

Bram frowned, which meant he wanted Jake to say more, but Jake didn't know exactly what to say.

Dragging a hand across his nape, he came up with just about the most brilliant thing he'd ever said. "Molly likes the horses. Wasn't scared of them at all."

"'Orse." The child clapped her hands, leaning toward Nugget.

"We can come out tomorrow—" Emma broke off then resumed in a less-than-steady voice. "We can see Nugget again, all right?" She hugged the baby to her, glancing in Jake's direction. "She won't be underfoot."

"Emma—"

Bram interrupted, scowling at Jake. "Everything's fine."

She didn't respond. Jake saw the doubt in her eyes and realized she didn't know anything had changed. That *he* had changed. "Emma, could I talk to you for a minute?"

She stiffened as if he'd threatened to take a switch to her. "Of course. May I get Molly ready for bed, first?"

"I'll do it." Bram took the little girl, hitching her in the crook of one arm.

"Oh, no, please don't!" The brunette looked panicked. "I'm sure I won't be long, then I can take care of her."

"I want to do it. And I don't want you to give it another thought." His brother's gaze shifted to Jake. Whatever he saw in Jake's face had his focus returning to Emma and contemplating her. "No one expects you to do everything, all the time. She'll be clean as a whistle and ready for bed by the time you get back to the house." Bram lifted the little girl over his head and blew on her belly. She shrieked with laughter, kicking her feet.

Bram left, chuckling when his murmured words to Molly had her shrieking, "No!"

After a long moment, Emma faced Jake. In the slant of late-day sunlight, he could see the apprehension on her face. His gut tightened. She was no doubt still concerned about his giving away the baby.

He cleared his throat. "I should've told you this the other night, but—"

"You found another family for Molly?" Emotion trembled beneath her words.

"Yes." He couldn't miss the devastation that crumpled her features. "I mean, no."

She bit her lip, her hands pushing so hard against her pockets he was surprised the seams didn't give.

"I wasn't thinking too clearly after I returned from Abilene."

She made a small sound of distress.

Jake figured he'd better spit it out. "What I'm tryin' to tell you is I want her to stay."

Emma drew in a sharp breath, searching his face. After a long moment, she said, "You wouldn't tease about this."

"Hel— Heck, no."

Hope shone in her eyes briefly. "But what about…"

"What I said about Delia and my baby?"

She nodded. "If you don't think you can love Molly, you should let me take her to town and help you find another family for her. Don't let her get any more attached to all of you."

"She belongs here, Em." Cupping the petite woman's shoulders, he turned her fully toward him. Though afraid he might see blame, he forced himself to look into her green eyes. But behind her spectacles was only concern and caution. "When I went to Abilene, I found a family for Molly. Good churchgoing people. They really wanted her and I agreed."

Beneath his hold, Emma flinched. Tears filled her eyes.

"But I didn't get a mile outside of town before I knew I'd made a mistake."

Her gaze jerked to his; he could swear she stopped breathing. "Why?"

"I told myself it was because the man didn't know a horse

from a mule." Even though he was serious, he hoped that might coax a smile out of her, but it didn't. "Now I know the real reason, but the other night in the barn, I didn't."

Too much whiskey, for one thing. Silence ticked between them for a long moment. Jake's nerves prickled.

"Are you sure?" Emma asked shakily, staring at his chest. "Really sure?"

He waited until her gaze rose to his. "Yes."

Looking as if she finally believed him, she closed her eyes. The relief on her face was so great that he wanted to kick himself for taking so long to figure things out.

"Thank you." She reached for the nearest stall, curling a hand over one of the slats.

Her voice was soft, calm, but she looked as if her legs might give out at any second. The white of her knuckles alerted Jake to the death grip she had on the wood. He cupped her elbow. "You okay?"

She started to speak then simply nodded.

His thumb brushed the skin of her inner arm, just below the bend of her elbow. "You look wobbly."

"I'm fine. Just relieved."

The word hardly seemed to describe the reaction Jake was witnessing.

"You're absolutely sure?" she asked.

"Yes." He could tell she was going to ask again. Chuckling, he swept his thumb over her soft skin. "I'm sure, Em."

When he'd first told her he had changed his mind, she'd looked startled, but also…guilty. Why would she look guilty?

He must have read that wrong. Because right now she looked so pleased that Jake called himself nine kinds of a fool for taking so long to admit he wanted the baby to stay.

"You made the right decision." Emma's soft smile stole his breath. "You're perfect for each other."

She was steady now and didn't need his support, but he didn't want to let go.

She half turned to him, releasing her tight-fisted hold on the stall. "What about your family?"

"You know they all want her. I'll tell them I've changed my mind about her staying."

"Thank you," she whispered, clasping his hand between both of hers. "Thank you so much."

He smiled. "No doubt we're getting the better end of this deal."

Her eyes went liquid, the way they had after he'd kissed her, and Jake had all he could do to keep from pulling her to him.

"I want to tell Molly." With a squeeze of his hand, Emma hurried out of the barn, calling over her shoulder. "Thank you!"

He half expected to feel panic or a sudden pull in his gut that would tell him he'd made the wrong decision. Neither happened. Nor was he hit with the mind-numbing need for a drink.

For the first time since Delia's death, Jake saw something in his future besides guilt. He'd never thought he would want another child, never thought he'd be given another chance. But he had and he wasn't going to waste it.

If Emma had stayed out there another second with Jake, she would have thrown herself into his arms. She had planned to leave with Molly tonight, after the family was asleep. Their things were packed. All that remained was to write the note explaining that Molly was her sister and that they couldn't stay. She would tell as much as she could without saying anything about her mother's murder or mentioning Orson.

But now they didn't have to go!

If Jake thought it was silly that she wanted to tell the baby, he didn't let on. Just smiled the smile that turned her upside down. Lately, she'd questioned her decision to follow him from Abilene, to choose his family for Molly, but she'd been right. They loved the child and her sister was most definitely attached to them.

Now Emma could unpack the valise. Now Molly could keep the little dress and bonnet Josie Holt had made for her.

That night, Emma slept without having any dreams. Over the next week, the family fully embraced the little girl and Emma could see how glad they were that Jake had changed his mind.

Georgia rocked the baby and sang her to sleep every night. Ike put Molly on his knee while he worked on the books, though he didn't get a lot done because he had to keep her hands out of the inkwell and off his ledger. Bram was good about taking care of the little girl in the evenings after supper.

And he was as dead set as Jake on turning her into a horse-woman. The brothers insisted on taking her out every night, one or the other of them sitting her on the saddle in front of them as they rode the perimeter around the house. Jake and Bram had been riding since the age of four and they wanted that for Molly. She had a natural instinct, Jake said.

Emma was grateful every single day for every gesture, every kindness. Molly had a home. She was loved. She was safe. Emma felt safe, too, though she knew she wasn't.

Two months had passed since she and Molly had escaped Orson. There was no word that the cruel senator was looking for them, no word of him or his man, Sharpton, being anywhere near Whirlwind. It was easy to imagine staying here herself, but Emma knew, if she did, there would always be the chance that Orson would find Molly.

Still, it was several days before she could force herself to think about leaving. As she worked in the kitchen a week later, Emma knew she had to make a plan. Peach-pie filling cooled on the counter to the right of the stove. The sweet fruity aroma filled the room as she rolled out crusts for four pies.

The September temperature was mild so she had opened the wooden door that led outside, allowing the cooler air to come through the screened door. Even so, working over the stove had her perspiring. Her spectacles slipped down her nose for the hundredth time. She hated wearing them, but now she felt as if something were amiss if she didn't. She'd braided her hair and wound it into a coronet to get the heavy mass off her neck. Her faded pink calico was damp between her breasts, down the line of her spine.

Molly played on the floor close to the screened door, banging a spoon against the small saucepan Emma had given her. Working on the long counter to the right of the stove, Emma laid the crusts in the pie dishes and crimped the edges. Mama had always insisted on crimped edges. The memory put a lump in Emma's throat. And brought her thoughts back to her stepfather, what he'd done to her mother. What he would likely do to her if he found her.

The thought of leaving Molly filled Emma with dread. And the thought of leaving the Rosses left her feeling more hollow every day. Damn Orson Douglas!

Deciding the filling was cool enough, Emma picked up the stew pot and began spooning the sugary mixture into the first pie dish. She had to make sure her sister's clothes would fit through the winter. Who would the Rosses find to care for the little girl after Emma left?

She choked back a sob. Using the back of one flour-dusted hand, she swiped at the tears welling in her eyes.

"Something sure smells good in here."

Starting violently at the sound of Jake's voice, she cried out and lost her grip on the heavy pot. The door opened and clattered shut as the object hit the edge of the counter.

She managed to catch the pot, but not before pie filling splattered all over her apron and a few places on the pine floor.

"Sorry." Jake was beside her immediately, taking the ironware and setting it aside.

Molly crawled toward him as fast as she could, her wooden spoon clacking against the pine floor. "Yake!"

"Hey, little bit." He scooped her up and turned back to Emma.

Using her apron hem, she wiped at the sticky globs that dotted her bodice and one sleeve of her pink calico.

Feeling his gaze on her, she gave a self-conscious laugh. "That was clumsy. I don't know what's wrong with me."

"It was just an accident." He bent over the pot and inhaled deeply, his hard shoulder brushing her arm on the way. "Peach pie?"

His breath washed against the back of her hand, causing her skin to tingle. "It was almost floor pie."

He chuckled.

She tried to match his lightness. "You wouldn't have thought it funny if you'd lost your dessert."

Mercy, he smelled good. Like the outdoors and leather and a faint tang of sweat.

"You mean, Bram could've lost *his*. You'd never make me go without dessert, would you?"

She wanted to smile, to flirt with him, but every breath of his clean, masculine scent reminded her that she had to leave. The sight of him—white shirt molded to broad shoulders and big arms, his hat pushed carelessly back to reveal his sweat-dampened hair falling over his forehead, those hot black eyes—was branded on her brain.

He looked like a mountain, solid, sheltering. After she left the Circle R, when she felt lonely or afraid, she would call this image of Jake to mind. She bit her lip to keep it from quivering.

"Emma?"

Dragging her attention back to the mess she'd made, she knelt to clean the floor.

"I'll do it." Jake carried a wiggling Molly away from the sticky goo and put her down next to her saucepan then returned. "Let me clean it up."

"No, no, that's fine." Emma was starkly, acutely aware of him and it was a struggle to keep her voice steady.

Using a clean towel she'd tucked into the waist of her apron, she quickly wiped up the filling and rose. "There, all done."

The baby smacked her spoon against the wall, happily jabbering nonsense.

Emma picked up the iron pot of filling and tucked it under her arm for better stability.

"Here, I'll hold it and you fill the crusts."

She let Jake take the container, then dipped out the mixture with an unsteady hand and spooned it into the pie dish. As she moved to the next one, Jake ran a finger around the inside edge of the ironware then licked off the filling. "Mmm, that's good."

He said it in the same intimate tone he had used the night he'd come to her room, and a shiver skipped down her spine.

"You sure are a good cook. We lucked out when you answered our ad."

So had she and the baby. Emma distributed the filling evenly in the dish. "I'm glad you like it."

She turned her face away, fighting the urge to confess the truth to him. She couldn't do it. It wasn't smart. But, oh, how she wanted to.

Trying to steady her trembling hand, she ladled the fruit mixture into the next dish.

He swiped another taste. "I came in to tell you that Russ Baldwin stopped by with a message from Haskell."

Emma stiffened. Earlier, she'd heard a horse and had looked up from the stove, but had only managed to glimpse the rider's back. She knew Charlie Haskell owned the general store in town. Why would he need to send a message to the ranch? Why would it concern her? Her mind raced. Haskell's was a main gathering place. The merchant could've heard Orson was looking for her. Or he could've even seen her stepfather.

She hoped her voice didn't betray the apprehension battering at her. "Oh?"

"Molly's bed is in."

At the sound of her name, the child said loudly, "Ma-wee!"

"Oh." Emma gave a silent sigh of relief. She'd forgotten about the bed. She didn't know if it was Jake's thoughtfulness in ordering the furniture that had her heart clenching or the fact that his news brought crashing home to Emma exactly how many things she would miss out on with Molly.

Stop it, she ordered herself. Better to miss out on her sister's life than to risk Orson's rage if he found them. The thought of it had Emma's hand shaking and she dropped half of the filling on the edge of the crust and the rest onto the counter. "Emma?" Jake asked over the banging of Molly's spoon against the saucepan.

"Sorry. I'm just clumsy today."

His intense regard affected her like a touch, raising goose bumps on her arms. Emma tried not to let him see how he flustered her and managed a smile. "Are you hoping for another taste?"

"I reckon I am," he murmured.

In that instant, tension charged the air between them. His heavy-lidded gaze dropped to her mouth and Emma knew he wasn't talking about pie filling. He wanted to taste *her.*

Heat flushed her entire body and she forced herself to move to the last pie crust. Jake went, too, his big body brushing her side.

"Next time I'm in town, I'll pick up Molly's bed."

"Okay." Standing so close to him, smelling his woodsy scent mixed with the spiced fruit put flutters in Emma's stomach. Her hand jerked involuntarily, cracking the spoon against the side of the iron pot.

"Emma?"

There would be no more of her and Jake. She wouldn't be making any more peach pies. Wouldn't get to see Molly sit her first horse alone. Or learn to read.

"Is everything okay?"

His sharp tone got her attention. He was frowning and she realized he must have asked her the question more than once.

"Yes. Why wouldn't it be?"

"That's what I'm trying to figure out."

"Everything's fine. Really." She made herself look at him.

When she did, she caught his gaze sliding down her body, then back up. He paused on her mouth.

Want tugged sharply in her belly and she dropped the spoon right into the pie. Try as she might, she couldn't look away from him.

"Em." His voice sounded choked as he reached out and grazed the corner of her mouth with his index finger.

Sensation streaked down her entire right side, from her neck to her toes and she froze.

"Pie filling," he explained as he moved his finger over her lips.

His gaze turned fierce and wanting, making her legs go to powder. Emma wasn't sure exactly what was going on, but her blood hummed. Her breasts grew heavy and she had this urgent, insistent need for him to touch her, to take her in his arms. It was dizzying. And a little frightening.

"There's more," he said in a velvet-over-rock voice.

She couldn't tear her gaze from him. He caught her hand in his and turned it palm up, revealing a dab of pie filling on the inside of her wrist.

Before Emma could even think about cleaning it off, he bent his head and kissed her there. His mouth was whisper-soft against her skin, his tongue warm and wet. She made a sound in the back of her throat. Her fingers involuntarily tightened on his and she realized his other hand rested at her waist.

Black fire burned in his eyes. "You taste good."

Her breath backed up in her throat before she stammered, "It—it's the peaches."

He leaned close, breathing against her ear. "It's you."

Her legs nearly gave out. More than anything, she wanted him to kiss her. But it wasn't right. There could never be anything significant between them.

He searched her face and she saw the moment he became aware of her conflicted feelings. He asked quietly, "No?"

"I—I don't think we should." Despite the tremor in her voice, she looked at him. Part of her wanted to pull away and leave the room. The other part wanted to put her arms around him and never let go.

He didn't release his hold on her. "Because you work for my family?"

Because she couldn't tell him the truth, she nodded. Emma

reminded herself why she was here, who she had to protect. And that she wouldn't be staying.

His gaze never left hers as he brushed one finger across her lips. "Remember how it felt?"

Just that. And she knew exactly what he meant. "Yes."

"I'd sure like to change your mind," he said in that gravelly voice she'd heard the night he had kissed her.

Emma swallowed hard, recalling the feel of his mouth on hers, wanting to feel it again. All she had to do was lift up, touch her lips to his. But her choice couldn't be about what she wanted. It had to be about her sister.

For Molly's safety, Emma had to go soon. If not, she wouldn't be able to make herself leave the Circle R—*Jake*—at all.

Chapter Ten

By the way Emma's green eyes darkened, Jake could tell she was thinking about kissing him.

She stared at his lips for so long that his body drew up tight. He stood motionless, trying with everything in him to let her decide. But, hell, he wanted to put his mouth on hers.

C'mon, sweetheart. Say yes.

Her tongue peeked out to touch the center of her bottom lip and he fought a savage urge to pull her hard into him and kiss her breathless. He didn't think she was even aware of what she did to him.

The delicious aroma of peaches and pastry and Emma's fresh scent wrapped around him. A pretty pink flushed her cheeks and her pulse fluttered rapidly in the hollow of her throat.

She still had her hand in his. He was able to keep his hands where they were, but he couldn't do one thing to stop the throbbing in his body. Though it felt like an hour, it was probably only seconds before she lifted her free hand and cupped his face.

Staring in arrested silence at him, her touch skimmed his

jaw. Want flared in her eyes. He felt it in the slight trembling of her hand. Saw it in the invitation on her face. "Em?"

She nodded, shifting in a way that had her breasts brushing his chest.

Yes! Exhilaration flooded him. Before he could do more than smile, his brother's voice boomed from the front room. "Jake!"

Emma gave a little squeak and jumped back guiltily, dropping her hand from his face, dislodging his from her waist. Jake closed his eyes in frustration and bit off a groan. He wanted to skin his brother!

When he opened his eyes, Emma backed up another step. "I'll finish the pies."

She turned away and Jake barely stopped himself from hitting the wall.

"Jake!"

"Yeah, I'm comin'," he growled. He managed to level his voice when he said to her, "Emma, I want to—"

"I'm just going to put these pies in to bake and try to get Molly down for a nap." Her hand fluttered to the side of her neck in a nervous gesture.

He wanted to sweep her up and kiss her. He was going to kill Bram! "I was going to say, I mean, ask you—"

"Ah." His brother appeared in the doorway between the kitchen and dining area. His gaze paused on Emma then moved to Jake. "When I smelled those peaches, I should've known I'd find you here."

Jake scowled at the other man. It was plain by the mischief sparkling in Bram's eyes that he knew he'd walked in on something. From where Jake stood just behind Emma's shoulder, he could see that a blush still crested her delicate features. She busied herself laying strips of crust across the tops of the pies.

"Bam!" Molly dropped her spoon and pushed to her feet, starting toward Jake's brother.

Emma scurried around Jake and picked up the baby, moving closer to the door and keeping the stove between them.

Bram tugged off his work gloves and tweaked Molly's cheek as he said to Emma, "Any chance I can get one of those pies?"

"They're not baked yet. They'll be ready after supper."

Jake was glad to hear her sound as if she couldn't quite catch her breath. He sure as hell felt winded.

"I have to miss supper tonight," Bram groaned. He glanced at Jake. "I'm going back out with the Baldwins."

He frowned. "More rustling?"

His brother nodded, looking wistfully at the fruit pies resting on the long counter.

"I'll save you one," Emma promised.

"You will?" Bram asked eagerly, handing over the glove Molly was tugging on.

Emma nodded.

"You'll have to hide it from Jake."

She gave him a little smile. "I can do that."

"Hey!" Jake eased up beside her.

"Thank you." Bram winked at Emma.

Jake didn't like that. She belonged to him. He knew Bram wasn't hot for Emma, but he didn't see any reason to let his brother fan the flame Jake had started.

He closed a hand over the other man's shoulder and pushed him out of the kitchen. "I'll go with you and the Baldwins. We can cover more area that way."

"Good."

"I'll wrap up something for you both to take with you," Emma said.

"Appreciate it." Bram gave Emma another wink.

Jake elbowed his brother in the ribs, urging him along.

When they were almost to the front door, Bram glanced behind him then asked in a low voice, "What was going on in there?"

"Nothing."

Snorting, the other man stopped. "It didn't look like nothing. It looked like something. A brand-new something."

Jake looked over his shoulder to see if Emma was close enough to hear. No sign of her. Still, he propelled his brother out to the porch and closed the door. "Why were you watching?"

"I wasn't doing it on purpose. Not at first, anyway." He grinned. "I was coming to see what smelled so good. Instead, I see you about to start lovin' on the baby nurse."

Jake glared. "Thanks to you, that isn't gonna happen. Not anytime soon, anyway."

Bram hooted. "I knew it! I knew something was going on."

They both stopped at the edge of the porch, staying out of the sun. His brother eased down onto the railing. "Are you serious about her?"

"I figure since I was ready to beg for a kiss in there, that's about as serious as it gets."

Bram looked taken aback. "How long you been feelin' like this?"

"Awhile, but especially since she told me that if Molly left, she would, too."

His brother scowled. "Is that why you decided you want Molly to stay?"

"At first, I wasn't sure." Emma's saying that had jolted him into thinking and he'd realized that what he felt for her wasn't only lust. He liked her soft ways and how she always put the baby first, willing to stand up for Molly even when it was obvious she was afraid of what might happen. "I've been considering the real reason I want Emma to stay and it's not about the baby at all. It's all about Emma. I don't want her to go. Ever."

Bram was silent for a minute. "This is more interest I've seen on your part for any woman since Delia died."

"It's the first I've felt." She'd come here on her own, possibly to escape something in her past. He admired her. And he wanted more than a mattress dance with her.

"From what I saw, those feelings go both ways."

"She doesn't think it's a good idea." Jake moved a few feet away and leaned one shoulder against the split-wood column.

Bram swung one booted foot. "Why not?"

"Because she works for us."

"Shoot, nobody'll care about that."

He nodded. "That's what I plan to tell her."

Bram peeled a splinter of wood off the railing and tossed it to the ground. "So, you're going to do something about it?"

"Yeah. I'm gonna change her mind."

Bram laughed. "You stakin' a claim?"

"Yeah."

His brother started, gripping the railing to keep his balance. "Well, I'll be. You really are sweet on her."

"I aim to have her."

"Is that right?"

"I'm going to court her."

"Maybe you should ask her to the pecan harvest dance or to dinner, first. Find out if you want more."

"I already know I do. A lot more."

"I see your mind's set."

"Yeah."

The other man looked as pleased as if he'd bested Jake in the rope-throwing contest. "Good for you."

"I'll have to go slow." Jake stared at the little plumes of

red dirt stirred up by the breeze. "I think she's been hurt in the past."

He thought about her nightmares of her mother's death, the vague information she gave about herself. There was no mistaking her fear of him the day of the wagon accident or her wariness around men in general. He, Bram and Ike were the only ones he'd ever seen Emma comfortable around and that had taken some doing.

"Going slow is probably a good idea for you, too," his brother said quietly.

"Maybe so." Jake didn't care how slow he and Emma went. He wasn't some green boy who couldn't wait for what he wanted. "I figure it'll take some persuadin' before she comes around, but that's okay."

"I guess you didn't have to do that with Delia. The two of you just always…were."

Jake nodded.

"Good luck."

"Thanks." He was going to win her over somehow.

Bram straightened and stepped off the porch. "You coming?"

Jake got to his feet and followed.

"I'll saddle your gelding if you want to go check on our supper." The other man turned with a cheeky grin. "And say bye to Emma."

"Okay. I'll meet you in the barn." He headed eagerly for the kitchen door at the side of the house, grinning like a fool.

Emma tried not to resent that Bram had interrupted her and Jake in the kitchen because his walking in was for the best. Jake didn't need to know how close she'd come to kissing him. But she was having a hard time corralling her emotions. Especially the disappointment.

Even two days later as Jake drove her, Georgia and Molly

into Whirlwind, Emma was still thinking about it. She should've let him kiss her, then she could've forgotten about it. She thought. She hoped.

Ever since he'd said he wanted to change her mind about getting involved with him, she'd tried not to notice the way he looked at her, hungry and determined. As if he meant to have her.

She knew she couldn't stay—she'd told herself that at least ten times a day since the incident in the kitchen—but Jake was making it difficult to hold on to her resolve. The last two mornings she'd found flowers on the kitchen counter next to the sink and this morning she'd answered a knock on her bedroom door and he'd given her a steaming cup of coffee.

She wasn't sure what to think about his gestures, but her body was in a state all the way into town. Relief edged through her when he reined up the double buckboard in front of Haskell's General Store.

This morning, when he'd said he was going to Whirlwind for Molly's bed and a visit to Sheriff Holt, Emma had asked to come along. Having left her and her sister's coats in Topeka, they both needed one. She wanted to get them before she left the Circle R; from Josie Holt if she could. The leftover money would be used to get her as far back east as possible.

Josie's shop was in a back room of the mercantile. Jake helped Georgia down from the wagon and she started toward the store. Moving to the second seat, he held up a steadying hand for Emma and Molly.

Even after Emma's feet touched the ground, his hand lingered on hers. "I'll load up Molly's bed then I need to see Davis Lee. He'll probably want to know if you're willing to try again to identify the thief."

"I am. Whenever he wants." That was just another thing she had to do before she left Whirlwind. She held firmly to her sister as the little girl twisted this way and that to see the people moving in and out of businesses and the horses hitched to posts on both sides of Main Street.

He gave Emma's hand a light squeeze. "I'll take you for lemonade after we finish our business. If you don't spend too long in the dress shop," he tacked on with a grin.

Emma murmured her agreement, barely able to look at him for fear he'd see how badly she still wanted to kiss him. They walked into the store, Jake close enough behind her that his denims brushed her skirts.

Once inside, it took a moment for her eyes to adjust from the bright fall sunshine. A wood-burning stove and a couple of chairs in the center of the big room welcomed customers. The smells of leather and perfume and apples blended. Next to the door stood a wooden crate of brooms and a display of molasses jugs. At the back of the store, shovels were stacked against the wall. Bolts of fabric were arranged neatly on two long tables that ran in front of shelves holding canned food. Boots covered a table in the corner.

Jake followed the proprietor, Charlie Haskell, out the front door and around to a wagon parked beside the building. Jake had told Emma that Charlie's nephew had picked up Molly's bed from the railroad depot in Abilene and had brought it by wagon to Whirlwind.

As Emma and Georgia stepped through the curtained doorway that separated Josie's shop from the mercantile, the seamstress looked up from her sewing machine branded in gold letters across the front as a Singer. The space was large and brightened by sunshine pouring through two windows on the back wall.

A heavy oak wardrobe stood against the left wall and held

frothy, lacy items that Emma determined were undergarments. A standing oval mirror and a wire-framed mannequin wearing what looked like a half-finished coat sat in the far corner. A long table for cutting had a place beneath the two windows. Within easy reach of Josie's sewing machine was a small table with a pair of scissors, a pleater, goffering iron, tailor's iron, a fluting iron and a sadiron. Above her chair was a shelf that held two hat frames. In the corner behind Emma were numerous bolts of fabric, everything from calico to satin to wool.

Josie greeted them warmly, removing her foot from the machine's pedal and rising from her chair to come around and hug the two women.

She stroked a hand over Molly's blond curls as the little girl wiggled in Emma's arms, wanting down. She let her sister stand, but stayed close to make sure the youngster didn't get into anything she shouldn't.

"Did Jake bring y'all today?" Josie asked.

Emma nodded, holding the baby's chubby hand as she toddled around the room.

As Georgia fingered a piece of navy woolen serge, she said nonchalantly to Josie, "Jake's taking Emma for lemonade after this."

Emma turned. "He's taking all of us."

Georgia smiled conspiratorially at the seamstress. "Jake knows I don't really care for lemonade."

"Ah." The other woman's eyes sparkled at Emma. "So, something's going on with you and Jake."

"No." Flustered, she scooped up her sister before she grabbed a pincushion at the corner of the small table.

Georgia beamed. "He brought her flowers the last two mornings. Daisies the first day and whirling butterflies today."

"Oh, I love those!" Josie exclaimed.

Emma flushed. She had liked the daisies almost as well as she'd liked the delicate white flowers, but she had tried not to attach any significance to them. She wished Georgia wouldn't.

"And he made coffee for her this morning," the other woman shared.

"He's sweet on you, Emma," Josie declared.

Molly grabbed at Emma's spectacles and she moved the baby's hands away. "I think he's just being nice. Those things, um, that coffee was for everyone."

Josie laughed softly.

Emma had told Jake they couldn't get involved. She thought he'd agreed, although now she realized he hadn't said so.

Georgia's gaze met hers. "He smiles so much more since you came."

"That's because of the baby."

The other two women laughed. So did Molly, crowing and clapping.

"It's you, Emma," Josie said. "I think it's wonderful."

She didn't know what to say. What *could* she say? Jake's interest excited her, but it also saddened her because she couldn't stay around to see where it might lead.

She heard Georgia tell Josie that Molly needed a coat. Emma opened her mouth to protest that she couldn't let the Rosses buy something like that for the little girl and barely managed to stop herself.

They were Molly's family now, she reminded herself. They would provide for her from here on. Speaking around the sudden lump in her throat, she said, "I need to see about a coat, too."

Ruffling Molly's blond hair, the seamstress pointed to the mannequin in the corner. "I've started a couple of women's coats. One is over there and the other is hanging in the wardrobe. You look at them and see if one suits you. If not, we can start fresh. Let me show Georgia a couple of fabrics for Molly's coat then we'll start on yours."

"All right."

As Josie walked to the corner where the older woman waited, a feminine voice came from behind Emma. "I can take care of the baby while Josie fits you."

She turned to see the tall, red-haired girl who worked for Josie.

The seamstress glanced over. "Emma York, this is Zoe Keeler."

"Nice to meet you."

"Hello. Hi, Miz Georgia." The young woman leaned down to Molly. "What's your name?"

Emma jiggled the toddler gently. "Can you tell her your name?"

"Ma-wee," the baby said.

"Hi, Molly." Zoe looked at Emma. "If she'll go, I can take her outside."

Emma wasn't sure about letting her sister go too far from her. Then she realized she would soon be much farther away from Molly.

"Or we can just go to the front of the store," the girl amended quickly.

"All right." She looked at Molly. "Want to go?"

"No!" The little girl grinned and leaned toward Zoe, who looked confused.

Emma laughed. "That's her favorite word right now. Half the time it means *yes.*"

The young woman grinned as she took the little girl and turned to go.

"Bye, Emma!" Molly said loudly, waving. "Bye, Jo-Ja!"

That was the closest they'd gotten to the pronunciation of the older woman's name.

Georgia decided wool would be the best choice for a child's coat, so Josie pulled out a bolt of slate-blue, a bolt of gray and a bolt of red.

Five minutes later, Georgia had selected the slate-blue wool and told Emma she would be at the Pearl Restaurant. Emma and Josie were left alone in the shop. Josie turned back with a wide smile. "That whole family feels blessed to have both you and the baby. Georgia says you do almost everything at the house and let her have a nap every afternoon."

Emma's lips curved. "I don't think she's once gone to sleep."

"It's the thought," her friend said kindly. "Did you look at the coats?"

"Yes. I think this gray one." The wool was plain and serviceable. Black buttons and black velvet trim at the hem and cuffs dressed up the wrap.

As Josie helped Emma into the half-finished garment, she looked longingly at a deep blue silk dress hanging in the wardrobe. Too bad she didn't have money for a new dress. She'd left a lot of nice clothes in Topeka, but they had all been purchased for the purpose of making it look as if Orson took good care of his new family.

Settling the coat on Emma's shoulders, Josie pinned and smoothed and repinned, then helped Emma out of the pieced material. "I should be able to have both coats ready in a few days."

Emma watched Josie rearrange the coat on the dress form. "That's quick."

"I'm caught up on some things and, the truth is, no one wants me to make them anything right now because they're afraid it will be stolen. It's rather annoying to have my work

snatched and taken who knows where for who knows what."
The brunette glanced over. "What's Jake doing while you're in
here?"

Remembering Josie's earlier assumption about her and the
rancher, Emma felt her neck heat. "He picked up a bed he
ordered for Molly and said he planned to stop by and talk to
your husband."

Her friend grinned. "I know they do law business, but
sometimes I think they just swap stories and play cards over
there."

A laugh bubbled out of Emma.

"You're doing a fine job with Molly. She's a sweetheart."

"Thank you." Emma's heart squeezed at the wistfulness
in the other woman's voice. "I guess I should relieve Zoe.
That was nice of her to take Molly for a bit."

"Zoe's a dear. She and her brother and sister have had a
hard time of it, though you can't tell by talking to her."

"What do you mean?"

"Their parents were killed in a twister several years back,
when Zoe was fourteen. She was left to take care of Zeke and
Dinah. Dinah's older by three years, but she's deaf and Zeke's
a little slow so most of the work fell to Zoe. Not that I've ever
heard her complain."

"That's awful," Emma murmured. "Jake told me a little
about them."

As she walked to the door with her friend, a thought hit
Emma. "I wonder what would become of Molly if something
happened to the Rosses?"

"Davis Lee and I would help any way we could," the petite
woman said immediately, her green eyes earnest. "I wouldn't
want to uproot Molly from another home, but, if it came to
it, we would take her in a heartbeat."

Emma really wanted to know what would happen when

she left, but she couldn't ask that directly. Still, she was slightly reassured knowing the Holts would step in if necessary.

She and Josie moved into the store, teased by the scent of fruit. Zoe had the baby across the room, at the end of a table that held blankets and washtubs. Emma walked over to the young woman and stopped in the open doorway. Josie followed.

Russ Baldwin leaned against the wooden counter, studying the candy jars filled with peppermint sticks, horehound drops and licorice whips. A dark haired man just as big stood beside him.

That man swept off his cowboy hat and moved around Russ to come toward Emma. His hair was a shade darker than Russ's and he didn't have a mustache, but the twinkling eyes were the same sapphire-blue. "You must be Miz York."

"Yes."

He hooked a thumb over his shoulder at Russ. "My brother tells me he met you at church. A pity you couldn't have met me, first. I might've been able to forestall your bad opinion of my family. I hope you won't judge me by him."

Emma started. "Oh, no, I don't have a bad—"

"Ignore him, ma'am." Russ shouldered his way in front of his brother.

Josie laughed. "Emma, don't take either of them too seriously. The one you haven't met yet is Russ's brother, Matt. Most of what he says is in jest."

"Jest?" Russ snorted. "It's pure bullsh—um, I mean, jest."

Emma smiled at the brothers, taking the baby from Zoe and thanking her.

"Wasn't no trouble. She's a doll."

Josie eyed the Baldwins as they, too, gathered in the doorway. "What are you gentlemen doing in town today?"

"Just taking in the sights." Matt's gaze appreciatively swept them all. "A man can only stand so much of looking at other men's faces."

Russ pushed his hat back on his head. "I was over talking to Davis Lee. Two brand-new chisels were stolen from my hotel last night."

"More things!" Josie exclaimed. "There was another corset stolen last week. From Catherine Blue." She touched Emma's arm. "She's married to Davis Lee's cousin, Jericho."

"He's a Texas Ranger," Matt put in.

"Retired," Russ added.

Josie leaned close to Emma so she couldn't be overheard by the men. "Catherine doesn't need her corsets right now because she's expecting, but I'm sure she'll need them after the baby comes."

Russ folded his arms across his broad chest. "I just heard that Pearl Anderson's fancy dishes were returned last night."

Zoe's eyes grew wide.

Emma wondered if Jake had asked the sheriff yet about her trying to help him again.

"Not a scratch on 'em." Matt leaned one hip against the counter that held soap and trinkets at the corner opposite the candy jars. His gaze settled on the baby for a moment and Emma caught a flash of fierce emotion in his eyes.

Josie spoke up, "I heard about that, too."

"Now, what do you suppose is going on?" Russ stroked his mustache.

"Yeah," Matt said, "who steals something and brings it back?"

"Maybe it's not the same person," Zoe ventured.

"It has to be." Matt looked thoughtful. "Otherwise, wouldn't the person returning the things know who the thief is and turn them over to the law?"

Emma murmured agreement.

"It doesn't make a lick of sense." Josie huffed out a breath. "If they're going to start returning things, I wish they'd start with my corsets. No one is indecent if they're missing a handsaw, but an undergarment is a different matter."

"Aw, now, Josie, that would ruin our fun." Matt winked. "We've been betting on who's wearing their— I mean, who's had their unmentionables stolen and who hasn't."

"Matt Baldwin!" Josie sounded scandalized even as a smile tugged at her lips.

"The whole thing is strange," Russ said.

Emma stepped over the threshold to leave, smiling at the small group. "I'd better find Georgia. It was nice to meet you, Matt. And you, too, Zoe."

Josie walked out with Emma and whispered, "You'll have to tell me what Jake does next."

Emma flushed, glancing at her friend.

The seamstress gave her a quick hug. "I'll let you know at church on Sunday how far I've gotten on your coats."

"All right. Thank you."

Matt lifted a hand in farewell. "Pleasure to make your acquaintance, Miz York. I'll look forward to seeing you Sunday."

"Well, that's a surefire way to get her not to come," Russ drawled.

Amused, Emma said goodbye, checking to see if Jake or Georgia were at the wagon, but they weren't.

"Bye! Bye!" Molly waved, repeating the phrase over and over.

The adults laughingly responded.

Emma stepped out from under the wood awning and into the street, hugging the baby to her. "That lemonade sounds good, doesn't it, Molly?"

"No!" She bounced in Emma's arms, grinning broadly.

Emma chuckled. "You've got to get another favorite word soon."

A man in a wheelchair came toward them and Emma stepped back out of his way, surprised when he stopped in front of her. He looked to be about Jake's age, maybe a little older. He wore a thin mustache, his straight coal-black hair neatly trimmed. He was handsome in a haunting kind of way, though the sun-burnished skin pulled taut over his sharp cheekbones gave him a harsh look.

He stared at Emma for so long that his intense regard sparked her paranoia. Why was he studying her so hard? Was he looking for her? The thought had her stiffening.

"Hi!" Molly flapped her hand at him. "Hi!"

"Hi." He laughed, a rusty sound that indicated he didn't do it often. His gaze went to Emma. "Your daughter?"

"She's my...charge. I'm her baby nurse."

"I don't believe we've met." His voice was deep and friendly, totally at odds with the emptiness in his brown eyes. "You must be new to Whirlwind."

"Yes." She faced him fully and behind him, she saw Josie standing in the doorway with both Baldwins, watching.

"Nice to have you here. I work for *The Prairie Caller*."

"Oh." Oh, no! Emma glanced at the building next to the mercantile. Was he talking to her because he wanted to print something about her? All Emma needed was for some article about her to show up in a newspaper, even a paper that served only Whirlwind.

The man considered Molly for a moment then spoke to Emma. "Did you come from Abilene?"

Wishing she could politely extricate herself, she nodded. That wasn't a lie. She *had* come from Abilene. She just wasn't *from* there.

"You been in Whirlwind long?" He must have registered her reluctance to answer because he gave her a sheepish grin. "Sorry. My curiosity gets the better of me sometimes. I usually write up bits for the paper and everyone always wants to know about our newest residents."

"I see." She clutched Molly closer to her, noting that the Baldwin brothers now looked concerned and had moved outside to the edge of the store's porch. The weight of her derringer in her pocket was reassuring. Who was this man?

"Are you here with the rest of your family?"

Just as she wondered why he would ask that, she realized he'd spied her wedding band. She didn't get the feeling he was interested in her romantically, but there was definitely something about him that made her anxious. "I'm…a widow."

Sympathy flared in his eyes and he rolled closer. "I'm sorry to hear that, Miz…"

"York. Emma York." Oh, why had she let him fluster her into saying that? It wasn't her real name, but sweat slicked her palms, anyway. The baby grabbed for Emma's spectacles and she dodged her sister.

"Nice to meet you, Miz York. I'm—"

"Quentin." Jake was suddenly beside Emma, his voice flat and hard in a way she'd never heard. His hand slid across her lower back to her waist and rested there.

"Jake." The other man's eyes went cold.

This must be Quentin Prescott, Emma realized, noting absently that Matt and Russ backed slowly into the store. Tension arced between Jake and the man Emma decided was his brother-in-law. A tension pulsing and heavy enough to have her pressing into Jake's side.

The man's eyes narrowed at Emma's movement.

"Yake!" Molly lunged for the rancher, chattering some incoherent words.

He easily caught her, holding her in the crook of his other arm. His attention never wavered from Quentin.

The other man's voice was clipped. "So, this must be the little one you found on your doorstep?"

Jake curled the fingers of his free hand more firmly into Emma's waist. If he thought she might pull away, he was wrong. She was staying right here. Molly looked from the stranger to Jake, uncertainty flickering on her little face.

Quentin looked again at the baby and his eyes softened, causing Emma to feel a confusing tug of compassion. Then his gaze turned as sharp as a blade. "I was just asking your nurse here where she was from."

"We have to get going." Shielding Emma with his body, Jake eased her back, giving Quentin a wide path to pass in front of them. The baby wrapped her chubby arms tightly around Jake's neck.

His brother-in-law rolled around them, then paused on the street between the store and the newspaper office to look at Emma. "Nice to meet you, miss. Maybe I'll see you again."

Jake's hold clamped hard on her and she felt his entire body go rigid. Quentin didn't frighten her exactly, but she felt better with Jake putting himself between her and the other man.

As the handicapped man wheeled the short distance to the ramp in front of the newspaper office, Jake cupped Emma's elbow and guided her to their wagon.

After a long moment of watching Quentin make his way inside, Jake glanced at Molly, who had laid her head on his shoulder, then he looked down at Emma. There was no mistaking the fierce possessiveness burning in his eyes. His index finger stroked above her elbow, sending a shiver through her. "Are you okay?"

"Yes."

He looked her over, anger flushing his features. "You're sure?"

"He didn't do anything," she reassured him. "Just asked questions."

"I don't like him talking to you. How long was he here?"

"Maybe a couple of minutes before you arrived."

Georgia hurried up to them from behind, looking worried. "What did Quentin want? Did something happen?"

"Nothing I couldn't handle." Jake's face went carefully blank as he watched the paper's office door close.

Emma wanted to know what was going on, but she sensed now wasn't the time to ask.

"Still want to get that lemonade?" he asked neutrally.

Quentin Prescott's questions had rattled her, shattered any sense of security she'd felt. And left her with a renewed sense of urgency to leave.

"Maybe another time?" she asked uncertainly, knowing there might never be another time.

He helped her into the wagon's backseat. "Sure. Whenever you want."

Emma knew from Georgia's sidelong glances that she was concerned about what had just happened with Jake and his brother in law. But the older woman didn't pursue it so Emma didn't, either.

As the wagon rocked through the browning prairie grass toward the Circle R, she told herself to think about her own business, but she was more concerned with why Jake was even quieter than usual. More concerned with the heaviness that had come over him.

That was when Emma knew how strong her feelings were

for him. She'd planned to leave after Molly's birthday, but now, despite the threat to her and her sister, Emma wasn't sure she could make herself leave at all.

Chapter Eleven

Emma had to talk to Jake. The unease she'd felt with Quentin Prescott had grown, and not just for herself. The drive from Whirlwind had been mostly quiet. Once they'd arrived at the ranch, Jake had situated Molly's bed in Emma's room then washed up for supper.

During the meal, the family was subdued. Emma hadn't thought it possible for Jake to become even quieter than usual, but he did.

After supper, she and Georgia cleaned up while the men went outside. When night fell, Bram and Ike came inside, but Jake didn't.

Even after everyone said good-night and Emma put her sister to bed, there was still no sign of Jake. She had to make sure he was all right. The business between him and his brother-in-law was none of hers, but she didn't care anymore. She hadn't imagined Georgia's misgivings or the fact that the Baldwins had stayed close to her until Jake had arrived. Quentin Prescott was a threat, but it was his blaming Jake for the past that had anger mixing with concern.

She wrapped her third loaf of freshly baked bread in

cheesecloth and went to the screened kitchen door for the fifth time to see if the lantern still glowed in the barn. The light bobbed toward the house and Emma could make out the dark outline of a man's shoulders, the denims and boot on his left side. Jake, finally. She hurried to put another layer of cloth on the loaf before storing it in the bread safe, but a few minutes later, she still hadn't heard him come inside.

Placing the dining table's burning lamp at the end gave her ample light to see her way to the front door. Her shadow wove in and out of the spread of amber light on the pine floor. From outside, she heard a noise—two quick taps, pause, two quick taps.

Opening the door, she stepped out and closed it behind her. The back of her gingham skirts brushed against the straight-backed chair sitting to the side of the door.

Jake was on the porch in a matching chair at the top of the steps. A lantern rested at his feet and he was hunched over something on the wood floor that Emma finally identified as a boot lying on its side. A curved awl and needle lay beside his chair.

He looked up and slowly straightened, his eyes glittering, his face half in shadow. "Hi."

"Hi." This was one of the first cool nights they'd had since her arrival, but the chill she felt was from nerves, not temperature. Sliding her hands into her skirt pockets, she took a couple of steps toward him. "What are you working on?"

"Flattening the stitches on the boot tops I just replaced. What are you doing?"

The combination of leather and Jake's woodsy scent was heady, but it was the pleasure in his eyes at seeing her that put a hitch in her pulse. "I wanted to thank you for the flowers and the coffee."

"You're welcome," he said gruffly.

He melted her heart. She knew she'd embarrassed him. He didn't like making a fuss; he just preferred to *do*. Emma had never known anyone like him. How was she going to walk away?

He braced his left hand on his thickly muscled thigh and dangled a hammer between his knees with the other. "You okay with me doing that?"

She paused, then said, "Yes."

"But?" he prodded.

She hoped he couldn't see her blushing. "People are starting to talk."

"What people? Georgia?" He chuckled. "And what is my cousin saying?"

Oh! She'd gone into that all wrong. "Well…"

He cleared his throat. "That I'm sweet on you?"

The deep rumble of his voice sent a shiver down her arms. She was grateful for the veil of dim light when heat flushed her cheeks. "Um, yes."

He stared at her for a moment, his gaze dropping to her mouth. "Hmm."

Hmm? What did that mean? It didn't matter, she told herself. *Focus on why you came out here.*

But, before she could ask him about Quentin, Jake cleared his throat. "Have you had a lot of suitors?"

She looked down at the floor, her hair falling over her shoulder. "One, but that didn't last long."

"Why not?"

"My st—" She broke off. "He wasn't very interested, I guess."

"Lucky me." What was wrong with the men in her town? She blinked. "Lucky?"

"If he'd been interested, you probably wouldn't have come to Whirlwind."

"Oh."

He figured she had a reason for seeking him out and she'd get around to it. In the meantime, he meant to enjoy the fact that she was here.

"I realize this is none of my business…"

"Go on."

"Are you okay? You've been quieter than usual since we got home."

"You thinkin' it's because of Quentin?"

"Yes."

Emma usually didn't question things that had nothing to do with Molly, and Jake was surprised she was asking about his run-in with the newspaper man. "Don't be afraid, Em. He's probably no danger to you."

"I'm not worried about me!" She stepped closer. "He's your brother-in-law, isn't he?"

The gentle breeze teased him with her body-warmed scent. He cocked his head, admiring the golden mix of amber and moonlight on her cheek, the line of her jaw. "How did you know that?"

"I heard his name that day at church, when you and Sheriff Holt were talking about Quentin's saws being stolen."

"Did he upset you?"

"He upset all of us."

Jake's gaze caressed her face as he murmured, "I won't let him hurt you, Emma."

"That isn't what concerns me. I'm afraid he'll hurt *you.*"

Jake was silent for a long minute, not because he didn't want to tell her, but trying to decide how. Bluntly was the best way. "He tried to kill me for what I did to his sister."

"What?" Emma breathed, moving closer in a quiet swish of skirts. "He blamed you *that* much? Enough to try and kill you?"

"Yes."

She frowned. "What happened?"

He told her how Quentin had attacked him that day, had accused him of killing Delia. Then had started shooting. "He fired. After a while, I fired back."

"In self-defense."

"He was as torn up over Delia's death as I was."

"Maybe so, but *you* didn't try to kill *him*."

Emma was so sure, so trusting. He didn't want to destroy that, but she needed to know it all. Shifting his gaze to the floor, he placed the hammer on the boot between his feet.

"My bullet hit his spine. The doctor said Quentin would never walk again and he's been in that chair ever since."

"Oh," she said softly.

He couldn't look at her, didn't want to see horror or disgust on her pretty face. Resting his elbows on his knees, he studied the wash of moonlight across the toe of the boot he'd been repairing.

Locusts droned over the occasional chirp of a cricket. In the distance, he heard a cow bawl. "For a while, I felt like I'd taken both their lives."

"You didn't!" She turned and grabbed the other chair, dragging it next to his. "What happened to Delia wasn't your fault."

"Most of the responsibility is mine."

"No, it isn't."

"And what I did to Quentin cost him the ability to do his job. He used to work on the railroad."

"You lost your wife," she said fervently. "That counts, too."

"I had Bram and Georgia and Ike. Quentin had no one after Delia went."

Emma started to speak, then stopped, looking uncertain.

On a deep breath, she said, "If Quentin had told you about the doctor's warnings, you wouldn't have… Delia couldn't have gotten with child and she and the baby wouldn't have died."

Jake's gaze swerved to Emma's. It was true Quentin had known what Jake hadn't.

It felt wrong to shuck his responsibility for what had happened, but Emma's words kept playing through his mind.

"Did I speak out of turn?" she asked solemnly.

"No." He realized she'd slipped her arm through his and he put his big hand over her much smaller one to keep her there. The look of compassion and anxiety on her face made him want to pull her a hell of a lot closer than this.

"Do you want me to go?"

"No, I don't." He grazed his thumb across the back of her knuckles.

Seeing Quentin circle around Emma had snapped something inside Jake, brought it into sharp focus. "You know, before I met you, I would've headed straight for a bottle after seeing Delia's brother, but I didn't feel the need for a drink today."

"Really?" She flushed with pleasure.

"Yeah." After returning to the Circle R, Jake had unharnessed and brushed down the horses, then had started toward the loft for his whiskey. But he hadn't wanted a drink. Even more amazing, he hadn't *needed* it. The hole inside him had been filled, by Emma and the baby. "What you said a minute ago got me thinking."

"Is that good?"

He grinned. "I guess that depends on who you ask, but I think so."

"I don't understand how people can do such horrible things to someone they love."

The ache in her voice tugged at him. Who had hurt her? What had happened? "You ever been in love?"

She hesitated. "No."

Jake held her gaze until she looked down, following the shifting pattern of lantern light on the wood beneath her feet.

He didn't press. She had trusted him enough to come and ask him about one of the most painful things in his life. That was a bold step for her.

He caught her hand in his, the one still curled through his arm and lifted it to brush a kiss across her knuckles. "Think you ever might be? In love, I mean."

Despite the half light, he could see a flush darken her pale skin. "I don't know."

More than anything, he wanted to kiss her. Before he could talk himself out of it, he leaned forward and brushed his lips lightly against hers. Only that little bit, he cautioned himself, recalling that he'd told her he would take things at her speed.

But, when he made to pull away, she curved her soft hand around his neck and pressed her mouth firmly to his.

Heat shot through his veins. Pulling back slightly, he murmured against her lips, "You sure?"

"Yes." Her breath feathered over his skin. "I've been sorry ever since I stopped you in the kitchen."

That set off an explosion in his blood. When he settled his mouth on hers, she slid her other hand into his hair and parted her lips. She leaned into him, her breasts pressing against his chest.

Damn, she felt good and he wanted to feel her all over. Tugging her into his arms, he slid her from the chair and into his lap. There was a moment he thought she might protest, but, instead, she wrapped both arms around his shoulders.

He cradled her head, with one hand buried in her silky hair, letting himself get lost in the honeyed heat of her mouth. Careful of her glasses, his other hand skimmed her velvety cheek, the delicate line of her jaw. She was so fine, so daintily built. The rapid pulse of her blood fueled his own.

He cautioned himself to go easy, but he was starving for her, hammered by a savage churning in his blood he'd never felt. His entire body was hard, especially between his legs where her bottom pressed against him.

One of her hands slipped from his neck, trailed lightly over his whisker-rough cheek to his mouth, tracing his lips where they joined hers. She shyly touched her tongue to his and he barely bit back a groan.

Trying to hang on to his control, he dragged his mouth from hers and buried his face in the warm fragrant curve of her neck. The scent of musky woman made his pulse go wild.

She had two fingers in the shallow vee of his shirt where the placket was unbuttoned, petting him. Dragging his tongue up the tendon at the side of her neck, he licked the shell of her ear. She wiggled, her movement sending a shock of pure sensation down his spine. Hellfire.

He knew he should slow down. Stroking the sweet curve of her collarbone, he put his mouth there and sucked lightly.

She whimpered, her hands a soft fire as they stroked his back beneath his shirt. Capturing her lips again with his, barely able to calm the savage need pounding through him, he lightly rested his hand on her breast.

She lifted into his hold, but it wasn't enough. He wanted to feel real flesh, not the edge of her stays. Damn that corset he'd bought. She'd probably worn it because they'd gone to town today.

Compelled by a raging need, he opened the front of her bodice with an unsteady hand. The white of her chemise peeked over the top of her corset. In the fractured light, he could barely make out the shadowed swells of her breasts. There was no thought, only a desperate longing to touch her, claim her.

His hand easily spanned her rib cage and he squeezed the edges of the busk lightly, freeing the first five hooks with one motion.

He tugged the satin ribbon of her chemise and slid his hand inside the loosened garment, curving his work-roughened hand carefully around her perfect velvety flesh. Her nipple tightened against his palm and she moaned.

Lust drove through him like a spike and he moved his mouth back to hers, kissing her deep and long and slow as he grazed her sweet taut flesh with his thumb. He lifted his head so he could look at her. The dreamy expression on her face made his muscles quiver with want at the same time it cracked open something inside him.

"You're mine, Emma York," he whispered. "Mine."

Looking dazed, she opened her eyes, searching his face. He could feel the heat of her blood just beneath the surface of her skin.

A shudder rippled through her as realization spread across her face and cleared the desire from her eyes.

"Em?"

Plainly unnerved, she sat up and scrambled off his lap, one hand covering her mouth as she trembled before him. Concerned, he reached out. "Did I hurt you? Tell me you're okay."

She backed toward the front door. "We can't. I can't."

He rose, fighting the want thundering through his body. "Emma."

Her chest heaving, she held the edges of her open bodice. The satin ribbon from her chemise fluttered between the gaping fabric. "Jake, I c-can't," she said on a sob.

It was driving him out of his mind that he didn't know the problem. "Are you hurt, Em? Tell me."

"No, no."

Relief made him dizzy for a second. "I went too fast."

"It isn't that."

She was lying. The wariness behind those spectacles was every bit as stark as it had been the night he'd come upon her after that nightmare. "What, Emma? Tell me what I did."

"It isn't you," she said brokenly as she retreated another step. "I just can't."

Her lips were still moist from his and there was an ache bordering on pain in his groin. "Why? Because you work for me?"

"No. I mean, yes."

He said hoarsely, "Sweetheart, you're the only one who cares about that."

"It's not a good idea for us to get involved that way."

"After what just happened between us, I'd say it's a damn good idea. You felt it, too." He moved closer.

Smelling of soap and sweet woman, she stood with her back to the door looking trapped, her body rigid. "Please stop."

He did immediately, her plea striking at a place deep inside him where he'd thought to never feel pain again. "It's more than the fact that you work for me. Can't you tell me?"

For one heartbeat, he thought she would relent, but then the frightened, wary look returned. She shook her head, her eyes overly bright.

Wanting to reassure her, he stepped forward and she shrank away. Even though he knew she wasn't afraid of him, her withdrawal ripped at him. "It's okay, Em. I won't do anything you don't want."

"I know. You're so—so good," she choked out, patting her chest as if she couldn't breathe. "I'm sorry."

With that, she slipped inside the house.

The door shut quietly in his face. Trying to cool his blood, still the urge to go after her, Jake braced one arm on the door frame and hung his head. He didn't know whether to cuss himself or shoot.

What had started out as lust had turned into more. He didn't only want her; he needed her. Something frightened her and Jake was pretty sure it wasn't him. So, what was it, then?

He didn't know, but he had to change her mind about him. About them. He wasn't giving up.

They'd been swept away by impulse, Emma decided. She spent most of Friday night telling herself that Jake's kisses hadn't changed anything, but they had. They had changed *her.*

She'd never felt that kind of consuming want—a wild recklessness that burned away all her reservations. Her common sense. There had been nothing in her head except Jake and what he made her feel. She had wanted to give herself to him, right then, on the porch. Not only because she wanted him, but because she wanted a life with him. It hadn't been his desire that frightened her; it had been her own. *That* was why she'd run away.

He had to think her the most naive kind of ninny.

Emma thought her behavior would've discouraged him, but he didn't act discouraged in the least Saturday morning when he came through the kitchen on his way to breakfast and whispered in her ear how pretty she looked. She'd nearly put pepper in the coffee. The man *wanted* her and it flustered her crosswise because she wanted him, too.

If it weren't torturous enough to catch him looking at her with the same blatant possession he had on the porch, she couldn't stop replaying the feel of his mouth on her mouth, on her skin. Just the memory had her blushing. She'd probably melt clean away if he did it again.

Kissing him, touching him had been a mistake. Not because it felt wrong, but because it made painfully clear what she'd be walking away from.

There was no longer any reason for her to stay except Molly's birthday. No one had mentioned the upcoming date and Emma was determined to be with Molly on that day. She had put off talking to the family about marking the little girl's first year because it emphasized just how little time she had left with her sister. With Jake.

But on Sunday, after the family had returned from church and swept her and the baby out to the creek behind the house for a picnic, Emma knew she had to broach the subject. The afternoon was beautiful. Evergreen trees and brush dotted the rolling landscape that had begun to brown for fall. Fat clouds floated in a pure blue sky. Every so often, the breeze would sweep down the little hill where they had spread their blanket.

Bram and Jake took turns riding Molly on their shoulders or taking her to the edge of the water. Ike slept against a scarred scrub oak, his hat pulled low over his eyes. Emma felt secure and happy for the first time since Mama had married Orson. It wasn't the meal and the sunshine that had contentment stealing through Emma; it was Jake. Occasionally he would plop down next to her on the quilt and tell her what checker to move against Georgia. He didn't seem to care that she didn't need his help, and she didn't care, either.

Every time he sat beside her, Emma's body hummed with awareness. An uncommon urge to touch—his chest, his face, his hand—came over her every time. She knew the smart thing to do was to keep some distance between them, but, when she left the Circle R, she wanted to take as many memories as she could, so, when Jake asked her to go walking with him, she accepted eagerly. Despite the meaningful smiles exchanged between his brother and cousin, despite the fact that Emma could barely look at him without blushing clear to her toes.

As they strolled along the bank of the creek, away from the family, she could hear Bram talking to the baby. Molly sat on his lap, her chubby hands gripping the cane pole he supported for her. The creek gurgled, sparkling in the sunshine, and water bugs skidded along the surface.

"Quentin wasn't in church," Jake said.

"Good." Emma hadn't attended services, too unsettled at the possibility of seeing Jake's brother-in-law again. Not only because of his curiosity about her, but because she grew angry every time she thought about his blaming Jake for Delia's death.

Still, she was concerned enough about Quentin's questions that she had asked Georgia when *The Prairie Caller* was published. The older woman had told her new issues came out every Wednesday. Emma planned to get the next one and check for any mention of her or Molly.

Jake had gone with the family this morning because he'd needed to speak to the sheriff.

"Did you talk to Davis Lee?" she asked.

"Yeah. He said to thank you for offering to come into town tonight and try again to help him identify the thief. It's a good thing you already agreed to go because Haskell's was broken into during church."

"What?"

"A couple of pairs of boots were taken, a pair of spectacles and a blanket."

She touched her own glasses. "Again, right under everyone's noses."

"Yeah. This is getting darn aggravating. You and I will get to town after sunset, like before."

"All right."

"Just so you know," he muttered, "I think Davis Lee's going to join us this time."

The scowl on Jake's face had Emma laughing. "Can't you make up your mind? First, you want him with us, then you don't."

"I think you know what I want," he said huskily.

Her body went soft. With the way she'd been wishing more had happened between them the other night, it was a good thing they wouldn't be alone.

Ravens and mockingbirds chattered raucously overhead and from some of the trees shedding their leaves along the water.

Jake's dark gaze met hers. "Davis Lee and Josie are going to Abilene tomorrow for an early anniversary trip."

"Oh, good! Josie was hoping she could talk Davis Lee into going. That's a lovely gift for their one-year anniversary."

"Well, he owed her something extravagant. Instead of a church wedding, they were married by Reverend Scoggins in Davis Lee's house the day after he'd been shot and they weren't able to take a honeymoon trip."

"Josie told me." Her friend had almost cried at the memory of Davis Lee's being nearly killed by Ian McDougal, the outlaw they'd both been chasing who had murdered Josie's parents and former fiancé.

"While they're gone," Jake said, "I'll be workin' days at the jail. Cody Tillman, one of Riley's hands, will take the nights."

She had met Davis Lee's brother, a handsome strapping man, but her thoughts were fixed on the fact that she wouldn't see much of Jake in the next several days. Disappointment stabbed at her.

He stepped over a deep, rock-studded fissure, and gripped Emma's elbow to help her over. The faint scent of wildflowers and grass and earth drifted past on the breeze.

Shoring up her resolve, she forced herself to address the subject she'd avoided all week. "Molly's birthday is in a couple of weeks."

She could tell he only then remembered. "I reckon that's right."

"It probably wouldn't do to have a party for a little girl, but maybe I could make a cake. It would be nice if you—if everyone could be there."

"Count me in. The rest of 'em, too. That's a good idea." Admiration lit his eyes. "Good thing we have you to remind us of things like that. You can't ever leave or we'll be up a creek."

"Y'all would've remembered." Emotion ached in her chest. "Or at least, Georgia probably would have."

"Maybe."

His gaze caressed her face for so long that she felt herself flush. She glanced away, trying to control the quiver of anticipation in her stomach.

"Her birthday's the seventh?"

"Yes. A week from Wednesday."

"I'm glad it isn't while I'm workin' at the jail. And I just remembered Bram and Ike will be gone a few days this week to a meeting of the Cattleman's Association, but they should be back before then."

"About the rustling?"

He nodded, flicking a grasshopper off his denims. With the four buttons of his shirt undone and his sleeves rolled up to reveal muscular forearms with black hair, he looked more relaxed than she'd ever seen him. His hat was pushed back, revealing the strong, whisker-shadowed jaw and a lone strand of dark hair that curled stubbornly just behind his ear.

In certain places where the grass grew more than knee-high, Jake skimmed his hand along the browning tops. Twice he pointed out a butterfly, one a monarch and one a smaller, vivid blue.

They reached a small stand of trees. Across the water, the bank sloped higher. Just ahead, past the pines and oaks on a thickly grassed knoll, sat a headstone and beside it another one Emma almost missed. She slowed and so did Jake.

Following her gaze, he answered her unasked question, "Delia."

"And the baby?" Emma pointed to the smaller stone.

"No, I thought the baby should be with Delia."

Emma's chest felt tight as Jake cupped her elbow and turned her back the direction they'd come. "The other one belongs to Aunt Rose."

"Ike's wife?"

Jake nodded. Usually the mention of Delia brought a heaviness over him, but Emma didn't sense it today.

"How did you and Delia meet?" Emma knew he wouldn't answer if he didn't want to, but she hoped he did. She planned to hoard every scrap of information she could learn about him.

With a light squeeze, he released her elbow. "We always knew each other. She was just a friend, like Davis Lee and Riley, then one day I looked up and she was a woman."

"And you fell in love with her?"

"Yeah." He plucked a long piece of drying grass and fiddled with it. "What about you? There's never been anyone special?"

Not until you. "No."

"Can't imagine that lasting much longer."

The mix of tenderness and heat in his black eyes had her stomach dipping. Oh, how she wished she could stay and see if this thing between them went anywhere. A hawk spiraled overhead. "Do you think you'll ever marry again?"

"I plan to." He looked straight at her and the frank intent in his rough-velvet voice sent a jolt straight through her. "I spent the last five years beating myself up over Delia, but talking to you the other night helped me with that. It riled me up more at Quentin, but you helped what I felt about Delia."

Her eyes widened. "I did?"

"Yep."

She paused next to a pine, swallowing around the sudden lump in her throat. "That's one of the nicest things anyone's ever said to me."

"There's plenty more where that came from."

Heat burned her cheeks and she shifted her gaze to the spot ahead where they'd left the family. There was no sign of them or the colorful quilt they'd brought or the two hampers Ike and Bram had lugged from the house. Or her sister.

"Where is everyone?" She couldn't help a pinch of anxiety. "Where's Molly?"

"I told them to go on to the house."

Pushing up her spectacles, Emma started in that direction. "Molly's probably ready for a nap."

"I don't want you to worry about it." Jake drew even with her. "I mean it. That baby's perfectly fine."

"I know." She glanced at him, slowing down. She was surprised at just how certain she was.

"I asked them to leave us alone. I wanted to talk to you about the other night."

Emma's mouth parted on a silent "Oh". She searched his face, struggling to keep from remembering how it had been between them.

"Feel like I should apologize."

She didn't want that. Nor did she want him to regret it.

Tilting her head at him, she smiled. "You've apologized for not kissing me and now you're apologizing because you did?"

He chuckled. "Bringing that up, huh? I guess you make me so crazy I don't know up from down."

That was certainly how he made her feel. This was probably her one chance to tell him. She made herself look him in the eye, wanting it to mean as much to him as it did to her. "I'm the one who's sorry, for running away. I wanted you to kiss me. Please don't apologize."

"Okay." He grinned. "I probably wouldn't have meant it, anyway."

She laughed softly, falling back into step with him. His denims and her skirts made swishing noises against the drying vegetation. This was the best day of her life and Emma planned to enjoy it. It was all she would have to keep her company in the future.

In the distance, the house and barn came into view. Jake slid a look at her, then said slowly, as if weighing his words, "If you ever need someone to talk to, you can come to me, Em. Anytime."

"I know." She might want to confide in him, but she definitely couldn't. The sun grew hot on her nape, where her skin was exposed because of her chignon.

"Are you still having nightmares?"

"Not in a while."

"You never said what happened to your ma."

She faltered on a perfectly flat patch of ground and his hand shot out, closing around her wrist to steady her. Why was he asking about Mama? Emma couldn't tell him anything and that made her feel guilty, especially since he'd shared with her about Delia and the baby. And Quentin.

She swallowed hard. "It's too hard to talk about."

Still holding her wrist, he brushed his pinkie finger against the back of her hand. "Maybe someday you can tell me."

She only had two weeks of someday left. The wariness she'd cultivated over the last couple of months warred with a growing desire to tell him the truth. "Maybe."

"And maybe you'll tell me what brought you here."

She stilled, hardly breathing. The fact that she couldn't confide in him caused her stomach to knot painfully.

"And maybe," his voice lowered, "you'll tell me what happened to make you so skittish of men."

The tenderness in his dark eyes invited her to share. "I'm not afraid of *you*."

"And I'm darn glad, but I know there's something that haunts you, Emma."

Tears stung her eyes. If she told him, he would most likely understand. Protect her even.

"That business with Delia was haunting me and I don't regret telling you about it. I'm holding out for the day when you trust me like that. Hey." He reached out to brush his thumb against the corner of her eye, catching a tear Emma didn't realize had fallen. "But, even if you don't, that's fine. Whatever happened doesn't matter to me."

He tucked a windblown strand of hair behind her ear, then took her hand, moving again toward the house. She truly believed he wouldn't hold her lies and deceit against her.

But this was about Molly. Emma wasn't trying to be coy or mysterious. Telling Jake, involving him would be too dangerous. Not only to her and her sister, but to him, as well. Emma cared for him too much to involve him.

When she tried to imagine her future without Molly and without Jake, all she could see was a long stretch of lonely.

As they walked back in silence, she glanced over. He

didn't act uncomfortable or even put out with her, but Emma felt unhappy. Trapped by what she must do. She didn't want to let go of Jake, ever.

And, in less than two weeks, she would have to.

Chapter Twelve

That night, Emma's second attempt at identifying the thief was as unsuccessful as the first. She didn't spot even one unfamiliar face, let alone the man she'd witnessed stealing from J. T. Baldwin's saddlebag. Jake was disappointed, as was Sheriff Holt, and Emma was discouraged because her time here was nearly gone.

Monday morning, Jake headed into Whirlwind and reported for his daytime watch at the jail during Davis Lee's absence. He returned home so late that night Emma didn't see him. That was the pattern for the next three days. Despite there being five people at the house, it seemed empty without him.

Emma was surprised to realize just how often she found herself listening for his boot steps on the porch or his deep, quiet voice. Though he was out of sight, he was very much in her thoughts, thanks to the little reminders he left for her.

On Monday, it was a flower outside her bedroom door. A jug of lemonade, clearly marked to her from him, was waiting in the kitchen on Tuesday. Wednesday, a copy of *Godey's Lady's Book* and *Harper's Monthly* had been slid under her door. She hadn't read either of them in months.

She loved every gesture and every one tore at a piece of her heart. She should discourage him, but how, when she never saw the man?

On the fourth day, Jake sent word to the ranch by way of Russ Baldwin that Cody Tillman had come down with the croup. Jake would stay in Whirlwind until the other man was well enough to relieve him at the jail or Davis Lee returned, whichever came first. For the next two days, Emma didn't see him or find anything from him.

When he returned Saturday night well after supper, Emma found herself wanting to throw herself into his arms, but, of course, she didn't. His absence, along with Bram's and Ike's, had left the men with chores on top of chores. For the next three days, they left before sunrise, taking whatever food Emma had packed the night before. They showed up late for supper, all of them looking so tired she thought they might fall out of their chairs at the table. She wanted to see Jake, talk to him. And say what? *Goodbye. I'll be running out on you the night of Molly's birthday.*

When that Wednesday dawned, Emma wanted to hide under the covers and pretend today wasn't the day. With a heavy heart, she pulled back the blanket and started her daily routine. Thinking ahead, she made extra biscuits so the family would have something to eat with their fried ham, at least the first day she was gone. In the barn, she checked to make sure her mare was fit to travel. She took special care with a cake for Molly.

Everything was ready except for Emma.

She couldn't bring herself to pack. Her few belongings could be thrown into her valise and ready within minutes. Tonight, after everyone was asleep, she would ride out for Dallas. From there, she would take the train or stage to Fort Smith and keep going through Arkansas. She thought she could make it to Tennessee before she ran out of money. She had no family there, no reason for Orson to even suspect she'd gone east.

Before she knew it, it was time for supper. All the men made a point to wash up and come in as Emma was getting food on the table. She'd expected to feel a trifle self-conscious around Jake after their discussion of the night on the porch and his invitation for her to confide in him, but she didn't. What she felt was a longing to talk to him alone, even for just five minutes. Her heart hurt at the thought of leaving but she knew she had to hide her upset.

Georgia invited her to join them at the table and, this time, Emma accepted. Seated across from Jake, Emma felt a belonging with the Rosses she hadn't felt since her mother had married the senator.

In her high chair beside Emma, Molly happily banged away at the tray with a spoon. She would probably not remember that Emma was here for her first birthday; she probably wouldn't remember Emma at all. But Emma would remember.

After supper, she brought out the chocolate cake she'd made while Jake moved Molly and her high chair to the center of the table. The little girl clapped when she saw the hair ribbons from Emma. And squealed at the doll bed from Bram that went with the doll Ike had bought for her. From Georgia, Molly received a new winter coat.

They sang "Happy Birthday" in one of the more off-key attempts Emma had ever heard as Molly bounced in her chair and chattered incoherently. The knot in Emma's chest grew harder, hotter.

After the gifts were opened, Jake scooped up the little girl and told everyone to follow him outside. Emma wondered what he intended, but her questioning look at Bram only resulted in a secretive smile.

Georgia and Ike didn't appear to know any more about Jake's plan than Emma. They stopped at the corral and Emma drew up to the fence between Jake and Georgia.

Molly pointed her chubby finger at the palomino fillies and waved. "'Orse!" she squealed.

Nugget sauntered over, bumping her nose against the fence rail then Emma's arm. She rubbed the mare's nose, her attention going to the frolicking babies. One of them came up to the fence.

Jake smiled at Molly, taking her hand and stroking it down the filly's nose. "This filly is yours now, Molly."

Emma gasped while Ike and Georgia murmured their approval. Bram beamed.

"After she's saddle-broke in a couple of years, we'll teach you to ride her."

Molly only cared that she was petting the animal, but Emma was overwhelmed at Jake's complete acceptance of the little girl. Her sister was now a Ross. Emma had known he loved the child, but she hadn't been certain that Jake knew it.

"You'll be in charge of her care, tadpole, when you're old enough. Until then, we'll help you."

Emma wanted to laugh and cry at the same time. Jake glanced over his shoulder. "Do you think this is okay? Not too much?"

"It's definitely too much, but wonderful."

He grinned and opened the corral gate, carrying Molly inside. The mare came up to him while the foals hung back by Nugget's flanks. The more adventuresome of the babies, who now belonged to Molly, eased her way up to Jake and let the toddler pat her head a couple of times before she spun in a cloud of dust and pranced to the other side of the corral.

"'Orse!" Molly clapped. "'Orse!"

Emma memorized the joy on her sister's face. She would probably never see Molly again. Never see Jake or his family, who had accepted her more than the man who'd claimed to love her mother.

When Molly began to get sleepy, Emma rocked her longer than usual then put her to bed. Ike, Georgia and Bram came to Emma's doorway, each of them looking in on the little girl before saying good-night. But Jake didn't come. And an increasingly anxious part of Emma hoped he wouldn't.

She wanted to see him but she didn't know how she would be able to pretend that this was a night like any other.

As she leaned against the door frame watching her sister sleeping in her new bed, a hot fierce anger boiled up. She was the one running, when it should've been Orson Douglas for what he'd done to Mama. Because of him, Emma would miss Molly's growing up. Because of him, she was walking away from a man she knew she could easily love. She was half-afraid she already did.

Someone came up behind her and Emma knew it was Jake by the clean soap scent of him mixed with an intriguing hint of the outdoors.

He braced one arm over her head and leaned around to look into the room. "She asleep?"

"Yes."

He wasn't touching Emma, but he stood so close she could feel his warmth, the powerful width of his chest, the faint impression of a shirt button. She wanted to turn around and lay her head on his shoulder.

"She had a big day today," he said quietly, bending down so that his cheek brushed Emma's.

She nodded, trying to force away the image in her mind of them putting Molly to bed together every night, as a family. "Your gift was lovely, if extravagant."

"Humph, it was practical." His breath feathered against her ear, causing a little shiver. "A lot more practical than that doll bed from Bram. She's a Ross. If there's one thing she's gotta know, it's how to ride."

Trying to hold on to her composure, Emma laughed shakily. "She's a lucky little girl to have found such a good home."

"This is your home, too," he murmured against her hair as his big hands came up to bracket her waist. "I thought my family was never gonna go to bed. Feels like I haven't seen you in a month of Sundays."

It felt that way to her, too. Her heart clenched painfully. He nuzzled the spot behind her ear bared by her upswept hair and she shivered. Completely ignoring convention and her common sense, Emma relaxed into him.

"I missed you."

He said it so quietly she almost didn't catch the words. Throat tight, she turned to face him, lifting her hand to stroke his jaw. How could she leave this man? She'd never expected to complicate things even more by having feelings for him, but there was no denying she did.

His dark eyes glittered at her. "Come outside with me?"

With no thought of refusing, she put her hand in his. Once they were on the porch, he lifted her and sat her on the railing in front of him.

"Jake!" She gripped his forearms in an effort to get her balance on the narrow seat. "What are you doing?"

"I wanna talk and I wanna see you while I do."

"You can't see me if I'm standing?" she teased.

"Nope." He grinned.

The night was chilly, the sky clear black with shimmering stars scattered like beads across a velvet canvas.

The purely masculine interest in his eyes gave her a little chill and she swallowed hard. "Nothing new on the thefts?"

"Those boots turned back up in Haskell's store and so did the spectacles and the blanket."

Surprised, Emma laughed. "What do you think is going on?"

"I have no idea. What I don't like is how long it's taking us to figure this out. This stealin' is going on right under our noses and we can't see any of it."

She murmured agreement, hit by a sudden thought. If Jake and Davis Lee were having this much trouble finding a thief who was stealing in plain sight, couldn't Orson be having this much trouble finding *her* if he were still looking?

It had been over two months since she'd left Topeka with Molly. The senator knew by now that Emma hadn't gone to the law and accused him of murdering her mother. And that, by now, she probably wouldn't. She was no longer a threat to him. And she was bone tired of being frightened. She felt safe here with Jake. She knew Molly was safe. Why shouldn't Emma stay and raise Molly in Whirlwind? Why couldn't they both start fresh?

She let herself consider the idea and a tight band around her chest eased. She felt as if she could get a full breath for the first time since finding her mother dead. This was right. Staying with Jake and his family was right. And Emma was going to do it.

She knew there was a chance she'd have to leave if Orson showed up, and she would. But, for now, she could stay. The burst of joy inside her had Emma almost throwing her arms around Jake's neck. She settled for taking one of his hands and squeezing it between hers.

He smiled. "What's that for?"

"For everything." She could barely contain her excitement; her voice trembled slightly. "For being so kind to Molly."

"It's no hardship." The softness in his voice matched that in his eyes.

Emma stared up at him, overwhelmed by her decision to stay, by the relief, by *him.* It was sheer impulse that had her brushing a lightning-quick kiss against his smoothly shaven cheek.

He blinked. "What did I do to deserve *that?*"

"That's for being kind to me, too."

Looking at her speculatively, he chewed the inside of his cheek. "So, if I asked you to the horse races this weekend, would you go?"

"Yes."

"Hmm." He settled both her hands on his chest and put his back at her waist. "And the dance after? Just us?"

"Yes."

His gaze dropped to her mouth and his jaw clenched. "And if I wanted to kiss you?"

A thrill raced through her. "Now? Or then?"

"Definitely now."

She pretended to think about it. "All right," she breathed, feeling his heart jump beneath her palms.

Flattening one hand low on her back, he pulled her into him. She would pretty much do whatever he wanted, though she had no intention of telling him that. He bent his head and kissed her, a sweet slow kiss that had her eyes drifting shut and her arms going around his neck. She pressed into him, enjoying the feel of his hard angled body so different from hers. The top button of his trousers nudged her stomach.

When he lifted his head to change the angle of the kiss, she screwed up her courage and whispered, "I missed you, too."

That set off something inside him. Almost roughly, he slanted his mouth over hers and lifted her, holding her tight with one arm low across her back and the other at her nape. He kissed her and kissed her until her head swam.

When he finally drew away, they were both breathing hard and there was an unfamiliar buzzing in Emma's blood. He rested his forehead against hers. "Does this mean you've changed your mind about us?"

She nodded.

"Good." He nuzzled her neck. "I didn't know if I could hold out much longer."

Emma held him tight. If this was a mistake, it felt more right than anything she'd ever done.

During the days leading up to the horse races and dance, Jake made it clear to Emma that she was being courted. He took her for a drive in the buggy. Another evening, they walked to the creek then she sat out in the barn with him and talked while he repaired the cheek billets on a bridle.

Though he never did more than kiss her, he wanted to and he thought she did, too. He was in love with her, but he kept that to himself. If she knew the whole of his intentions, she'd probably run like a buckshot coyote.

She was slowly opening up, but still wouldn't confide in him about her past. She'd blossomed. He'd thought her pretty before, but now there was a serenity about her that brought a glow to her alabaster skin.

Saturday found them in town with his family, most of the citizens of Whirlwind and even some folks from Abilene who'd come for Whirlwind's biggest racing day of the year. There was a race to be had for every level of skill. Jake entered a couple and won one, but Cora Wilkes was the star of the day. Since being unmasked at a competition almost two years ago as the mystery rider who'd beat every contestant, she and her mare, Prissy, raced openly now.

The fall sunshine was bright, heating up the day. Money exchanged hands; challenges were issued; spirits were high. In the early evening when the temperature began to cool, people gathered outside the church to eat under the trees on blankets or in wagon beds or the church steps. Desserts were waiting inside the Pearl Restaurant, to be served throughout the dance. The adults visited while the children played marble games as well as Blindman's Bluff and Fly Away, Pigeon.

Emma acted as if she enjoyed herself. Jake kept her close until Josie swept her off after supper to introduce her to more townspeople. She met Jericho Blue's mother, Jessamine, as well as Charlie Haskell's wife, May, and Cal Doyle's Lizzie. Emma visited with Cora for a while.

Jake couldn't take his eyes off her. Little tendrils of her upswept hair escaped to brush her nape, the side of her face. The matching bodice of her blue gingham had been exchanged for a dressy white shirtwaist with long sleeves. Over the past couple of months, she'd put on some much-needed weight and the garment fit snugly over her breasts and nipped in at her waist. It was growing more difficult for Jake to keep his hands off of her.

Which explained why, for the first time in his life, he was impatient for the dance to start. He could hold her all he wanted then. An hour after dark, the dance was going strong and he knew it would likely continue until morning. He and his family wouldn't stay all night, because of the baby and because he, Bram and Ike had been gone so much last week, but right now he was enjoying the sight of Emma with Josie and Susannah Holt, along with their cousin by marriage, Catherine Blue.

Catherine's raven hair and Susannah's blond were dramatic contrasts to Emma and Josie's brunette locks. The four women together were striking, but Jake only had eyes for

Emma. He'd never seen her so animated. For the first time since he'd met her, she looked young and almost carefree, the nearly constant watchfulness on her face appearing only when she met someone new.

The Pearl's tables and chairs had been moved to make room for dancing. The piano, brought over from the saloon, was in the corner. Cal Doyle played the piano and was joined by his brother, Jed, on the fiddle for a reel danced to "Buffalo Gals." Situated between Riley and Jericho, Jake stood at the edge of the dance floor.

Riley's lemonade gave off a strong odor of liquor, no doubt provided by Pete Carter, who owned the saloon. Jake and Davis Lee had both declined so they would be alert in case there was another theft or trouble of any kind.

Emma twirled around the room with J. T. Baldwin, then Charlie Haskell, followed by his nephew, Mitchell Orr. Jake didn't much care for her steady stream of partners, but he had cautioned himself not to claim her for every dance. Still, the longer he watched, the more convinced he became that he'd made that decision when he was booze blind.

He'd shared four dances with her and was starting onto the floor for number five when Russ Baldwin appeared and whirled her away.

Jake halted, folding his arms across his chest.

Davis Lee walked up, draining the last of his punch. "Looks like Emma is enjoying herself, getting to know people."

"More like the Baldwins are getting to know *her.*" Jericho Blue, the Holts' cousin, made his observation from behind Jake's left shoulder.

"You know how they are. They don't mean anything by it most of the time." Riley sounded lazily unconcerned until he saw Matt Baldwin make a beeline for Susannah. The rancher snapped to attention and started across the crowded floor, straight for his wife. "I'll be back."

Jake laughed along with the others, but he was beginning to understand Riley's possessive nature, especially where the Baldwins were concerned. They'd all been friends for years and Jake trusted both of them to have his back, if the occasion warranted. Until now, he hadn't given their fast ways much thought, but as he watched Russ dance Emma past him, that changed.

Davis Lee cleared his throat and asked in a low voice, "How well does Russ know Emma?"

"Not that well." Jake glanced at him. "Why?"

The sheriff shrugged. "The way he's whispering to her."

Jake's gaze narrowed on the couple, spinning around the floor to the lively tune of "Turkey in the Straw." He didn't see anything improper in Russ's behavior.

"I'd be more concerned about how close he's holding her," Jericho remarked in his usual quiet tone. "Neither one of those men will be puttin' their hands on Catherine."

Jake had no doubt about that. Despite the injury to Jericho's gun hand caused by a shootout with the McDougal Gang, the former Texas Ranger was still a better marksman and a faster draw than anyone in five counties. Jake's muscles clenched as he watched Emma and Russ. This polka *was* a mite fast to hold one's partner so close.

Riley rejoined them, looking satisfied at having diverted Matt's attention from Susannah.

"I'm not sayin' this means anything," Davis Lee said, "but Russ's hand seems to be sittin' a little low on Emma's back for this dance."

"And I think he just moved it *lower*," Riley observed incredulously. "One or both of those boys will be tryin' to steal a kiss before the night is through."

Something inside Jake snapped and he growled, "Don't y'all have your own women to watch?"

His friends burst out laughing and he shot a look at them, only then realizing they'd been trying to goad him. And they'd succeeded.

He grinned, reminding himself he was the man going home with Emma, but that didn't settle the churning in his blood. Or soothe the growing restlessness he felt as he watched her in Russ's arms.

She wasn't flirting with the big man, but the thought that one of the Baldwins might try to kiss her had Jake half out of his mind. As the song ended, he caught sight of Matt stepping up to take his brother's place. Jake strode across the floor.

He clapped a hand on his neighbor's shoulder. "This dance is already spoken for, Matt."

The younger Baldwin looked questioningly at Emma, who nodded and gave him a smile that made her eyes glow like emeralds.

"My loss." He graciously stepped aside.

Once Emma moved into his arms, Jake pulled her close, closer than he probably should have.

A blush pinkened her cheeks as she folded her soft hand in his. "Everything okay?"

"It is now." She belonged to him. Matt, Russ and every other man here needed to know it. She smiled up at him, so sweetly that his gut knotted.

Thanks to his lessons at Susannah Holt's charm school a couple of years ago, Jake was a fair dancer. He swept Emma around the room, thinking how pretty she looked with the flush of lamplight on her skin. Beneath the mouthwatering aromas of dessert, he caught her soap-fresh scent. "You having a good time?"

"Yes. Are you?"

"It could be better."

"How?"

"If I was kissin' you."

"Jake!" Her gaze darted to the couples nearest them.

He grinned. "The music's plenty loud. No one heard me."

A shy smile curved her lips, which made him want a lot more than a kiss.

Neither Matt nor Russ would ever force themselves on a woman, but they would do their damnedest to convince her that she wanted what they wanted. He didn't want Emma to be available for convincing so he decided to sort it out right now.

"Go for a walk with me?"

"All right."

"Where's Molly?"

"At the Whirlwind Hotel with Jericho's sister, Deborah. Probably asleep by now."

"Good." Jake threaded his fingers through hers and walked toward the front door. A quick glance around found his brother across the floor next to the table holding punch and cake. Jake inclined his head, silently telling Bram that he and Emma were going outside and Jake wanted to be alone.

Bram nodded to show he understood.

Emma preceded Jake outside and they startled J. T. Baldwin and Cora, who stood talking in a deep pocket of shadow. They all said hello as Jake guided Emma off the end of the porch and into the street.

The cool air was welcome after the heated crush of bodies inside the restaurant. With the fiddle playing "The Blue Danube," Jake led Emma into the alley between the Pearl and the jail. "You cold?"

"A little."

Pulling her into him, he braced his shoulders against the

wall of the building and wrapped his arms around her. "You look real pretty tonight."

"You said that already." She snuggled into him. "But thank you."

He tipped her chin up for a kiss, teasing her lips with his tongue until she let him in. He sank into the honeyed warmth of her mouth, his world narrowing to the feel of her curves against him, the hot velvet of her tongue.

When they came up for air, she looked at him dreamily. "Mr. Ross, did you bring me out here to compromise me?"

"Yes'm."

She laughed, the moonlight caressing her face. Tenderness welled up in him and he kissed her again, softer this time.

He brushed his knuckles along her cheek. "I didn't like you dancing with all those men tonight."

Looking bemused, she tilted her head. "I danced with you more than anyone else."

He adjusted his stance so that she had to lean into him for support. She did, her palms flexing on his chest as he buried his face in her neck. "It wasn't enough."

"How much is enough?"

"Every dance."

A soft laugh escaped her. "You're teasing me."

"A little." He had planned to go slow with this courtship, but seeing her with those men made him realize he couldn't. Patience had never been a problem for him, but the closer he got to Emma, the more impatient he became.

It wasn't only that he wanted her, though he certainly did. It was that he needed her gentle ways and fierce love, just as Molly did.

There were things in her past she hadn't told him and he had hoped she would by now, but once she believed that the past really didn't matter to him, she would share her secrets.

Though he hadn't planned to do this tonight, he couldn't think of one reason why he shouldn't.

He pulled back so he could see her face, hoping he wasn't fixin' to spook her. "Emma, I've fallen in love with you."

"Jake," she breathed, going completely still, her eyes huge as she stared at him in arrested silence.

"Too soon?" Damn. "I'm sorry. I should've waited—"

"No." Her fingers curled into his shirt. "It's all right. You just surprised me."

"In a good way?"

She nodded as tears filled her eyes.

Lifting one hand, he cupped her face. "I sure didn't mean to make you cry."

"I can't help it. No man has ever said that to me."

Satisfaction flared in his eyes. "I like that I'm the first. It probably seems sudden to you, but I've felt things for a while now. I hope that doesn't make you jittery."

"I have feelings for you, too." The fingers she stroked down his face were trembling. Would he still feel the same if he learned the truth?

Looking relieved, he let out a deep breath. "Good."

Could this really be happening? How had she been so lucky to find the perfect family for Molly and the perfect man for herself?

"You belong here with me."

If she hadn't already decided to stay, the husky promise in his voice would've convinced her. She nodded, fascinated by the mix of hunger and tenderness on his strong features.

"I want you to marry me, Emma."

Drawing in a sharp breath, she studied him. The moonlight slashed across his face, emphasizing the strong jaw, showing the desire in his eyes.

She wanted to say yes, but accepting his proposal would

mean she'd no longer have the option to leave if Orson ever showed up.

He stroked his thumb across her lower lip. "You don't have to answer me now."

He'd opened his home to her, his heart. And she couldn't do that for him. She'd seen firsthand how protective Jake was of her. If she told him about Orson murdering her mother and that he had abused Emma, she was afraid Jake would go after her stepfather.

He would be no match against the senator's money or power or willingness to hire men to do anything, even kill. If Jake went after Orson, Emma was afraid the man would kill Jake, just as he'd killed her mother. She couldn't take the risk. She couldn't tell him the truth about herself, but she also knew she could no longer fight her feelings for this man.

He must've taken her speechlessness for uncertainty. "Em, I know there's something in your past that hurt you real bad."

"Jake—"

He stopped her with a finger on her lips. "If you're worried about telling me, don't be. It's okay that you can't talk about it yet, but someday I hope you will. What I want you to know right now is that I'll take care of you, no matter what."

She knew if she said yes, if she gave in to the feelings for him that grew stronger every day, she'd be taking a tremendous risk. Not only for herself and Molly, but for Jake, as well.

"I think you have feelings for me, Em, but, if you don't, you can tell me."

"I do." She touched his face. There was no protecting her heart now. "Yes. The answer is yes."

He hugged her to him, kissing her with increasing intensity. Her palm curved around his nape and she flattened the other on his chest, over the heavy thud of his heart.

The feel of his arousal against her caused a tug of sensation deep in her belly. He pulled his mouth from hers, nuzzling her cheek, her neck.

A gasp caught in her throat when he raked his teeth lightly down the side of her neck, then bit her gently on the spot where her neck met her shoulder. Her knees wobbled and she had to grip his shirt to keep from falling. Had that moan come from her?

With light touches, she explored his face, his chest, rubbed her fingers across his belly. When her hip pressed his erection, his whole body went tight and he froze.

After a moment, he lifted his head, breathing hard. As was she, Emma realized.

"We gotta stop, Em, or I won't be able to. And the first time I love you is not going to be in an alley."

"All right." Though she blushed at his words, there was no denying the thrill of anticipation that shot through her.

His gaze soft on her face, he squeezed her tight. "You said yes. You can't back out."

"Neither can you." She slid her arms around his neck.

Laughing, he kissed her quick and hard. "Let's go tell the family."

It wasn't impulse that had her saying yes; it was the fact that her heart was talking a whole lot louder than her head. She was tired of running, tired of denying her feelings for Jake.

Marrying Jake meant that Orson's chances of finding her and her sister would increase, that moving on wouldn't be possible if Orson did catch up to her. It also meant that by following her heart, she could be putting Jake in danger.

No, no, she reassured herself.

They'd been fine these past two months. She hadn't even brought her derringer tonight. Chances were good that her stepfather had stopped looking altogether, that her past was no longer a threat. As she held tight to Jake, Emma prayed she was right.

Chapter Thirteen

They settled on a wedding date three weeks away. Emma would've done it much sooner, but Jake wanted her to have a wedding dress made and he needed the time to work on the surprise he had planned.

The days before the wedding were taken up with preparations. In addition to caring for Molly and the house, Emma had fittings for her dress and new undergarments. And she dyed her hair again, a chore she was beginning to despise.

Jake made a trip to Abilene for the marriage license then spent the rest of the time working at the ranch or on the old cabin Uncle Ike had built when he'd first settled here. With the help of his uncle and brother, Jake was able to finish Emma's surprise in time.

At straight-up noon on Saturday, he waited at the church in Whirlwind with Bram, who was his best man. He was clear-headed and sure and chomping at the bit for the wedding to be over. Emma was with Josie, Susannah and Catherine at Josie's shop, out of sight so Jake couldn't see her before the ceremony.

Davis Lee had offered to check on Quentin and Jake had

gratefully accepted. Jericho had escorted his mother and four sisters to the church, then gone with Riley to move tables and chairs at Pearl's restaurant, where people would gather after the ceremony. Georgia and Ike sat in the front row with Molly, who was currently toddling from one end of the wooden seat to the other. She wore a navy-blue velvet dress Josie had made special for today; the matching bonnet hung down her back.

Jake had never seen Whirlwind's little church this fancied up. Thick white ribbon and some kind of white gauzy material swagged from pew to pew. The aisle was spread with white all the way to the front where Jake and Emma would stand. Small bunches of gold, russet and purple wildflowers were tied to the ribbon on the first two pews on either side of the aisle.

As he waited, he saw Cora slide into a seat near the front beside her brother, Loren Barnes. She'd been the one to organize dressing up the church, which also served as the school. Josie had told him that all the women in town had pitched in because they were so happy for him and Emma.

Finally, everyone was seated and Emma was coming down the aisle toward him in a gown of sage-green silk trimmed with lace and satin. Jed Doyle's fiddle played softly in the background but Jake couldn't care less about the song. His every sense was taken up by the woman who would soon be his wife.

The tightly fitted, high-necked bodice emphasized her breasts and her small waist. The straight flow of the gown gave her a slim silhouette. Her brown hair was swept up into a chignon and crowned with a thin wreath of whirling butterflies like the ones he'd given her. Behind her spectacles, her eyes glowed like emeralds.

Jake had told Emma to get a white dress if she wanted, but, ever practical, she'd settled on something that could be worn more than once. Might be practical to her, but she was so beautiful Jake had to make a concerted effort to lock his knees so his legs wouldn't give out. That woman belonged to him.

His heart started pounding hard.

"Will you look at her?" Bram breathed beside him.

"How 'bout if *you* don't?" Jake said out of the side of his mouth as Emma neared.

Folding her hand in his, they faced the preacher and Jake repeated his vows as best he could with her sweet scent tantalizing him. As he slid on the wedding band he'd bought her, she said hers quietly, without any doubt in her voice. And then they were husband and wife. When the reverend told Jake to kiss the bride, a pretty blush pinked her cheeks. He kissed her softly, whispering he'd give her a real one when they got outside.

He escorted her up the aisle and out the church door. Once on the landing, he hooked an arm around her waist and pulled her into him. Emma held his face and kissed him back, more confidently than she ever had. Only when someone jostled him did Jake realize that people were coming out of the church. Or trying to.

Meeting Davis Lee's amused gaze, Jake pulled Emma with him to the side so the guests could pass. Everyone hugged them and wished them well. Under Jake's watchful eye, the Baldwin brothers each bussed Emma, on the cheek. Jake had agreed to stop by the Pearl for a toast and some cake, but then he wanted to get on with the honeymoon.

Reverend Scoggins was the last one out. Jake shook the slender balding man's hand. As the preacher headed for the restaurant, Jake stepped back and looked at Emma, catching her hand and twirling her in a circle.

The graceful curve of her neck tempted him to put his

mouth there. His hands itched to touch her all over. Not much longer now. "You about made my heart stop when I saw you comin' down the aisle."

Giving him a little look that made him think about leaving right then, she touched the buttoned-up collar of his white shirt, then the black vest of his three-piece suit. "You about made *my* heart stop when I saw you in that suit."

"Because I wore my Sunday clothes and not my denims to our wedding?"

She laughed with him as they started down the church steps. As they reached the ground, Jake's gaze was caught by a lone figure beneath the copse of trees just northeast of the church. Quentin, in his wheelchair. Even from this distance, Jake could tell his brother-in-law was staring daggers at him. He hadn't come to the wedding, for which Jake was glad, so why was he here? Did he plan something?

If he thought he was going to talk to Emma again, he was dead wrong. Quentin didn't move. Jake tucked Emma's arm through his and started across the street to the Pearl.

This was his wedding day. Nothing was going to ruin it. He easily put Quentin out of his mind, but it wasn't so easy to dismiss the foreboding that slithered up his spine.

Late in the afternoon, Jake and Emma left Whirlwind in the buggy and headed for the cabin.

He'd replaced all the rotten floorboards, repaired two holes in the roof and gotten a new mattress—one filled with feathers, not husks. Georgia had dusted the entire place, made up the bed with new sheets and a blue-and-white quilt and hung light blue curtains in the windows that now sparkled. The cabin was still used occasionally as a shelter from bad weather, and Jake had decided it would be perfect for his and Emma's honeymoon. Bram's, too, if he ever got hitched.

It was private, but not too far from the ranch in case of emergency.

Even in the dusky light, the orange, gold and red fall leaves stood out against the green cedars and pines. Ike and Jake had finished Emma's surprise only last night. He couldn't wait to see the look on her face.

The cabin was beyond the ranch house and as they started across Circle R land, she looked at him uncertainly. "Where are we going?"

He laughed. "Not to the ranch."

"Good," she said, looking relieved. "So, are you going to tell me?"

"Just hold your horses. You'll see."

They passed the creek where they'd picnicked and the family headstones. The worn trail gave way to grassy, hilly pasture. The buggy bumped its way up the creek bed and around a bend. The cabin came into view.

"Oh!" Emma exclaimed, grabbing his knee. "What is this?"

"It's a cabin, Miz Ross." Jake grinned, reining up at the door and hopping down to come around to her side.

She gave him a look as he lifted her down from the buggy. "I can see it's a cabin."

"Uncle Ike built it when he and Aunt Rose first settled here."

Emma smiled at the bouquet of wildflowers Georgia had hung on the front door. Amazement spread across her face. "Is this what you've been doing the last three weeks?"

"Not the decoratin', but everything else." Taking a lantern from behind the buggy's seat, he struck a match and set the light on the porch.

"It's wonderful."

"Wait till you see the rest." Without warning, he scooped her up in his arms.

"Oh! Are you carrying me over the threshold?"

"Yep."

"I like that."

Jake liked *her*—the feel of her, the scent of her. He was mighty tempted to start gettin' off her clothes right here, but he was trying not to jump on her like a wild animal. He angled his body so she could lean down and open the door.

On an indrawn breath, she looked around the front room. A Franklin stove sat in the corner behind Jake's left shoulder, along with a dry sink and short work cabinet. Straight ahead, the bedroom door was open.

He put Emma on her feet and she looked up, eyes sparkling. "This is wonderful."

He thought *she* was wonderful and gave her a kiss that went on for a bit before he stepped out to pluck up the lantern then returned to urge her toward the bedroom. "There's more."

Once inside, she stopped short at the sight of the bed in the center of the room. Jake set the lantern down and put his hands on her waist, angling her toward the right rear corner.

Her jaw dropped. "A bathtub!"

"With hot and cold water."

She looked doubtful until he walked over and turned the porcelain knobs.

When water gushed out, she came to him with an awed look on her face, putting a hand under the faucet.

"I wanted us to have a nice place to honeymoon that wouldn't be too far from Molly." He passed her a towel from the stack beside the tub then turned to start a fire in the small heat stove behind him.

Her lips curved. "You did all this for us?"

He nodded. "It needed sprucin' up. I figure we'll use it

more than once and Bram might even have a need for a honeymoon place one day."

"You're a very thoughtful man, Jake Ross."

Closing the stove door, he stood and winked at her. "Well, I've got ulterior motives."

She lifted a brow.

"I thought you might want a bath after the drive out here and I was hopin' you might let me watch."

Color rose high on her cheeks and she swatted at him.

When he tugged her close, she leaned up and kissed his cheek. "It's very nice. I love it."

All the frustration and cussing it had taken to figure out the plumbing was worth it.

He brushed his lips against her temple. "You go ahead and get in, if you want. I have to take care of the mare, then I'll be back."

"All right." Her gaze slid uncertainly to the bed.

He tipped up her chin. "You scared?"

"A little."

"We'll go slow, as slow as you want." *As slow as I can,* he amended silently.

She looked somewhat reassured, but if he was going to keep his word, he needed something to take the edge off.

Walking over to the bedside table, he lit the kerosene lamp. "After I hobble the horse, I'm gonna wash off in the creek."

"But it'll be cold!"

"That means I'll be washin' fast, so don't dillydally."

She laughed. "All right."

His gaze slid down her body, then back up to her breasts, straining against her bodice and its small satin buttons. "Need me to help with your dress?"

She wrinkled her nose. "I don't think I trust you to do that."

"Pretty and *smart.* Guess I found myself some wife."

After grabbing a towel, he took a tin of soap and the lantern then headed outside.

He unharnessed the horse and led her to the creek; she drank and grazed while he bathed. The cold water had him jumping in and out quicker than a bullet with feet. He dried off and pulled on his shirt, trousers and boots, bundling up the rest of his clothes and stuffing them under his arm so he could carry the lantern.

As the mare followed him back to the cabin, he toweled his hair. Pale yellow light from the bedroom was visible through the cabin's front window. Jake hobbled the mare a few yards away, growing impatient to get back inside.

He stepped into the cabin and barred the door, then doused the lantern. Yellow light spilled out past the bedroom door. No sign of Emma. Maybe he *could* catch a look at her in the tub.

Jake shucked his boots and dumped his clothes on the small sturdy dining table he and Bram had made when they were ten and nine. He padded barefoot to the bedroom and stepped inside, intending to call out to Emma. Her name slid back down his throat.

The lamp beside the bed cast her shadow on the wall and Jake froze, taking in her silhouette. From her slender shoulders to her narrow waist and over the gentle flare of her hips. She raised her arms and began to take down her hair. When she turned slightly to lay her hairpins next to her glasses on the bedside table, smoky golden light shone straight through her gown.

Jake could see every soft dip of her body, the full underside of one breast, the flat of her belly. His throat went dry.

He wanted to go to her, but he couldn't move. Hell, he could barely breathe. He'd never seen anything like her in all his born days.

Silky brown hair tumbled thick and straight down to the

middle of her back. His gaze lingered on the rounded curve of her bottom. He finally found his voice.

"Emma?"

She gave a tiny start and turned, smiling shyly. "Hi."

She looked nervous. And so beautiful all he could do was stare.

Because of the halo of light behind her, Jake couldn't see the blush he was almost certain was there, but he could see plenty more.

The gown was transparent, made of some finely woven ivory cloth that shimmered and looked soft at the same time. The square neckline was cut lower than anything he'd seen her wear, baring the beginning swells of her breasts. Baring enough to have him going from the thinkin' stage to the doin' stage in a heartbeat.

"Hell. Fire." His gaze returned to her face. Without her spectacles, she looked younger. Her big wide eyes and finely arched brows complemented the straight line of her nose.

Her hands were clasped together so tightly in front of her that bone shone through. She was more nervous than he'd first thought.

That slapped some sense into him. He took a step toward her, unable to stop staring at her thinly veiled curves. "You're so beautiful, you're making me stupid," he said hoarsely. "Where'd you get that?"

"Josie made it for me."

"I shoulda known." He started to reach out, then dropped his hand.

Emma fought back a flutter of panic. Was he displeased? Disappointed? "Did I do this wrong?"

"There is no wrong way, Em. It's just…" He gave a gruff laugh. "You look like spun sugar. I'm afraid I might touch you too hard."

She breathed a sigh of relief. "You won't."

He frowned. "Why are you shaking? Cold? I can stoke up the fire."

"No, I'm not cold."

Taking her hand, he pulled her close. He stroked her neck, her skin still slightly damp from her bath. She smelled fresh and sweet. "What is it?

She wrapped her arms around him. He was hot and big and hard everywhere. "I'm afraid…."

"Of me?" He slid his hands up and down her back, spreading warmth through her limbs. "Of the first time?"

"No." She drew back to look at him, blushing to the roots of her hair. "Because you've done this before and I haven't."

Did she have any idea what it did to him to know he'd be her first? "Are you worried about what's gonna happen?"

"No, I know about that. I just don't want to disappoint you."

Particularly, she didn't want him comparing her to Delia and she felt helpless on top of nervous because there was nothing she could do about that.

He framed her face in his hands. "There's no way that can happen, Em. All that matters is that I make you feel good."

"Aren't I supposed to do that for you, too?"

He gave her a crooked grin. "Just touching you is probably gonna blow my boots off."

She doubted that, but smiled anyway. His eyes burned so hot she thought she might melt.

"Want me to leave the lamp burning or not? It's your first time so I want you to be completely comfortable."

"Not burning?" She watched his eyes for any sign of disappointment. She didn't see any.

He turned and put out the light. Darkness settled around them and Emma's eyes began to adjust. Dipping his head, he touched his lips to hers, soft, teasing, until she spread her palms on his back and leaned her slight weight into him.

Only then did he coax her mouth open with his. He held her face and kissed her for a long time, sometimes hard, sometimes soft, turning her boneless. He tasted faintly of lemonade and smelled like fresh air and soap.

He finally lifted his head, breathing hard, as was she. Threading his hands through her hair, he brushed his lips across her cheek, her jaw, a ticklish spot just below her ear.

She squirmed and he chuckled. His hands smoothed over her shoulders, glided down her arms. When he lifted her hand and pressed his mouth to the inside of her wrist, a vibration raced up her arm. Even in the silvery light, she could see the hot glitter of desire in his eyes.

She stroked his chest between the open placket of his shirt and he released her long enough to pull the slightly damp garment over his head, dropping it on the floor.

His torso and shoulders were hard, striated muscle, covered by skin she knew was browned by the sun. She flexed her fingers in the dark hair on his chest. Nestled against him, she breathed in the scent of man and soap. She ran her hands up his sides, feeling the scar he'd gotten from the barbed wire.

He cradled her head with one hand and slid the other to the small of her back, pulling her lower body into his. He throbbed against her stomach and excitement zipped through her. She went to her tiptoes trying to fit herself better to him. Shifting his head, he took her mouth again.

Her hands moved to his hair, the strands silky and damp against her skin. Gliding her palms down his chest, she halted at the waist of his pants and the undone first button.

"Emma," he said hoarsely. "I want to go slower, but I'm not sure I can."

"I like this just fine," she whispered.

Slanting his mouth across hers, he stepped her back to the bed until her knees bumped it. He pulled away and set his hands on her waist. The emotion blazing in his eyes tugged sharply at her heart. Features tight with need, he reached around and jerked down the quilt and sheet. Emma sank to the edge of the mattress, her heart beating wildly. Her gaze dropped to the front of his trousers and the part of him that was so different from her.

Fascinated, curious, she touched him there. The hard muscles in his belly clenched and she looked up to find his eyes closed, pleasure on his face. He liked this, she realized with delight. So did she.

She undid his trouser buttons as he murmured encouragement, but when her knuckles brushed against his hot rigid flesh, he froze.

She glanced up quickly. "Did I hurt you?"

Jaw tight, he shook his head, his hand on hers indicating she should continue.

He'd left his drawers off after bathing and the flap of his pants parted to reveal the pale smooth skin below the dark tan of his waist. This time when she stroked him, he shoved off his pants and urged her back onto the bed.

Coming down beside her, he took her hand and pressed it against his cheek. "Kiss me."

As she did, his hand went to her ankle and slid up the inside of her leg, gathering her gown on the way. Baring her knees, her thighs, her hips. And every place he uncovered, he kissed. She was aching by the time he cupped her between the legs and slid one big finger into her heat. Tension gripped her down low, a lovely tension that pulsed between her thighs then coiled tight. Reflex had her legs squeezing together.

"Let me touch you," he whispered in a labored voice.

As he worked her slowly with his hand, an amazing sensation began to throb there. He slid in another finger, stretching her uncomfortably and, after a while, a third, this one almost painful. When she strained against him, he moved his mouth to her breast, curling his tongue around her through the sheer fabric. "Try to relax around me, Em."

She did, sliding her hands to his shoulders, holding tight as she shifted restlessly. "Jake."

His fingers pushed deep and she moaned. The sensation was too sharp, too much and somehow not enough. Her gown came off and his lips returned to her breast. Before she could do more than register the feel of his rough-velvet tongue, he drew hard on her nipple while touching a hot knot of nerves between her legs.

The coil of sensation inside her snapped, took her over and she was aware of nothing except a throbbing heat until Jake settled his big body between her legs.

"You know this will probably hurt the first time?" he asked in a guttural tone.

She stroked his face. "Yes. My mother said it gets better with the right man."

"That man is me, Emma."

Her answer was lost on a gasp as he reached between their bodies and touched the same place he had before. Tiny urgent flutters started inside her and Emma slid her arms around him.

Jake thrust hard. There was a tearing and a sharp pain and she involuntarily shied away.

"I'm sorry, Em. That's the worst of it."

She didn't see how that could be because he was still inside her and he felt huge.

"I promise." Keeping his lower body still, he brushed his lips across her eyelids, the tip of her nose, her chin. There was a fiery friction at the place where their bodies joined and, when his weight pressed her into the mattress, she arched up.

The most amazing sensation streamed through her. "Oh!"

"Better?" he murmured against her flesh.

"Yes," she said in wonder, experimentally tightening her muscles. Though there was still an uncomfortable tightness, she felt her body began to soften. "It's…almost good."

He gave what could've been a groan or a laugh.

Nuzzling her breast, teasing her with his tongue, his big hand curved gently around her soft flesh and he thumbed her nipple. He stayed inside her, heavy and hot, and after a bit, she shifted against him, wanting something more, not knowing what.

Sliding his hands beneath her hips, he tilted her slightly and started a slow steady pumping. He hit a spot up high with his body and it felt as if the bottom of her stomach dropped out.

"Oh!"

Lifting his head, he fixed his gaze on her. "I love you, Emma Ross."

Tears stung her eyes and she clasped his face between her hands. Unable to look away, she let him guide her body into his rhythm. Everything was in his eyes—love, desire, tenderness.

"C'mon, sweetheart," he urged in a labored voice.

And, when she came apart in his arms, moaning his name, he groaned and throbbed into her.

Breathing heavily, her skin damp, she held him tight, frightened at how much she felt for him. He'd given her every bit of himself. His whole body, his whole heart, the pain, the past, all of it. She'd given him very little in return.

He rolled to his side, holding her close. Cushioned against his hard, sweat-dampened chest, she drifted off.

* * *

Emma slept and Jake couldn't help a grin as he studied the dark sweep of her lashes against her cheek, the small, slim hand resting on his chest. He'd never seen anyone drop off to sleep so fast. One second she was stroking his chest, the next she was out cold. She shifted onto her stomach, burrowing under him so that he lay half on top of her. He inched over, giving her more room, then propped himself up on one elbow to look at her.

The sheet draped low on her hips, baring the sleek fluid line of her back, the dent at the base of her spine. Her petal-smooth skin glowed in the silvery moonlight.

With her head resting on her arm, her hair spread across the pillow and her back in a silky curtain. He stroked his hand through the thick mass. How could a man be so lucky? He hadn't expected to have another chance like this after Delia, after he'd learned that she had kept things from him. *What* she had kept from him. He hadn't thought he would ever want another chance, but with Emma, he did.

Taken with the ivory velvet of her skin, he grazed his thumb along her shoulder. He bent to put his mouth there. Her skin was wonderfully soft and he skimmed across more of her flesh. Moving her hair aside, he set his teeth on her nape and raked lightly.

She shivered.

Starting at the delicate top knob of her spine, Jake pressed hot, open-mouthed kisses down her back.

She made a sleepy noise and arched up against his mouth for more. "That tickles."

"Mmm." He laved her with his tongue, surprised when he felt a ridge of skin. Then another.

She froze at the same time he sat up and reached to light the lamp.

Between her shoulder blades was a ragged patch of scars that had healed to almost the same tone as her skin.

Emma sat up, bringing the sheet with her and starting to turn toward him.

He held her in place with a firm but gentle palm against her shoulder. "These are scars."

"Yes."

"Burn scars."

Spine rigid, head down, she nodded.

He pushed her hair completely out of the way and she winced. He paused. "Do they hurt?"

"No."

He skimmed a finger over them. "What happened?"

"It was a long time ago." She had gone perfectly still, as if she were trying to disappear into the sheet.

Jake studied her back. Some of the scars were long and bumpy, like a wax dripping from a candle. Some were shaped like drops. "Was this an accident?"

"No." Her voice was small, almost a whisper.

No. The word rang in Jake's ears. "Who did this to you?"

She looked away.

He waited. Nothing. A searing black fury erupted and he got out of bed. The air was cool against his bare skin, but he felt hot all over. "Emma?"

She shook her head, barely a movement.

His fists were clenched tight enough to make them ache. Every part of him was screaming to find out who'd hurt her, then kill them. "Tell me who did this and I promise they'll never lay a hand on you again."

Clutching the sheet to her breasts, she scooted around to face him. "I'm all right now."

He scrubbed his hands down his face, trying to keep some thread of control, but all he could see was Emma burned,

Emma hurting. "Emma, I'm supposed to take care of you. Let me."

"Nothing needs to be taken care of." She gave him a wobbly smile.

Fighting a swirl of vicious anger, Jake struggled not to lose his temper. Why couldn't she trust him? Would she ever be able to? "These scars have to do with what or who hurt you in the past."

Her gaze skittered away. In the rumpled bed, half covered in a sheet, she looked fragile. Her voice was thin, frantic. "You said I didn't have to tell you. You said it didn't matter."

"That was before I saw what some bastard did to your back!"

She flinched and pulled her knees up, wrapping her arms tight around them.

The haze of rage cleared enough for Jake to realize he was yelling. Tears rolled down her pale cheeks and her delicate features were anguished. She was trembling, shaken.

He was a jackass. Immediately, he climbed in beside her, relieved when she didn't flinch or move away. His behavior had done nothing to merit that trust. He pulled her onto his lap and she curled into him as the sheet fell away.

Somebody needed to kick him! "I'm not mad at *you,* Em."

"I kn-know," she stammered.

Her small plump breasts pressed against him, warmed him, but the rest of her skin was cold. He felt a tremor run through her. What had he done? Holding her tight, he rubbed her back, murmuring, "I didn't mean to upset you. I don't want to start this way."

"Neither do I." The words sounded choked out of her as she looked at him with tortured eyes. She swiped at a tear.

What had happened to her? Chest aching, Jake lay down,

taking her and the bedclothes with him. His heart turned over in his chest. "I'm sorry."

"I'm sorry, too." Her voice was raw, hoarse. "I just can't—"

A tear landed on his chest, then another, burning his conscience. All he wanted was to make her feel safe and happy. He wished he could love those memories out of her. "Shh, easy now. It'll be all right."

She didn't know if it would. After a long moment, Emma kissed the underside of his jaw. He was the only person she trusted completely. What if he decided he didn't want her? What if he couldn't forgive her for keeping this from him?

With gentle hands, he stroked her back, his body warm and strong against hers. They were naked, as close as two people could be and yet there was an invisible barrier between them. Emma had put it there.

Witnessing his fury over her scars, she knew she'd been right not to tell him that her stepfather had thrown a pot of boiling water at her for daring to defy him, that the only reason her entire back wasn't burned was that her mother had knocked her out of the way. Emma might never be able to tell him.

Guilt dug in deep. She was keeping a secret from Jake, just as his first wife had done. Delia's secret had killed her and nearly destroyed him.

But Emma was trying to keep him and Molly safe. How could that be wrong? As much as it hurt her to do it, as much as it bothered Jake not to know, Emma would rather have things that way than him dead.

Chapter Fourteen

Emma's unwillingness to talk about her scars grated on Jake, but after seeing how much his questions had upset her, he let her be. The terror and agony he'd seen in her eyes that night was something he didn't want to see again; he sure as hell didn't want to be responsible for putting it there. What kind of person could burn another, especially someone as sweet-natured as Emma?

Jake wanted to know and he figured that, once she'd calmed down, once she'd gotten used to the idea of his seeing her scars, she would explain about them. But, after a week of his wife acting as if the incident on their wedding night had never happened, Jake began to wonder if she would ever tell him.

Disappointment rode him hard, as did frustration. He'd hoped that having this secret between them would bother her as much as it bothered him, but it didn't appear to.

Those scars were a shadow of her past and clung like smoke to both of them. So to curb his gnawing need for Emma to tell him about her past, Jake focused on what was good and gave thanks for the woman he loved more every day. His life hadn't felt this right in a long time. He knew a second chance when he saw one and he wasn't going to piss it away.

A week and two days after their wedding, Jake watched his wife from the adjoining doorway of the small bedroom he'd fashioned from part of his and Delia's after learning she was expecting. It hadn't been opened in the last five years, but once he and Emma had settled in to his room, she had cleaned the smaller one and moved Molly.

Emma finished singing to the toddler then gave her a kiss on the forehead. Looking at the two of them put a hard knot of emotion in his chest.

She rose and took the lamp, moving gracefully toward him. The play of shadow and pale gold light couldn't hide the weariness on her face. After she stepped into their bedroom, he shut the door behind her and carried the lamp to the bedside table.

He returned, drawing her into his arms. "Hi," he said.

"Hi." She slid her arms around his neck, meeting his kiss.

Inside her mouth was like liquid velvet and Jake let himself sink into it for a moment. She smelled like cinnamon and sugar and the Ivory soap she loved. Nuzzling her neck, he gave her a squeeze. "I'm gonna take care of you tonight."

"What do you mean?" Her voice was ragged with fatigue.

"You'll see." He'd already taken off his shirt and boots and he began undoing the buttons down the front of her gray bodice.

Smiling, she smoothed her hands across his bare shoulders and down his chest. "Is this going to be the same way you've taken care of me every night?"

"I can see where you might think that." He grinned, pushing her dress off her shoulders and holding her hand while she stepped out of it. "But, no."

The skepticism on her face had him chuckling and he gave her a quick kiss as he tugged at the ribbon on her chemise. He pushed the garment off her shoulders and watched it slide to the tops of her breasts. Since they'd married, she'd taken to leaving off her corset as most women did while at home, for which Jake was glad. He coaxed her to remove the undergarment.

She did, although she left on her drawers. The pretty blush covering her body told him she was still shy about him seeing her in the altogether. He couldn't stop looking at her, his body drawing up tight as his gaze touched her face, her neck, lower.

"Jake Ross." The warning in her voice was ruined by a smile.

He loved seeing her smile, hearing her tease, taking care of her. Even though he didn't plan to make love to her, he had no intention of keeping his hands off. And he had to touch her right now. Against her fair complexion, his hands were big and deeply tanned. Work-roughened against her silken flesh. He skimmed his palms over her soft curves and back up to frame her narrow rib cage as he bent his head to kiss the swell of her rose-tipped breasts.

Her nipples tightened and she slid one hand into his hair, stroking his scalp languorously. Her little sigh of pleasure had all his blood rushing south, but he moved on.

Tonight was about what Emma needed, not him. Knowing it would distract her if he left her clothes on the floor, Jake scooped them up and hung them on the hook inside the dark mahogany wardrobe to his right.

"Drawers, too, Miz Ross. While I get the light."

As he stepped to the bedside table and doused the lamp, he heard the shuffle of her bare feet as she took off her undergarment. A thin wisp of smoke curled from the top of the lamp and the lingering burn of kerosene.

He returned to her, admiring her curves in the silver moonlight. Her gaze met his, her eyes dark in the shadows.

After slipping her sheer night rail over her head, he reached behind her and loosened her braid. He combed his fingers through the silky mass of her hair, separating the sections until it fell in a sleek dark curtain around her shoulders. His throat closed up as he watched pleasure steal across her face. The light was soft on her skin, gliding over the soft curve of her jaw, her graceful neck.

She rubbed her cheek against the back of his hand where it rested on her shoulder and he dropped a kiss on her forehead.

The circles under her eyes didn't diminish the sweetness of her smile, but Jake knew she was worn slick. Their nightly loving had lasted until well after midnight and, even though he would've been perfectly happy last night to go straight to sleep, Emma had had other ideas.

Jake had obliged, of course. He was no dimwit. If his wife wanted to lie with him, he wasn't about to refuse.

But tonight, as much as he wanted her, he wanted more to take care of her. She'd been up and in the kitchen by the time he'd gotten downstairs this morning at dawn and he knew she'd worked just as hard all day as he had.

He scooped her into his arms, turning for the bed.

She rested her head on his shoulder, reaching up to touch his face. "Mr. Ross," she chided. "This feels exactly like last night."

Grinning, he laid her on the bed and rolled her onto her stomach.

"What are you doing?" She turned her head toward him at the same time he began to knead her neck. "Ohhhhhh."

She sagged into the mattress and her eyes fluttered shut. The pale light shimmered down the length of her body, leaving her delicate profile half in shadow. The transparent fabric of her gown gave her skin a beautiful dewy sheen.

He worked the knots out of her shoulders until she lay pliant and boneless beneath his hands.

"How's that?" he asked.

"Wonderful," she breathed.

He put his lips on the sensitive patch behind her ear, drawing in her sweet scent. "Who's my girl?"

"Molly—oh!"

He goosed her in a ticklish spot just below her ribs. "Who?" he growled.

"Me," she amended breathlessly, giggling and squirming when he tickled her again. "Stop that!"

Chuckling, he moved his hands over the lean whisper of muscle in her legs then to the bottoms of her feet.

The little sounds of pleasure she made went straight to his groin, making him rock hard.

Leaning over her, he massaged her upper arms and nudged her hair aside to nuzzle her neck.

"Jaaaake."

She drew out his name the way she did when she found her release and he ached to slide into her. But he liked this, too.

Using his first two fingers, he rubbed his way down her neck. She lay loose-limbed and relaxed until he lightly grazed her scars.

When she stiffened, his heart sank. It didn't matter that he had already seen the marred and puckered flesh, touched it, kissed it. Emma braced herself every time as if it were the first.

He refused to pretend they didn't exist. Not only because he wanted every part of her body to accept his touch, but also because he wanted her to know he would protect her. No one would ever hurt her again.

He kept up a gentle massage until finally she melted again into the mattress. Only then did he move his hands to her lower back, to her legs. When her breathing finally became slow and even, he knew she slept. He rested one hand on her shoulder, stroking her downy-soft skin with his thumb for a moment.

After lightly kissing her cheek, he rose and removed his jeans along with his short drawers.

He slid into the bed and curved one arm under her breasts, rolling her toward him until they were spooned together, her bottom pressing into his groin. She snuggled into him trustingly.

Already, Jake had learned his wife preferred sleeping on her stomach so he knew she wouldn't stay like this for long, but he would enjoy it while he could.

Moonlight seeped through the white lace curtain. Feeling her satiny warmth, Jake grew drowsy as he drank in her scent, relished the soft weight of her breasts against his arm. Someday, she would tell him about those scars. Until then, he could be patient.

That was his last conscious thought until he was roused from sleep sometime later by Emma's voice. Groggy, it took him a second to sort things out. She was crying and talking.

"It burns, it burns," she panted frantically, thrashing on the bed. "Hurts!"

Coming fully awake, Jake sat up. "Em?"

She was curled away from him, sobbing. Having a nightmare, he realized.

"Jake," she moaned. "Jake."

"I'm here." He touched her shoulder and she cried out, rolling toward him.

In the silvery light, tears shone wetly on her face. Terror pinched her fine-boned features then an awareness of where she was. She reached for him with a choked sob. "Jake!"

Heart slamming into his chest, he pulled her into his lap. "I'm here, Em. I'm here."

Her entire body shook. She buried her face against his neck, and hot, wet tears slicked his skin. She locked her arms around him and pressed closer, as if she were trying to crawl into him.

Jake rocked her, murmuring soothing words as concern hollowed out a hole in his gut. She was every bit as frightened as she had been the night he'd found her in the alcove.

"Wh-what happened?" Her voice was raw.

"You were talking in your sleep. Something was burning you."

Taking a deep breath, she shuddered. "Don't let go of me."

"I won't." Jake fought back equal parts alarm and anger, sheltering her with his body.

One arm cradled her head and the other slanted across her back, holding her tight to his chest. Though her sobs were lessening now, he could still feel them rattle through her.

It was a long time before she quieted. Finally, she lifted her head to look at him. Her eyes were wet, her thick lashes spiky from her tears.

He touched his mouth to her forehead, shifting her in his arms so he could see her face. "Wanna talk about it?"

Her voice quivered. "It started out the same as always. Mama was calling for me, asking for my help and I couldn't find her. And then I saw you. I called and called, but you were… You were…hurt and you couldn't come to me."

She hugged him tight. No mention of the burns she'd cried out about. Replaying the fear in her eyes, feeling her slight frame tremble against him, Jake couldn't bring himself to ask about them.

Though still huddled into him, she was calm now, one

hand resting over his heart as he held her. Easing back against the carved walnut headboard that had belonged to his aunt and uncle, Jake stroked her hair with an unsteady hand.

Just before she fell asleep, she whispered, "I love you."

He didn't close his eyes. He held Emma and pondered until the moonlight gave way to the gray-pink of dawn. If the threat to her were eliminated, she would feel safe. Jake could do that for her, but he didn't know what—or who—was the threat.

The absolute fear on her face had put a hard lump in his chest. Emma might be able to go on like this for the rest of their lives, but Jake couldn't. He had to find out what had happened to his wife.

If Jake hadn't been with her last night, Emma didn't know how she would've handled the nightmare. It had started the same as it usually did, with her looking for Mama then finding her dead and Orson standing over her body. Then Emma had felt the scalding water on her back and, worst of all, Mama's dead body had become Jake's.

He'd been dead, not hurt as she'd told him. She hadn't been able to say it. She'd hardly been able to process it.

Even though Emma wasn't superstitious, that image had dread creeping up her spine. This morning, she'd woken in his arms, in the same spot where she'd fallen asleep. She was pretty sure he hadn't slept at all.

He'd encouraged her to talk about the nightmare, without asking questions. Since their wedding night, when she'd become so upset about his seeing the scars, he hadn't asked about them again.

But he didn't ignore them, either, as she wished he would. Every time he touched them, every time he kissed them, her guilt dug deeper. The scars were a physical reminder of the secret she was keeping from him. A secret she *had* to keep in order for him to remain safe, for all of them to remain safe.

It wasn't lost on Emma that the best thing for their safety was the absolute worst thing for their marriage, in more ways than one.

The guilt carved a bigger piece out of her every day. But she hadn't changed her mind; she wouldn't. If nothing else, the nightmare had reminded her how dangerous her stepfather was and what a threat he posed to Jake.

As she rode beside Jake in the wagon on the way to Whirlwind, Emma was fully aware that something was weighing on her husband. He was as kind and attentive as usual to both her and Molly, but there was a tightly leashed tension in his body, a soberness in his eyes. He was distracted and Emma was afraid it was because of her nightmare. She didn't feel as if she could ask. She wouldn't answer his questions; why should he answer hers?

The sense only grew stronger when he helped her and Molly down from the wagon in front of Haskell's General Store. He kissed her, telling her that, if she finished before he and Bram returned, they would be at Ef's smithy. Even Bram's parting wink didn't settle Emma's unease.

She watched as her husband drove the wagon down the wide main street toward the simple frame structure where Ef Gerard worked steel and metal. The glow of the constantly burning fire was visible through the wide-open doorway.

As she stared at Jake's broad, strong back, he jumped down from the wagon and shook the blacksmith's hand.

Molly's bouncing up and down jarred Emma out of her thoughts and she went inside Charlie Haskell's mercantile.

The tall thin proprietor was helping a customer and

he glanced over as she walked inside. "Be right with you, Emma."

"No hurry." She smiled, hitching Molly to her other hip. "We'll look at your fabric for a minute."

Once at the table holding bolts of cloth, she fingered a small checked gray-and-white flannel. "Think Jake would like a shirt out of this, Molly?"

The little girl, who'd begun another round of teething last week, stopped gnawing on Emma's shoulder. "Yake!"

"He'll be here in a bit." Emma moved to a red twill as her sister went back to gumming the shoulder of her dress.

"Zoe! Zoe!" A deep masculine voice had Emma looking up as a broad-shouldered man hurried past her and toward the curtained doorway of Josie's shop. "Zeke needs you."

Emma caught a quick glimpse of ragged brown hair and huge hands, noting he was almost as big as the Baldwin brothers.

"That's Zoe's brother, Zeke," Charlie explained to Emma as he stacked several boxes of soda crackers next to a jug of molasses on the shiny wooden counter. "He refers to himself in the third person a lot."

Emma gave a polite smile, her gaze returning to the doorway that led to Josie's shop. She remembered that both Jake and the seamstress had said the boy was slow.

On the other side of the curtain, his deep voice alternated with his sister's. There was something vaguely familiar about him. Had she met him before? At church maybe?

Church. Emma recalled the white shirt and brown pants. The ragged brown hair. No! Could it be?

The thief she'd seen rifling through J. T. Baldwin's saddlebags had worn a very similar white shirt and brown pants. And Zoe's brother was big, just like the man she'd seen, but a thief?

Keeping her thoughts to herself, Emma worked her way over to the doorway of Josie's shop and peeked through the opening in the curtains. She had to get a better look.

Jake and Bram helped Ef roll out the first of four newly banded wagon wheels, then began to stack them in the back of the buckboard.

Jake didn't know what to do about Emma. Last night, he'd made up his mind to get answers. But, when he'd seen her this morning, he'd changed his mind. He wanted to wait until she was ready to tell him about her past, but he couldn't forget the fear on her face or the desperation in her voice.

He'd crawfished on it all the way into Whirlwind and he was no closer to making up his mind now than he had been when they'd left the ranch.

He stared down the street at the open door of Haskell's where he'd left his wife. That nightmare had rattled him to his toes.

"Hey." Bram nudged his arm.

He glanced over to find his brother and Ef grinning as if sharing a private joke. "What?"

"Ef's asked you the same question twice."

"Oh." The back of Jake's neck heated. "What is it?"

The black man laughed. "You been married to that woman for over a week. You still mooning over her?"

"I can answer that," Bram said with a twinkle in his eye.

"Yeah, yeah." Jake turned to his friend. "What'd you want to ask me?"

"Do you still want me to make those pot hooks?"

He nodded. "And a new cutting edge for my ax."

"All right," Ef said in his deep voice.

Jake hooked a thumb over his shoulder toward the new

hotel. "You did a fine job on that ironwork for Russ. Real fancy."

"Thanks." Ef wiped his sooty hands down the front of his heavy apron. "It was a heck of a job."

"Beautiful work, as usual," Bram added.

As the three stepped under the overhang of Ef's shop, a stranger rode up and dismounted. He pushed back his bowler hat, his gaze settling on Ef. "You're wearing the apron, so I assume you're the blacksmith?"

"Yes, sir." The big man stepped over to him. "May I help you?"

"Could you take a look at my mare's left rear shoe? I can't find a rock or anything in her hoof, but she's starting to favor that leg."

"Be happy to." With an easy touch, Ef smoothed one large hand down the horse's side, to her flank, over her rump and down her leg.

Jake hefted another wheel into the wagon bed.

Bram rolled the last one to him. "Everything okay?"

"Yeah."

"Ya sure?"

"Yeah." He hoisted it up into the bed, turning to see concern on his brother's face. "Why?"

"You've barely taken your eyes off Charlie's store since you left Emma there and I don't think it's because you're moonin' after her."

Jake rubbed his chin then eased down onto the bed of the wagon. "There are some things about her that are bothering me."

Bram frowned. "What kinds of things?"

Jake explained about her nightmares and discovering her scars. "I know something in her past hurt her real bad, but before we got married, I told her she didn't have to talk about it if she didn't want. That it didn't matter to me, and I meant it. But you should've seen her last night. She was scared out of her wits. She scared *me*."

"And you think the nightmare has to do with the scars?"

He shrugged. "I don't know. This is the first one she's had since we married. She told me about another one and didn't mention burns or scars at all."

"Do you think she's afraid to tell you or does she just want to forget?"

Jake pulled off his hat and shoved a hand through his hair. "I think she's afraid. Not of me, but of something."

Bram thought for a minute. "She was pretty skittish around all of us when she got to Whirlwind. Maybe she still is?"

"We've moved past that."

His brother folded his arms, studying the mercantile. "And you haven't asked her about the scars since your wedding night?"

"No, but now I'm wonderin' if I should push her." When his brother didn't reply, Jake said, "If I don't force the issue, she may never tell me, and I don't think I can live the rest of my life not knowing what happened to her."

"Are you asking if I think you should press her?"

Jake fed the brim of his hat through his fingers. "I don't know. If I could find out who burned her, I'd make sure they paid for it and never did it again. Those damn nightmares would go away. I can't stand to see her back and not do something about the bastard who hurt her. Still, I did tell her she didn't owe me an explanation."

Bram was quiet for a long minute. "Well, I don't much like suggesting this, but I can try to find out somethin' if you want. That way you won't have broken your word to her."

"That's a pretty fine hair you're splitting."

"You're the one who has to decide." His gaze went over Jake's head and he straightened. "Here comes Emma right now. With Molly."

Settling his hat back on his head, Jake stood and turned as his wife hurried toward him. The sight of her pretty features drawn tight with anxiety had him recalling with gut-twisting clarity how terrified she'd been last night.

"Find out somethin', if you can," he said in a low voice to his brother.

Bram nodded as Jake stepped around the end of the wagon and met Emma. "You're in a hurry. Everything okay? Did you see Quentin?"

"No, not Quentin." She halted abruptly in front of him, dust swirling around her skirts. "The thief! I saw the thief!"

Alert, he scanned the street behind her, his hand settling automatically on the butt of his revolver. "Are you sure?"

"Yes, yes." She slid her glasses up the bridge of her nose. "He's at Haskell's. I thought I'd better come get you before he left."

She and Jake started toward the jail. Molly reached for him and he took the little girl, following Emma up the steps and into the sheriff's office.

When Emma relayed what she'd seen, Davis Lee grabbed his hat and followed her and Jake outside.

"Oh, no!" She stopped halfway down the steps, ignoring Molly's chattering. "He's leaving. Hurry!"

Jake paused beside her, his gaze going across the street to the general store. He saw Mitchell Orr, Zeke Keeler, Bram. He didn't see a big man matching the description Emma had given.

"There he is!" she whispered, easing up against him as Davis Lee made his way around them and off the bottom step.

Adjusting his holster, the sheriff followed Emma's gaze. He frowned. "Where?"

"There, right there." She pointed discreetly toward the three men in front of Haskell's store. "It's Zeke Keeler. He's wearing a white shirt and brown pants, just like that day."

"He's just a kid. Remember? I told you about him," Jake dismissed.

"That's him! He's the one I saw going through Mr. Baldwin's saddlebag."

Jake exchanged a shocked look with Davis Lee.

"It's him! He's the man I saw."

The sheriff looked skeptical.

Emma frowned up at Jake. "He's so big. That's why I thought he was a man. My description matches except for that."

"He's not even fifteen," he said.

Her voice was quiet and small. "Do you not believe me?"

"Of course, I do!" Jake's gaze swerved to her, noting the hurt in her eyes. "We're just surprised, Em."

"No wonder we couldn't find him," Davis Lee said. "All along, we've been looking for a man when we should've been looking for a big ol' kid."

Jake thought he caught a glint of tears in Emma's eyes.

"Guess we'd better go talk to him." The grimace on Davis Lee's face said he'd rather do just about anything else.

Still holding Molly, Jake walked with Emma and Davis Lee over to Haskell's. Zoe hugged her brother and turned to go back inside the store.

"Hi, Zeke." The sheriff stopped a few feet from the young man. "Zoe, can you hold up a minute?"

"Sure." Looking anxious, the redhead paused.

"Hey, Davis Lee. Hi, Jake." The boy stared unblinking at Emma for a long time. "Hi."

She smiled.

Davis Lee glanced at the boy's sister. "I'm afraid Zeke was seen stealing something out of J. T. Baldwin's saddlebag."

"What?" Zoe exclaimed. "Are you sure?"

"We have a witness."

Her face flaming, the girl turned to her brother. "Is Davis Lee right, Zeke? Did you steal something from Mr. Baldwin?"

The boy licked his lips nervously, apprehension blunting his ruddy features. "Yeah."

"Zeke." Zoe sighed.

Face falling, he looked between Davis Lee and Zoe. "Am I caught?"

"Yes," his sister said.

His brown eyes filled with tears. "I'm sorry. I'm sorry."

Emma pressed against Jake and he looked down to see the same compassion on her face that he felt.

Zeke touched his sister's hand. "I was only trying to help. You said you'd take care of Dinah, but you already take care of me and I wanted to help."

"I know." She hugged him, her gaze encompassing Jake and Davis Lee. "I'm sorry. I caught him one day, but we talked and I thought he understood that stealing was wrong."

"So, you were the one who returned the items?" Jake asked.

Zoe nodded.

"I was helping. Honest." Zeke's voice rose as he looked pleadingly at Davis Lee. "I was helping Dinah."

"It's okay, Zeke," Jake said quietly. The Keelers had already dealt with more in life than they should've had to at this young age.

Taking her brother's hand, Zoe met Davis Lee's gaze. "There may be other things at the house."

"They're safe. Under the floor," the boy offered earnestly.

Pulling Molly's finger from her mouth, Jake shifted the toddler to his other arm. "Zeke, do you remember what all you took?"

"Some dishes, a pair of boots, a mirror."

"And the corsets?" Davis Lee reminded. "Do you know how many of those you took?"

The boy turned beet-red and he ducked his head.

"It's okay, Zeke. We'll let Davis Lee look around and see what he finds."

He was visibly upset, tears welling in his eyes.

The young woman hugged her brother.

Davis Lee put a hand on the young man's shoulder. "Let's go on and see what we can find." He glanced at Emma. "Thanks. I appreciate you keeping your eyes open."

Zoe sent a long-suffering look in her brother's direction. "Zeke knows better. He just forgets sometimes."

The boy's eyes widened in alarm. "Am I going to have to stay in Davis Lee's jail?"

"We'll talk about that once I see your house, son," the sheriff answered. "You've returned most things. If you return the rest and there are no damages, and no one wants to press charges, I don't see any reason for this to go further."

"Oh, thank you, Davis Lee!" Zoe turned to Zeke. "Did you hear that? Sheriff Holt is giving you a chance to make things right."

"And then I can stay with you, Sissy?" he asked anxiously.

"Yes."

Davis Lee urged the pair forward. "Let's go see what we find."

The three of them walked across the street and disappeared into the alley between the jail and the Pearl.

Emma glanced up at Jake. "Who's Dinah? Why does Zoe need to take care of her?"

"She's Zoe and Zeke's older sister—she's deaf."

Emma recalled now that Josie and Jake had both mentioned Dinah. Regret colored Emma's voice. "Zeke didn't mean any harm."

"No, it doesn't seem so," Jake agreed.

"Poor kid." Bram shook his head.

Emma looked up at Jake. "What do you think will happen to him?"

He slid an arm around her waist as they turned toward their wagon. "Hopefully just a stern talkin'-to since it's his first time doing anything like this."

Bram walked up on Emma's other side. "If I know Zoe, she'll make him go to everyone he stole from and apologize, then have him make it up to them by working it off."

Emma was quiet until they reached the wagon. "What Zeke did was wrong, but his heart was in the right place."

"True." Bram held Molly while Jake handed Emma up into the wagon. "But the kid should've trusted his sister to take care of it. She always has."

"Do you think she'll ever trust him again?"

Something in Emma's voice made Jake wonder if she was comparing that to her own situation. And maybe he should ask himself the same question about his wife. If he let Bram try to find out about Emma, Jake would be destroying the trust they'd built.

Thanks to Delia, Jake knew how miserable that felt.

After Bram handed the baby to Emma, Jake and his brother met up at the rear of the wagon. As he checked to make sure the new wheels were tied into the bed securely, he said in a low voice, "Nevermind about Emma."

"Changed your mind?"

Jake nodded.

"I'm glad."

"Me, too." His heart ached a little as he watched his wife tuck the lap robe around her and Molly's legs.

He'd worked hard to gain her trust, but she needed to know he trusted her, too. Maybe he'd become paranoid after what had happened with Delia. Just because Emma was keeping something from him didn't mean it was something that would hurt her.

If Emma never told him about her past, Jake would have to find a way to handle it because he wasn't about to lose his wife over it.

Chapter Fifteen

Jake dreaded going to Quentin's for his biweekly visit, but it was time. When he rode into Whirlwind midmorning on Saturday, he went straight to the Prescott house to have done with his business.

There, he was relieved to discover his brother-in-law wasn't home. Good. Jake would handle whatever was needed then be on his way.

First, he took quick stock of the outside of the house. Thanks to his earlier repairs, the porch was fine and a check of the roof showed it was, too. But the window that looked out of Quentin's front room was cracked and with winter coming on, it needed to be replaced.

Jake would get a plate of glass the next time he went to Abilene, but, for now, covering the window with a piece of oilskin, used for rainwear, would keep out the wind. The material would still allow in some light.

After buying a box of tacks and the oilskin at Haskell's, Jake fetched Quentin's toolbox and got to work. He'd tacked the two top corners when he heard the squeak of wheels behind him.

Using the ramp Jake had built after shooting his brother-in-law, Quentin rolled up beside him. The other man had probably been at the newspaper office.

"Humph, wondered when you'd be back."

"I'm back."

"Didn't like me talkin' to your girl, huh?"

Jake leveled a gaze on him. After Quentin had approached Emma in town, Jake had sent Bram to the man's house for the next two scheduled visits. "Wasn't sure I wouldn't hurt you."

The other man looked pointedly at his legs then at Jake. *"Again?"*

Jake knelt to pull the material taut and tacked a bottom corner.

"Did you hear about Zoe Keeler?"

"You mean about her brother?"

Quentin was nearly vibrating with the need to talk. "Yeah, turns out he was the one stealing the corsets."

Jake slid a look at the other man. "How do you know?"

"I'm doing an article for next Wednesday's paper."

Quentin parked his chair at the front door.

Jake hoped the man would go inside, but he didn't.

Something was going on. Quentin never made conversation with him if he could help it.

"It's a real shame. The Keeler children have sure had it rough the last few years after losing their parents."

Quentin nodded.

Finally, Jake couldn't keep from asking, "Why're you telling me all this? We both know you never say more than ten words to me."

"'Cuz while I was writing up my article on Zeke, I had a visitor at the newspaper office."

Jake didn't see how that concerned him.

"A man named Sharpton stopped in, looking for his boss's daughters. One's about twenty years old, the other about a year."

The hair on the back of Jake's neck stood up, but he kept his face blank.

"His boss, Senator Douglas, lost his wife about three months ago and then his stepdaughter ran off with his little girl."

Apprehension snaked through Jake. "Hmm."

"Aren't you gonna ask who he's looking for?"

"No."

Quentin went on as if Jake hadn't spoken. "He's looking for Emma."

The hammer slipped and Jake barely managed to grab the tool before it fell. "I told you after that business in town that you weren't to talk about her."

"He said Emma is the senator's stepdaughter. Mr. Sharpton tracked her here, from Topeka to Baxter Springs, Kansas, through Indian Territory then by train to Abilene then Whirlwind. He just wants to find both the girls before something bad happens to them."

"You're lying."

"It'd be no less than you deserve after killing Delia, but I'm not."

Jake didn't know if it was all the years he'd taken this attitude or if he just wanted Quentin to shut up, but something snapped inside him. "I'm sick to death of your mouth, Quentin."

The other man's eyes slitted.

"You like to throw blame around so much, why don't you wear some yourself?"

"I'm not making up this stuff about your woman."

"I'm not talking about her. I'm talking about Delia." A

cold black fury moved through him and he stepped closer to his brother-in-law. "She told you about the doctor's warning, didn't she?"

"Yes." Satisfaction glinted in the other man's eyes.

"And you knew she intended not to tell me."

"Yeah." His smug smile faltered somewhat, as if suddenly wondering if Jake might be laying a trap for him.

Jake bent down, getting right in his face. His voice was soft, calculating. "Maybe if *you'd* told me she was warned not to have children, she might still be alive. Ever think of that?"

He turned to go.

Quentin's voice vibrated with fury. "Figured you wouldn't believe me about your woman. I asked for a description, but Mr. Sharpton did better than that. He had a flyer with Emma's picture on it."

She had said she was from Illinois. Was that a lie? If so, she had a reason. *Walk away, Jake. Just walk.*

"This picture is from a photograph taken a couple of years ago, at the senator's wedding to Emma's mother. It's your Emma, all right, Jake. Except her name isn't York. It's Douglas."

He shoved a piece of paper at Jake. Before Jake could move it out of his face, he saw the black-and-white picture. His whole body went still and he couldn't force his gaze away.

The woman's hair was fair and she wasn't wearing glasses, but she had the same pert nose, the same sweet smile. It was Emma. Jake crumpled the flyer and threw it back at Quentin. "Why in the hell would this man come to you?"

"He didn't. Not me specifically, anyway. He came to the newspaper office to ask about her. Said he's checked with every newspaper between here and Topeka, put out flyers at every stop. The timing fits. When your wife showed up here, the baby's age."

Jake didn't need his brother-in-law putting anything together for him. "You think what you want."

"All this man wants are his daughters back. You wouldn't want someone to keep your child from you, would you, Jake?"

Quentin's silky words had pain slashing through Jake, mixed with a growing anger. His brother-in-law would love to see Jake lose Molly. And Emma, too, for that matter.

"I told him I thought I knew who she was and that she was living right here in Whirlwind. Well, out at your ranch, but you know what I mean."

Jake wanted to plow his fist into the other man's face. Muscles quivering with restraint, he gritted out, "You told this man Emma was here?"

Quentin nodded.

"How do you know he's telling the truth?" Jake didn't know it *wasn't* the truth, but Quentin didn't know it was. "That he isn't planning to hurt her?"

"She's the one who stole a kid. Seems like she's the one who's hurting people."

"Where did Sharpton go after he left here?"

"I don't know."

"Did you tell him how to get to the Circle R?"

Quentin nodded. "Guess your little woman isn't who you thought, after all."

Jake wanted to pound the other man, but he needed to talk to Emma. "If that man poses any threat to her, you'll answer to me."

He dropped the hammer on the porch then stalked down the ramp and mounted up.

Despite Quentin's obvious pleasure at turning Jake's world upside down, there might be some truth to his story, but kidnapping a child? If what Quentin had said was true, Jake knew Emma had a reason for keeping this from him.

Why hadn't she told him? Why? The question pounded through his head with the rhythm of his horse's hooves. Jake had told Emma everything about himself, every ugly, painful thing.

Despite the full force of the sun, the autumn air was cool, scented with wood smoke from the Circle R's kitchen. As he galloped up to the house, he noticed the screened door was closed. He reined up at the porch, dismounted and was through the front door in three steps. "Emma!"

"In here."

She stepped out of the kitchen and met him at the dining table, wiping her hands on her white apron. A smile curved her lips. "What are you doing back so soon? Lunch won't be ready for an hour or so."

Trying to control his impatience, he shifted from one foot to the other. "I just saw Quentin and he told me some things about you."

She froze. "What things?"

"That your name isn't Emma York and you kidnapped Molly from your stepfather, a Kansas senator."

She drew in a sharp breath and gripped the table edge as if her legs might give out.

"Is everything okay?" Georgia's voice came from the top of the stairs.

Startled and annoyed at the interruption, Jake bit back a sharp retort. "I need to talk to Emma, cousin."

The older woman looked from him to Emma's stricken face. "All right," she agreed hesitantly.

Jake waited until he heard the door to her room shut before turning back to his wife. "Well?"

"I can explain."

"So, it's true."

"It's true that my name isn't York," she said hoarsely. "It's Douglas."

"And you're from Kansas, not Illinois?"

She nodded.

The sweet aroma of baked apples wafted into the room. Jake glanced around for Molly. She must be asleep or she would be near Emma. Jake fought both anger and hurt. He'd told her *everything* about himself. "And what about Molly?"

"She's my half sister."

"Does she belong to Senator Douglas?"

"Yes." Her voice was raw, her skin waxy. "How did Quentin find this out?"

"A man named Sharpton stopped in at the newspaper office this morning and asked a bunch of questions. He gave Quentin a flyer with your picture on it."

Right before Jake's eyes, Emma crumpled. She sank down into the closest chair. "No."

The word was choked out of her and Jake's concern ratcheted up another notch along with his irritation. She was scaring the hell out of him.

"What else did Quentin say?"

Jake forced back his anger, his hurt that she hadn't shared any of this with him. What mattered was that she tell him now. "I don't care what he says. I care what you say." With one knuckle, he lifted her chin. "Tell me what's going on."

She hesitated and Jake lost his patience. "Emma, there's a man looking for you! I know I said you didn't have to tell me about your past, but now I think we both know you do."

She looked trapped and panicked. For a second, he thought she might faint.

Jake jerked off his hat and threw it on the table. "Talk to me."

Her gaze darted around the room, as if she were seeking escape.

"I saw the picture. Your hair was blond, not brown. And you weren't wearing spectacles."

Still she said nothing.

He scrubbed a hand down his face. He was doing this all wrong. "Emma," he said quietly. "No more dodgin'."

Though visibly shaken, she looked him in the eye. There was no mistaking the terror in her colorless face. "Yes, Senator Orson Douglas is my stepfather."

Jake knelt beside the chair, folded her hand into his. That matched Quentin's claim.

She squeezed his hand tight. "About three months ago, he killed my mother. I have no proof, but I know it was him," she said fiercely. "One day, I walked into Topeka to fetch some clothes from the seamstress and, when I returned home, she was dead! She'd been planning to take us and leave him. For a couple of months, we hid money and clothes in a safe place. I think Orson found out and that's why he killed Mama."

A tear rolled down her cheek and she swiped it away. "My mother came between me and his temper more times than I can count. I was afraid of what Orson might do to Molly and to me so, on the day of her funeral, I took her and left that house."

"Your scars? From him?"

"Yes."

Jake cursed, trying not to crush her hand in his. "What happened?"

"He threw a pot of boiling water at me when I told him I wouldn't agree to the marriage he'd arranged for me. The burns would've been much worse if my mother hadn't thrown herself on top of me. As it was, she was scalded on her arm and one side of her face."

"What did he do to your mama? Why do you think he killed her?"

Her voice shook. "She took laudanum sometimes for a back injury he'd caused. I think he gave her too much. I tried not to let him see that I suspected what he'd done, but I believe he knew. He probably imagined I would go to the authorities."

"Why didn't you?"

"He's a powerful senator. They wouldn't have done anything. Orson was the one who got the sheriff in office."

"Did he threaten you?"

"Not verbally. He's careful about the way he does things. Appearances must be kept up." A bitterness Jake had never heard traced Emma's voice. "He watches, he intimidates, fools most people, then he moves, generally without warning."

And now he was here for Emma and Molly. Fear joined Jake's simmering anger. "Why did you come to Whirlwind? Why the Circle R?"

She explained about the day she'd seen his kindness to the little boy in Abilene. "When I took the job as your baby nurse, it was supposed to be only for a short time, to see if this was the right place for Molly. But it became harder and harder to make myself go. I was going to leave the night of her birthday and I couldn't, because of my feelings for you."

Jake didn't like the suspicion that slicked up his spine, but he had to ask. "Is that really why you married me? Or was it because it would make it even more difficult for your stepfather to find you?"

"No!" Hurt flashed through her eyes as she covered both their hands with her free one. "I married you because I'm in love with you."

He knew it was true; he'd seen it on her face many times. He saw it now.

Tears glinted in her eyes. "Don't you believe me?"

"Yes." He couldn't get past the black swirl of anger inside him. Anger at her. His jaw clenched. "Yes, I believe you, but that makes it even harder to understand why you didn't trust me with the truth. This man wants to kill you, Emma. If Quentin hadn't told me about this, Senator Douglas's man might've found you. You could be dead."

She winced and he realized he was yelling, scaring her. He didn't care. It was better she be scared than dead. His chest ached. "Why couldn't you tell me?"

"I was only doing what I thought was right!"

Jake stood, one hand curling over the back of her chair until he felt the wood bite into his hand. "I understand why you felt you had to keep your other life a secret and give yourself a new identity, but you should've told me. I can take care of you."

"I know that." Beseeching him with her eyes, she rose, too. She laid a hand on his chest.

Jake stepped away, hating the hurt in her eyes as he did so, but he was hurt, too. "Then, why keep this from me? Especially since you knew what happened because Delia kept things from me."

His mind had been circling for an answer to that. The one that popped into his head had his body going still. His voice cracked on the realization. "You didn't trust me to protect you."

Everything inside him broke open in a savage release—the guilt, the anger, the fear. He grasped her shoulders. "Do you think I can't protect you because I didn't keep Delia safe?"

"No! What happened to Delia wasn't your fault."

"You must think it is or you would've trusted me to take care of you." It *was* his fault Delia was dead. Maybe Emma would never be able to completely trust him.

"That's not it!" she cried out. "If I'd told you about Mama, about my scars, the danger Molly's in if Orson finds us, you would've gone after him."

"Damn straight."

"You don't know him. He wants me and Molly. If you get in his way, he'll kill you, like he did my mother."

Jake tried to take it all in. "You kept the truth from me because *you* were trying to protect *me?*"

"Yes." She clutched at his arm. "The nightmare I had the other night? In it, you weren't hurt. You were *dead!* Orson killed you. It may have been a dream, but it was no dream that he killed my mother. I'm not going to give him a chance to kill you, too."

"Dammit, woman, it's not your job to protect me! It's my job to protect you." He couldn't breathe; he had to get out of here. Pulling away from her, he grabbed his hat and stalked toward the door.

"Where are you going?" She sounded alarmed as she hurried after him. In the next room, Molly began to cry. Emma stopped, glancing back toward the sound. "Jake?"

"Quentin told that man, Sharpton, where you are. How to get here. I need to see if there's any sign of him. Signal my uncle and Bram to get back here."

"Jake, be careful. Sharpton is as dangerous as Orson."

The baby's cries grew louder, nearly drowning out Emma's words, but Jake caught them. He turned, pain digging deep. "Whether you believe I'm up to it or not, I can and will protect you and Molly."

Emma rushed into Molly's bedroom, soothing the crying toddler as she swept her up, then headed out the door. She'd hurt Jake deeply, but she couldn't worry about that right now. Not now that Sharpton had found her. Which meant Orson wouldn't be far behind. She had to make Jake understand how dangerous—vicious!—both men were.

He was standing halfway between the barn and the house, his mare's reins dangling loosely from his hands. Molly quit fussing as Emma approached Jake. His shoulders went rigid.

"I'm sorry." When he didn't move away, Emma drew in a deep breath. "I'm sorry I hurt you, but I'd do it again. I'd do anything to keep you safe."

"Yake?" Molly's voice was drowsy.

Before Jake could answer, the thunder of hooves had both him and Emma turning. Jake's mare stomped uneasily. A black horse and its rider approached the house. She couldn't see because of the sun, but as the man reined up a few feet away, she gasped. Sharpton!

"Well, Miss Emma, I'm glad to have finally found you." His gaze flicked over her and the baby.

Though his swarthy, honed features remained passive, Emma could see the ruthless determination in the thin line of his mouth, the cruelty in the stone-cold gray of his eyes.

"You look well." He shifted his attention to Jake. "Fred Sharpton. I work for Emma's stepfather." His gaze returned to Emma. "The senator's been worried sick about you and Molly."

Before Emma could refute that, Jake stepped forward, putting her slightly behind him. His mare's ears pricked forward. "I know who you are and I know the truth of why you're here, so you can get the hell off my land right now."

"I won't be leaving without the little girl."

"Yes, you will." Even as Jake reached for his revolver, Sharpton lifted his hand from the opposite side and fired a pistol he'd been hiding.

Emma could barely take it in. There was a loud crack. The mare shied and jerked out of Jake's grasp. Molly screamed then began to wail. Jake went down with a heavy thud. Blood gushed just above his ear and ran down his neck.

Emma cried out, automatically falling to her knees beside him as she jerked off her apron. "Jake, can you hear me? Please wake up!"

"Get up, Emma, and get on the horse."

"No!" Holding a sobbing Molly in one arm, Emma pressed the apron fabric to Jake's wound. Blood soaked the cloth, slicked her fingers. "Jake, please."

"I'm not telling you again," Sharpton said.

Heart kicking painfully in her chest, Emma leaned over her husband. He was so pale. He didn't move, didn't moan. Molly crawled higher on Emma's shoulder as she bent to put her ear against his chest to see if he was breathing. A solid click had her freezing in place, then she looked up to see Sharpton's gun pointed at her head.

He had dismounted and now kicked Jake's gun out of reach. "Up. Now."

Quaking and near panic, Emma moved automatically. She held her frightened sister close, trying to calm the little girl, trying to calm herself. Sobbing, trembling, Molly buried her face in Emma's neck.

Fear had Emma's throat closing up. At gunpoint, she climbed onto Jake's still-saddled mare with Molly and rode out with Sharpton leading them by the reins.

She looked back. Jake lay in the same limp position she'd left him, his stillness eerily reminiscent of her mother's the day Emma had found her. Shaken and afraid, tears poured down her cheeks. The only thought in her numbed mind was that Jake might be dead. Because of her.

Chapter Sixteen

"Dammit!" Jake roared at his cousin as she cleaned his wound with carbolic acid. His head hammered viciously behind his eyes, in his temples. "Hurry up!"

"I'm trying." Georgia had run out of the house after hearing the gunshot. "This would be finished a lot faster if you'd be still."

He sat in the spot where he'd fallen, pain shooting through his skull. The noontime sun had him blinking at its brightness. "I need to go. The longer I wait, the farther away they get."

"I know," the older woman said quietly. "But you'll get a lot farther if you're not bleeding like a stuck hog."

She was right, though that didn't make the delay sit any easier. He'd woken a couple of minutes ago, his cousin bending over him, his hat lying beside him. Blood covered his neck and one side of his face. Sharpton's bullet had plowed a furrow above Jake's left ear that Georgia had pronounced a deep graze.

"Tell me what happened. Who was that man? Why did he take Emma and Molly?"

Georgia worked as fast as she could with her one usable arm, but that didn't still the urgency coiling inside Jake. As his cousin wrapped a long strip of bandage around his head, he explained about Emma being on the run from her stepfather and how his hired gun, Sharpton, had tracked her to the Circle R.

"That son of a bitch pulled a gun out of nowhere," Jake spat. There was no way he or Douglas was walking away from this.

As Georgia tied off the bandage, Jake snatched his hat from the ground and struggled to stand. She held on to his arm until he steadied himself, then she gave him a hug. "Go. I'll fire shots for Ike and Bram."

A sharp ache drilled through his head. Cursing viciously, he headed for the barn.

"Be careful!" Georgia called behind him.

Tiny knives stabbed behind his eyes. Dammit, Emma was on his horse, the fastest one he owned. He'd take Nugget; she wasn't the fastest but she had the stamina of two horses.

Neither Ike nor Bram had shown by the time Jake had saddled the palomino and mounted. He couldn't wait. If either of them were within hearing distance of the ranch, they would come to the house and talk to Georgia. They would have no trouble following his trail.

It was easy to pick up Sharpton's trail. Jake tracked the man east, through the grass, up hills and down. He was heading north away from Jake's ranch, away from Riley's. After about a mile, Jake passed a dried creek bed.

Everything inside him wanted to give Nugget her head, but he rode carefully, searching the area. It wasn't wooded and Jake determined there was no ambush waiting for him behind a lone mesquite tree or in a small copse of oak trees and scrub brush. Sharpton was headed in the direction of Widow Monfrey's place. Jake hoped he might stop there.

The house had been vacant since her death a couple of years ago, except for the few days last year when the McDougal Gang had used it to hole up with their consumptive brother, Ian. The outlaws had forced Jericho's wife, Catherine, to come out and nurse the sick man.

As he rode, a sharp ache settled in Jake's chest. He couldn't lose either Emma or Molly. The little girl had worked her way into his heart and Emma... She'd helped him get past using Delia's memory as a crutch or carrying it as a burden. Her sweet quiet ways had soothed a still-raw part of him deep inside.

Both his girls were out there. Sharpton was a cold son of a bitch and Jake had no idea what plans the man had for Emma or Molly. He knew how much his wife loved that little girl. She would do everything possible to keep Molly safe, even die. Jake's heart squeezed at that. They'd both brought so much to his life.

The best thing he could do for them was to find them. His rage settled into an icy calm, narrowing his focus and clearing his mind.

He refused to believe he might have already lost the family he'd thought never to have again.

Jake! Emma needed to go to him, but all she could do was hold on helplessly as Sharpton forced Jake's mare to run alongside his horse.

She felt as if her heart were being pulled from her chest. What if Jake was dead? Emma wanted to break down and cry, but Molly was upset enough, nearly hysterical. It was all Emma could do to try and soothe the little girl when she could hardly soothe herself. She was terrified.

Her gun! She reached for her skirt pocket even as she realized it was empty. She'd stopped carrying the derringer because she'd felt safe.

"Where are you taking us?" she asked Sharpton.

"To meet your daddy."

That cruel, hateful man wasn't her father. Orson Douglas was a bully and a murderer. She wanted him to pay for killing her mother, but Emma didn't know if she'd live to see tomorrow, much less to see justice for Nola Douglas.

The most important thing was to keep Molly safe. To do that, Emma had to stay calm. That meant she couldn't think about Jake lying motionless in the dirt, blood spilling out of him. Or the way the energy had drained out of her upon leaving him.

As she'd ridden away, his strong, hard body had looked completely defenseless. She wanted to believe he was alive, but she just didn't know. Feeling panic well up, Emma tried to force her mind to this moment only.

Even if he was alive, he would be in no condition to come after her. She had to figure out how to get away from this man on her own.

Huddled into Emma's chest, Molly was quiet for the moment, her small body trembling, her arms locked tight around Emma's neck. A small white house came into sight and Emma shifted in the saddle.

Behind the house was a barn and a chicken coop. One sprawling oak tree, starting to drop its golden leaves, shaded the east side of the house. A few bushes ran along the same side. Peeling paint and a rotting porch step suggested it was vacant and had been for some time.

Sharpton slowed both horses as they reached the side of the house. The space between here and the barn provided no cover. There was only dirt and straw and leaves. But the line of trees behind the barn gave way to waist-high prairie grass beyond. If she had a chance to escape, she'd head there first. At least the grass was tall enough to provide some cover.

Over his shoulder, her captor said, "Scream all you want. Nobody lives around here."

Emma swallowed hard, her palms slick with sweat as she gripped the saddle horn with one hand and clutched her sister tightly to her chest with the other.

Molly whimpered Jake's name and Emma's heart twisted. *Please, oh, please let him be alive.*

The weathered gray barn had been badly neglected. Aside from weeds growing along and out from under the walls, both the wide front and rear doors sagged on their hinges. A roan gelding stood beside the barn.

The front door creaked and rattled as it slid open. Her step-father walked out in shirtsleeves and dust-covered trousers.

She'd only seen the tall, broad man without his tailored three-piece suit one other time. He was always immaculately groomed from his graying dark hair to his well-made shoes. His hands were huge, his legs as thick as tree trunks. And his eyes were a flat, dull brown.

Every gut-wrenching fear, every nightmare he'd caused rushed back to Emma and bile rose in her throat. Malice rolled off him, causing her to tighten her arm around Molly. The little girl burst out crying.

Orson's gaze skipped to Sharpton. "Well done, Fred. Were you followed?"

"No. I found her at that ranch and shot the man who was there, so we don't need to worry about him."

"Good." Orson's voice was still the same baritone she remembered. It was the calm in his voice, in his demeanor that had Emma's muscles clenching. This was the most danger-ous time to be around him. He would strike like a snake be-fore she ever saw it coming.

Every sense on alert, she sat quietly atop Jake's mare, her mind racing for any possible means of escape.

"Take the baby," Orson ordered Sharpton.

The other man dismounted and came toward Emma.

"No!" She reflexively pulled away.

Orson strode over to Emma's horse and held the animal in place. With his free hand, he grabbed her ankle and twisted until she cried out in pain.

Molly's sobs grew louder. Tears trickled down Emma's cheeks. Sharpton reached for the baby, who kicked out, shrieking. Her sister's hold nearly choked Emma and the baby's screams turned shrill.

The pressure on Emma's ankle increased, tearing at her muscles and finally she released her sister with a sob.

Molly's voice was piercing as she reached for Emma. Sharpton struggled to control the little girl's bucking body.

"Don't hurt her!" Emma cried. "Please don't hurt her."

"No one's going to hurt her." Orson's cold dark gaze drilled into her as he released her ankle. "But I can't say the same for you."

Emma went rigid, her heart aching as Molly continued to wail. *Think,* she ordered herself.

"You've caused me a lot of trouble," the senator continued over the noise. "But you won't be doing it again."

The horse was their best chance of escape, but she couldn't leave without Molly.

"Emma! Emma! Emma!" Molly's arms were open, her face red and frightened.

Emma thought her chest would burst. If she tried to take the child, there was no telling what Orson would do.

He motioned Sharpton over. "Give Molly to me."

When Orson took her, she strained away from him, her voice starting to go hoarse. The senator spoke loudly enough to be heard over her. "No shooting, Fred. I don't know if anyone's close."

"So how do you want to do it?"

After a few short seconds of staring into the cool darkness of the barn, he smiled in a way that made fear churn in Emma's stomach.

"Hang her. There's a rope on that saddle. Take her into the barn. Then we'll cut her down and say she fell off her horse, broke her neck."

Having no doubt that Sharpton would follow through, Emma choked back a scream. Seeing no way out, she nearly gave up then, but she had to do everything she could for her sister. She needed time to think.

Molly's wailing, the viciousness in Orson's voice made her ears vibrate. Tears blurred her vision. Desperation had words erupting out of her.

"You killed Mama yourself instead of having Sharpton do it. Why aren't you doing that to me?"

Her stepfather didn't answer, just motioned for his man to move into the barn.

"Why did you kill her?" Emma persisted.

Orson stared at her out of slitted eyes. "Who says I did?"

"We both know you did." Her chest ached with the effort to choke back more tears. "You found out she was planning to leave you and you gave her too much laudanum."

"Even if I were entertaining thoughts of keeping you alive—and I'm not—you'd never be able to prove your accusations." A smug light glittered in his eyes. "She simply took too much that day."

He didn't even care. There was no remorse, no regret on his smoothly planed features. Emma couldn't stop her tears. "Let me say goodbye to Molly."

"No."

"Please!"

"Emma!" Molly howled, flailing and thrashing in her father's arms, trying to escape his hold.

Sharpton hooked a hand under the cheek strap of Emma's mare and started forward. A shot rang out from the back of the barn. He jerked back then fell forward, dropping the reins.

Everything happened in an instant.

The mare reared up, front legs flailing the air. Emma lost her hold on the saddle horn and flew through the air, hitting the ground hard.

Winded, she scrambled to her hands and knees as her stepfather spun in the direction of the gunfire, holding Molly across him like a shield.

Who had fired at Sharpton? Emma's mind raced. Sharpton lay dead a few feet away, a gaping hole in his back seeping blood.

Emma dove for his revolver and yanked it from his holster. Orson swung around and fired at her.

She flattened herself to the ground. As her stepfather's slug plowed into the dirt beside her, she pulled the trigger. Her bullet hit him in the knee.

Blood spurted from the wound. His legs gave and he went down, dropping Molly. His scream of pain mixed with the toddler's.

Emma scrambled to her feet. She barely managed to grab her sister before her stepfather lunged up. Her heart stopped when she saw the gun aimed at her chest.

"Douglas!" a man hollered.

Jake! He was alive!

Orson glanced away for one second. Emma crawled away, but managed only inches before he swung back and leveled his weapon.

She covered her sister's body with her own, waiting in a suspended moment for the crack of the gun, for pain.

Two quick shots sounded in succession, then…silence. Through hers and Molly's sobs, she heard Jake calling her name.

She pushed herself up, cradling her sister tightly.

Jake raced around the corner of the barn. He paused long enough to kick Orson's gun out of reach before rushing to Emma and Molly. "Em!"

He dropped to his knees and wrapped them in his arms. Emma's tears flowed so fast and hard she could hardly see.

"Are you okay? Are you both okay?" Jake's heart had nearly stopped when he'd seen Emma's stepfather take aim at her.

He drew back enough to check for blood on Emma's pink calico and Molly's dark blue dress. Finding none, relief flooded him. He could hardly breathe past the ache in his chest. He hugged them close again and the toddler grabbed onto his neck.

Emma burrowed into Jake, shaking so hard he heard her teeth chatter. "Orson?"

"Dead. The SOB is dead. They both are."

She sagged against him, sobbing in relief.

"You're safe," he whispered fiercely against her hair, rocking her. "You're both safe."

She looked up at him, wiping her eyes enough to see. Beneath his bronzed skin, he was as pale as the white bandage showing beneath his hat. She raised a shaking hand to his face. "I thought he killed you. I thought you were dead."

"Takes more than a lead slug to dent my hard head."

He kissed her and she regained some measure of calm. Pulling away, he stood and helped her to her feet.

She glanced back, shuddering at the sight of her stepfather and Sharpton. "What about them?"

"I'll take care of 'em." Jake stroked her hair. "Once I get you girls settled, I'll get 'em ready to ride. Okay?"

"Yes," she whispered hoarsely, snuggling into his side.

As they walked toward his mare that had returned to pace nervously just beyond the house, Jake told her how he'd located them by following the sound of Molly's crying. He'd left his horse a short distance away and circled around to the back of the barn.

They stopped beside the house. Emma wrapped both arms around him and rested her head on his chest.

"Good thinkin' to shoot Orson in the leg. It got Molly out of the way and gave me a clear shot."

Hearing her name, the toddler planted a clumsy kiss on his jaw and he smiled.

Beneath Emma's cheek, Jake's heartbeat finally slowed. Everything about the last hour felt unreal, except for him, his steady strength, his warmth.

He rubbed her back, murmuring against her hair, "I'm sorry about earlier."

She shook her head, drawing away to look at him. "I'm the one who's sorry. I left my sister on your doorstep and lied to get the job as her nurse."

"You did that to protect her."

"I've been lying all this time, except about you and the way I feel. At first I was just trying to keep Molly and myself safe. And later, you. But, instead, I almost got all of us killed."

Jake hooked a finger under her chin. "You did what you had to, and none of that matters now."

"So you forgive me?"

"There's nothing to forgive. What matters is that you're alive. We're all alive." His black eyes went as soft as velvet and he brushed a kiss across her forehead. "I love you. Both of you."

"Ma-wee wuv." The little girl patted Jake's chest.

"I don't know what I'd do without either of you in my life," he said gruffly. "You *are* my life."

Tears filled her eyes.

"Let's go home."

"Yes, home." For the first time since her mother's death, Emma felt peace, a sense of belonging.

Her past was well and truly dead and she'd seen justice for her mother, all thanks to Jake. She and Molly had the home Emma had wanted for her sister, for herself.

Jake had given that to her, too. He'd given her everything.

* * * * *

Welcome to cowboy country....

Turn the page for a sneak preview of
TEXAS BABY
by Kathleen O'Brien
An exciting new title from Harlequin Superromance
for everyone who loves stories about the West.

Harlequin Superromance—
Where life and love weave together in
emotional and unforgettable ways.

CHAPTER ONE

CHASE TRANSFERRED his gaze to the road and identified a foreign spot on the horizon. A car. Almost half a mile away, where the straight, tree-lined drive met the public road. He could tell it was coming too fast, but judging the speed of a vehicle moving straight toward you was tricky.

It wasn't until it was about two hundred yards away that he realized the driver must be drunk…or crazy. Or both.

The guy was going maybe sixty. On a private drive, out here in ranch country, where kids or horses or tractors or stupid chickens might come darting out any minute, that was criminal. Chase straightened from his comfortable slouch and waved his hands.

"Slow down, you fool," he called out. He took the porch steps quickly and began walking fast down the driveway.

The car veered oddly, from one lane to another, then up onto the slight rise of the thick green spring grass. It just barely missed the fence.

"Slow down, damn it!"

He couldn't see the driver and he didn't recognize this automobile. It was small and old and couldn't have cost much even when it was new. It was probably white, but now it needed either a wash or a new paint job or both.

"Damn it, what's wrong with you?"

At the last minute, he had to jump away, because the idiot

behind the wheel clearly wasn't going to turn to avoid a collision. He couldn't believe it. The car kept coming, finally slowing a little, but it was too late.

Still going about thirty miles an hour, it slammed into the large, white-brick pillar that marked the front boundaries of the house. The pillar wasn't going to give an inch, so the car had to. The front end folded up like a paper fan.

It seemed to take forever for the car to settle, as if the trauma happened in slow motion, reverberating from the front to the back of the car in ripples of destruction. The front windshield suddenly seemed to ice over with lethal bits of glassy frost. Then the side windows exploded.

The front driver's door wrenched open, as if the car wanted to expel its contents. Metal buckled hideously. Small pieces, like hubcaps and mirrors, skipped and ricocheted insanely across the oyster-shell driveway.

Finally, everything was still. Into the silence, a plume of steam shot up like a geyser, smelling of rust and heat. Its snake-like hiss almost smothered the low, agonized moan of the driver.

Chase's anger had disappeared. He didn't feel anything but a dull sense of disbelief. Things like this didn't happen in real life. Not in his life. Maybe the sun had actually put him to sleep....

But he was already kneeling beside the car. The driver was a woman. The frosty glass-ice of the windshield was dotted with small flecks of blood. She must have hit it with her head, because just below her hairline a red liquid was seeping out. He touched it. He tried to wipe it away before it reached her eyebrow, though, of course that made no sense at all. Her eyes were shut.

Was she conscious? Did he dare move her? Her dress was covered in glass and the metal of the car was sticking out lethally in all the wrong places.

Then he remembered, with an intense relief, that every good medical man in the county was here, just behind the house, drinking his champagne. He found his phone and paged Trent.

The woman moaned again.

Alive, then. Thank God for that.

He saw Trent coming toward him, starting out at a lope, but quickly switching to a full run.

"Get Dr. Marchant," Chase called. "Don't bother with 9-1-1."

Trent didn't take long to assess the situation. A fraction of a second, and he began pulling out his cell phone and running toward the house.

The yelling seemed to have roused the woman. She opened her eyes. They were blue and clouded with pain and confusion.

"Chase," she said.

His breath stalled. His head pulled back. "What?"

Her only answer was another moan, and he wondered if he had imagined the word. He reached around her and put his arm behind her shoulders. She was tiny. Probably petite by nature, but surely way too thin. He could feel her shoulder blades pushing against her skin, as fragile as the wishbone in a turkey.

She seemed to have passed out, so he put his other arm under her knees and lifted her out. He tried to avoid the jagged metal, but her skirt caught on a piece and the tearing sound seemed to wake her again.

"No," she said. "Please."

"I'm just trying to help," he said. "It's going to be all right."

She seemed profoundly distressed. She wriggled in his arms, and she was so weak, like a broken bird. It made him feel too big and brutish. And intrusive. As if touching her this way, his bare hands against the warm skin behind her knees, was somehow a transgression.

He wished he could be more delicate. But he smelled gasoline, and he knew it wasn't safe to leave her here.

Finally he heard the sound of voices, as guests began to run around the side of the house, alerted by Trent. Dr. Marchant was at the front, racing toward them as if he were forty instead of seventy. Susannah was right behind him, her green dress floating around her trim legs.

"Please," the woman in his arms murmured again. She looked at him, the expression in her blue eyes lost and bewildered. He wondered if she might be on drugs. Hitting her head on the windshield might account for this unfocused, glazed look, but it couldn't explain the crazy driving.

"Please, put me down. Susannah… The wedding…"

Chase's arms tightened instinctively and he froze in his tracks. She whimpered, and he realized he might be hurting her. "Say that again?"

"The wedding. I have to stop it."

* * * * *

Be sure to look for TEXAS BABY,
available September 11, 2007,
as well as other fantastic Superromance titles
available in September.

HARLEQUIN *Super Romance*

Welcome to Cowboy Country...

TEXAS BABY

by Kathleen O'Brien

#1441

Chase Clayton doesn't know what to think.
A beautiful stranger has just crashed his
engagement party, demanding that he not
marry because she's pregnant with his baby.
But the kicker is—he's never seen her before.

Look for TEXAS BABY and other fantastic
Superromance titles on sale September 2007.

Available wherever books are sold.

HARLEQUIN *Super Romance*

**Where life and love weave together
in emotional and unforgettable ways.**

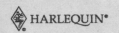

EVERLASTING LOVE™

Every great love has a story to tell™

Third time's a charm.

Texas summers. Charlie Morrison.
Jasmine Boudreaux has always connected
the two. Her relationship with Charlie
begins and ends in high school. Twenty
years later it begins again—and ends again.
Now fate has stepped in one more time—
will Jazzy and Charlie finally give in to
the love they've shared all this time?

Look for

Summer After Summer
by
Ann DeFee

**Available September
wherever books are sold.**

www.eHarlequin.com

HESAS0907

HARLEQUIN®

Mediterranean NIGHTS™

Experience glamour, elegance, mystery and revenge aboard the high seas....

Coming in September 2007...

BREAKING ALL THE RULES

by

Marisa Carroll

Aboard the cruise ship *Alexandra's Dream* for some R & R, sports journalist Lola Sandler is surprised to spot pro-golfer Eric Lashman. Years after walking away from the pro circuit with no explanation to the public, Eric now finds himself teaching aboard a cruise ship.

Lola smells a career-making exposé... but their developing relationship may force her to make a difficult choice.

REQUEST YOUR FREE BOOKS!

Harlequin® Historical
Historical Romantic Adventure!

2 FREE NOVELS PLUS 2 FREE GIFTS!

YES! Please send me 2 FREE Harlequin® Historical novels and my 2 FREE gifts. After receiving them, if I don't wish to receive any more books, I can return the shipping statement marked "cancel." If I don't cancel, I will receive 6 brand-new novels every month and be billed just $4.69 per book in the U.S., or $5.24 per book in Canada, plus 25¢ shipping and handling per book and applicable taxes, if any*. That's a savings of close to 15% off the cover price! I understand that accepting the 2 free books and gifts places me under no obligation to buy anything. I can always return a shipment and cancel at any time. Even if I never buy another book from Harlequin, the two free books and gifts are mine to keep forever.

246 HDN EEWW   349 HDN EEW9

Name	(PLEASE PRINT)	
Address		Apt. #
City	State/Prov.	Zip/Postal Code

Signature (if under 18, a parent or guardian must sign)

Mail to the Harlequin Reader Service®:
IN U.S.A.: P.O. Box 1867, Buffalo, NY 14240-1867
IN CANADA: P.O. Box 609, Fort Erie, Ontario L2A 5X3

Not valid to current Harlequin Historical subscribers.

Want to try two free books from another line?
Call 1-800-873-8635 or visit www.morefreebooks.com.

* Terms and prices subject to change without notice. NY residents add applicable sales tax. Canadian residents will be charged applicable provincial taxes and GST. This offer is limited to one order per household. All orders subject to approval. Credit or debit balances in a customer's account(s) may be offset by any other outstanding balance owed by or to the customer. Please allow 4 to 6 weeks for delivery.

Your Privacy: Harlequin is committed to protecting your privacy. Our Privacy Policy is available online at www.eHarlequin.com or upon request from the Reader Service. From time to time we make our lists of customers available to reputable firms who may have a product or service of interest to you. If you would prefer we not share your name and address, please check here. ☐

HH07

ATHENA FORCE

Heart-pounding romance and thrilling adventure.

Professional negotiator Lindsey Novak
is faced with her biggest challenge—to
buy back Teal Arnett, a young woman with
unique powers. In the process Lindsey
uncovers a devastating plot that involves
scientists from around the globe, and all of
them lead to one woman who is bent on
destroying Athena Academy...at any cost.

LOOK FOR

THE GOOD THIEF
by Judith Leon

*Available September
wherever you buy books.*

COMING NEXT MONTH FROM

HARLEQUIN®
HISTORICAL

- **KLONDIKE WEDDING**
by **Kate Bridges**
(Western)
When Dr. Luke Hunter stands in as the groom in a proxy wedding,
he doesn't expect to be *really* married to the bride! Luke's not a
settling-down kind of man, but beautiful Genevieve might be the
woman to change his mind.

- **A COMPROMISED LADY**
by **Elizabeth Rolls**
(Regency)
Thea Winslow's scandalous past has forbidden her a future. So why
does her wayward heart refuse to understand that she cannot have
any more to do with handsome Richard Blakehurst?

- **A PRACTICAL MISTRESS**
by **Mary Brendan**
(Regency)
She was nearly penniless, and becoming a mistress was the only
practical solution. The decision had *nothing* to do with the look in
Sir Jason's eyes that promised such heady delights....

- **THE WARRIOR'S TOUCH**
by **Michelle Willingham**
(Medieval)
The MacEgan Brothers
Pragmatic, plain Aileen never forgot the handsome man who
became her first lover on the eve of Bealtaine, the man who gave
her a child without ever seeing her face. Now that he has returned,
how can she keep her secret?